April's Man

Rosanna Rae

Copyright © 2013 Rosanna Rae

All rights reserved.

ISBN: 13- 978-1490363080

Hope you enjoy the story, Erna.

Rosanna Rae
27/3/2025

Contents

1. SISTERS 1
2. JUST ANOTHER DAY 7
3. RETAIL THERAPY 13
4. SPOILT FOR CHOICE 19
5. HAPPY DAYS 25
6. NOT SO HAPPY DAYS 32
7. SET UP 36
8. COMPLICATIONS 43
9. PATIENTS 49
10. CHANGES 56
11. I KNOW WHERE YOU LIVE 61
12. MOVING ON 66
13. UNLUCKY FOR SOME 73
14. FAMILY TIES 79
15. IT NEVER RAINS 85
16. SCOTT'S SOLUTION 92
17. THE DUST SETTLES 100
18. APRIL'S OTHER MAN 106
19. A DECENT PROPOSAL 111
20. DECISIONS, DECISIONS 117
21. THE LAST STRAW 124
22. RULES OF ENGAGEMENT 130
23. THE WEDDING PLANNER 138
24. DEAD END 143
25. NIGHTMARE 149
26. IT'S COMPLICATED 157
27. IT'S EVEN MORE COMPLICATED 163
28. THE BEST-LAID PLANS 170
29. THE ROAD TO DESTRUCTION 176
30. NO-MAN'S-LAND 183
31. THE BEST POLICY 189

32	STALEMATE	196
33	THE EVE OF DESTRUCTION	204
34	TRAPPED	211
35	SETTLING IN	221
36	MELISSA'S CHOICE	225
37	STRENGTH IN NUMBERS	233

1 SISTERS

The Carter household had been in a state of anticipation all day. The family had lived in the four-apartment semi-detached house in Yoker, Glasgow for twenty-five years. There had been good times and bad, but they had always managed to get by and had lived there quite happily. Now the three daughters were grown-up and their parents were excited today because their eldest daughter, April, was bringing her current boyfriend home to meet them. He was joining them for the evening meal and Mr Carter was still out at work, but Mrs Carter, in particular, was very excited about it because it wasn't like April to bring men home to meet her parents. Elspeth was sure that her daughter must be serious about this young man because she had invited him to her home. Normally, April's parents didn't even know who she was seeing and she had had a great many boyfriends since the age of fifteen, most of them for a very short period of time.

April Carter was in her mid twenties and had quite stunning good looks. She was very slim, but shapely, too, having what is normally referred to as a 'French figure'. She had a naturally full bust-line but was slim-hipped and had a mane of waist-length, blonde hair, which she achieved with only a little assistance in the form of highlights.

Her facial features were almost perfect. She had large, round eyes with well-shaped brows, long eyelashes, prominent cheekbones and a smooth, olive-toned skin. She never had any freckles, never broke out in spots and almost never looked flushed or flustered. Her nickname amongst her friends, not surprisingly, was 'Barbie'.

The Carters' second eldest daughter was sitting on the settee in the lounge with her arms folded across her chest and there was a moody expression on her face. Her brown hair was scraped back from her face in a pony tail, as it usually was, and she wore no make-up. She was watching her mother and her younger sister, June, running around preparing the food for their dinner. Such a fuss over a man! Honestly, it was only because it was *April's* boyfriend who was coming to tea, she was sure, that they were all running round in circles trying to pretend that the house was always this tidy and that they had a three-course meal every evening! She looked at June's pretty face and noticed she had put on more make-up than usual and that her very attractive auburn hair had been straightened to within an inch of its life! She sighed and her mother glared at her.

"I don't suppose there's any chance of you helping with the dinner, eh, May? You could at least offer to set the table."

"I've told you before, Mum – don't call me May. I'll lay the table if you want, but that's all I'm doing. He's April's guest, so why are *we* having to do all the work, as usual?"

"Don't start, May –" Elspeth warned, biting her lip as she realised she had again used her daughter's second name instead of calling her Belinda, which was her first name and was how she preferred to be addressed these days. When their first daughter had been born in the month of April, she and Pete hadn't been sure what to call her, so they had simply named her April; and when their second daughter had come along – in the month of May – they had done the same thing. But Elspeth had felt that

APRIL'S MAN

May was a little short and plain, so they had named her Belinda and had added May in as her middle name.

When their third daughter was born – in the month of June – it seemed only right to name her June! They hadn't set out to do that; it had simply happened that way. Family and friends were generally amused by this and had started calling Belinda 'May'. However, when she'd reached her teens, Belinda had rebelled against this and had demanded that everyone should call her by her first name. She felt that she was being made a fool of when people called her May, and also, she felt plain enough without having a plain name, too.

Elspeth privately thought it was quite unreasonable to expect people to start calling you by a different name after years of using another name. May was a perfectly good name anyway, she told herself. She couldn't really understand why her middle daughter didn't like to be called that. Seemed like a lot of fuss about nothing to Elspeth, who was well known for her pragmatism – and her quaint little sayings. She shook her head and pursed her lips, and then went back into the kitchen to mash the potatoes. It was nearly time for their guest to arrive and the large chicken was ready for carving.

June was busily putting the finishing touches to a substantial bowl of trifle and setting out the fancy new glass bowls her mother had bought specially for tonight. She didn't pay much attention to Belinda's grumblings because she was used to them and because she knew very well why she said things like that. Her sister was a very nice person, but she was a little on the plain side, whilst both June and April were very attractive girls. And, as if that wasn't enough, Belinda wasn't exactly brilliantly clever or blessed with any particular talents, either. She was envious of her siblings and it came out in these moods of hers, especially when any fuss was being made of either of her sisters. It didn't bother June at all. She understood it; *she* wouldn't want to be Belinda and she felt quite sorry for her. It must be difficult to be outshone in every department all the time. April was a very

3

successful model and June was about to start studying Arts at Strathclyde University.

Belinda had left school at sixteen and was on her feet all day in a local hair and beauty salon, cutting people's hair for a very low salary. She had nothing much going for her in life and she was very well aware of it.

The truth of the matter was that Belinda wasn't really such a plain-looking young woman. However, she didn't see any point in bothering very much with her appearance. Her sisters were so attractive that it seemed pointless to her to try to compete with them.

Just as everything became ready in the kitchen and the table was finally set for the meal, Mr Carter walked through the front door, threw his coat over the end of the banister and went into the kitchen to give his wife a little peck on the cheek.

"What's for tea, love?" he asked pleasantly, receiving an exasperated sigh as an answer.

"Chicken. I told you last night. April's bringing her young man home tonight – remember? And get into the hall and take that coat off of the banister, will you? Honestly, I don't know why I bother!"

Pete Carter smiled and shrugged, removing his coat and hanging it up in the hall cupboard. He then came back into the lounge and gave each of his daughters a quick hug. Just as he reached his customary chair by the fireplace and sat down, the front door opened again and April and her boyfriend came into the hallway.

Mrs Carter rushed out of the kitchen to greet them and looked expectantly at April, waiting for her to do the introductions, which she did with a carefree air.

"Mum, this is Scott. Obviously!" April announced, moving across to the hall mirror to check that the wind hadn't messed up her hair too much.

"Hello, Mrs Carter. Pleased to meet you!" Scott said pleasantly, holding out his right hand to shake hers.

Pete Carter had now joined them and so had June.

"Nice strong handshake!" Pete commented.

"You, too!" Scott replied, grinning.

June blushed slightly and fluttered her eyelashes a little as she offered their guest her hand and she could almost feel Belinda a little behind her, rolling her eyes heavenwards in disgust.

Belinda reluctantly moved forward to greet her sister's boyfriend and when she was right in front of him and shaking his hand, was immediately struck dumb by his appearance. He was, predictably, drop-dead gorgeous, and he also emanated a quiet, under-stated charisma. He was tall and slim, with dark brown hair and very dark eyes, and when he said "Hi, May!" to her, even his voice seemed to have a velvety, dark-brown quality to it.

"My name's not May – it's Belinda!" she replied sharply, causing him to raise his eyebrows in surprise. "My full name is Belinda May, but everyone keeps calling me May because it's easier. I prefer Belinda," she added, the tone of her voice brooking no argument.

"Belinda it is then," he answered smoothly, but the twinkle in his eyes gave away his amusement.

Belinda pressed her lips together in unreasonable annoyance and turned away towards the kitchen.

"I'm starving – let's eat!" she ordered, taking a deep breath and straightening her back. How much more punishment was she going to have to endure, she wondered as they all trooped into the kitchen and took their places around the dinner table? She was quite sure the rest of the evening was going to be more of an ordeal than a pleasure, so she decided to eat her food as quickly as possible and then escape to her bedroom as soon as she reasonably could without causing offence.

As the evening progressed, however, their guest kept them all very well entertained. He was a doctor, a G.P., and had a repertoire of little anecdotes about the antics and foibles of some of his patients, whilst still carefully respecting their anonymity. He was very attentive towards April, who simply smiled smugly and accepted his attentions as her due. June was obviously completely smitten with him, and it was obvious that Mr and Mrs

Carter could not have been more delighted with this young man. He was everything they could have wished for in a partner for their daughter.

Belinda, on the other hand, was in a state of complete emotional turmoil. Scott was handsome, charming and obviously a very nice person. She had never met anyone quite like him and she could have sat and listened to him talking for hours. She tried not to look directly at him in case she would find herself unable to tear her eyes away from his deep brown ones. She sat at the table for longer than she had intended doing, because his company was so entertaining and uplifting. She was actually enjoying herself and she didn't want him to leave. She said absolutely nothing because she didn't want anyone to guess how she was feeling. She was horrified by the strength of the emotions she was experiencing; she didn't want Scott to know how strongly she was reacting to him, nor did she want any of her family to realise that she had fallen madly – and hopelessly – in love with her sister's boyfriend!

2 JUST ANOTHER DAY

By the time she awoke the following morning, after a rather restless night's sleep, Belinda had managed to convince herself that she was imagining things. Of course she was smitten with this new man in April's life – he was gorgeous! Every woman who ever met him would fall at his feet. It was nothing personal to her. It had been obvious that June was feeling the same way, as she had gazed at him with rapt attention all evening. Belinda smiled at how silly she herself had been in thinking that she was the only one who would react to him in that way. June's reaction to him had been very similar to her own, she assured herself as she glanced across the room towards her sleeping sister's bed.

Belinda yawned and stretched and climbed out of her bed, padding across to the window to draw back the soft green curtains. She rolled the white Roman blind up just a little, so as not to disturb her sister. It was a lovely morning. The large bedroom she shared with June was at the front of the house, which was south facing. The sun was shining, the street outside looked the same as it always did, and Belinda felt quite certain that everything was going to be fine. She was making a drama out of a crisis and that wasn't like her. She decided it was time to give herself a mental shake and take herself off to work. She had a long, tiring day ahead of her. Working on Saturdays wasn't easy, as it was their busiest day, but then, she asked herself, what else would she do with herself if she wasn't working? She enjoyed meeting new people every day and had even become quite friendly with some of the regular clients. She went off into the bathroom for her shower, shaking her head slightly at her own silliness. Love indeed – what was she thinking?

As the morning wore on, Belinda relaxed even more and was quite chatty with most of her customers. One young woman in particular was making her smile. She usually came into the salon at the weekend, so Belinda presumed she was working during the week. She was a regular customer and her name was Melissa. She seemed to be around Belinda's age, in her early twenties, and always had a happy, smiling face. Her hair was like gold silk, and she wore it in an inverted bob style. It was a similar colour to April's hair, Belinda mused as she expertly worked with the styling brush and hair dryer. Melissa was chatting away to her about how she and her husband Cameron were going to his friend's birthday party that evening and how much she was looking forward to it.

"Are you doing anything nice tonight?" Melissa asked Belinda, looking at her in the mirror.

"No, but the family had a really nice time last night," Belinda replied. "My sister's new boyfriend came over for dinner and he was really nice – and very funny – and made us all laugh all night!"

Melissa raised her brows. "Wow. Sounds like he made quite an impression!" she commented.

"Oh, he did, and my wee sister June's quite taken with him, too," Belinda replied. "In fact, I'm sure if he asked my mum to leave my dad and run away with him, I think she would consider it!"

They both laughed loudly, making the other customers look over at them, wondering what they were laughing at.

Belinda really liked Melissa and on the spur of the moment, she asked her if she would like to go out with her some time, to do a bit of shopping and maybe have lunch afterwards.

"Oh, I'd like that," Melissa replied eagerly. "I don't have many friends of my own. We mostly mix with Cam's friends. When were you thinking of?"

"Maybe next Friday, if you're not busy. I have to work Saturday, but I often take Friday as my day off," Belinda explained.

"Right, that's fine then. Friday it is," Melissa confirmed, smiling as she stood up and went over to the till to pay for her hairdo.

Belinda felt really pleased and when Melissa left the salon, she waved her new friend off with a big smile, at the same time wondering why such a pleasant, easy-going woman would have any trouble making friends. She couldn't come up with any answer to that, so she simply shrugged and turned towards the next customer with a welcoming smile on her face.

*

When Belinda arrived home after work that day, she was pleased to find that everything seemed to have returned to normal. The only problem was that after they'd had their evening meal, which wasn't anything like as elaborate as their dinner had been the previous evening, everyone settled down on the two long, comfortable settees in the lounge and all of them seemed intent on discussing April's boyfriend, including April herself.

"So, what did you all think of him then?" she enquired, the self-satisfied smile on her face indicating that she was quite certain of their unmitigated approval.

Her father nodded. "Seems like a very fine young man, April," he stated. He was not a man to use more words than was necessary at the best of times, but he would have said a great deal more if there was anything he hadn't liked about her boyfriend.

Her mum wasn't so restrained.

"April, you've done really well there. He's very good-looking, of course, but he obviously has a great personality as well. I have high hopes for the two of you!"

June nodded. "He gets my vote, April – ten out of ten, but you know that already. He's a real 'keeper', that one. Don't go screwing things up with him. You won't get another one like him in a hurry, that's for sure!"

April simply shrugged and didn't look too concerned about it, one way or the other. She glanced at Belinda for her opinion, tilting her head enquiringly to one side.

"What can I say?" Belinda asked. "You know he's great." Then she asked, before she could stop herself, "When are you seeing him again?"

"Don't know. Probably tomorrow, but Max's been asking me out again, and I like him too," April replied, making them all stare at her in disbelief.

Max was one of the fashion photographers at the studio where she worked, and the two of them had had a very on/off relationship for the last few months. She knew he saw other women as well as her, so it suited her to take up with a new boyfriend, just to show him that she wasn't sitting around waiting for him to ask her out again. She smiled a very private smile as she thought about his mop of fair hair and his very impressive six-pack, achieved through spending a great deal of his time in the gym. He could have been a model himself if he'd wanted to. The last time they'd been together they hadn't even bothered going out anywhere. They had made love right there on the leather couch in the studio after everyone else had gone home.

Her father frowned but didn't comment on his daughter's statement. Her mother, however, didn't hold back on letting her feelings on the subject be known.

"You can't be serious, April!" Elspeth said, with an exasperated gasp. "That one will never settle down – you can be sure of that!"

"So?" April answered, pouting a little in annoyance. "Who wants to settle down anyway?"

Her mother simply shook her head in consternation.

"You can pass the doc over to me any time, if you're finished with him!" June declared, tossing her auburn ringlets in delight at the thought of it.

"That's enough of that now, both of you!" Pete Carter said warningly, to Belinda's great relief. She took charge of changing the subject by picking up the remote control and asking them all which programme she should switch to. That debate wouldn't have a fast or simple solution, she knew; it never did in such a full household!

*

By the time the following Friday morning arrived, Belinda was tired but was, nevertheless, in a good mood. It was payday and she was meeting Melissa for some shopping, some lunch and possibly one or two glasses of wine. She was looking forward to it and it would help to take her mind off things a little. She knew April was going out with her new boyfriend again that evening and Belinda didn't relish the idea of spending any more time in his company than she had to, because she didn't want him to start being aware of the effect he had on her. She decided that if her afternoon activities carried on into the evening, she would be quite pleased because there would be less chance of bumping into him when he came to collect April.

She threw her wardrobe doors open wide and gazed appraisingly at the contents. She didn't want to be too casually dressed, as Melissa was quite a well-dressed person – even her casual clothes were very chic. At the same time, she didn't want to be too dressy in the middle of the day. She took her time deciding and finally chose a pair of chocolate brown jeans and a clingy, cream v-necked top, which had a row of brown buttons at the neck and the wrists. She added a topaz-coloured pendant to complete the look. As she dressed carefully, she wished she'd had some highlights put into her hair, as it would have lifted her appearance quite considerably. All the girls at the salon benefited from staff discounts on the hairstyling prices, but she simply hadn't got round to arranging it yet.

Later, as she set off to meet Melissa, with a picture of the woman's glossy, golden mane in her head, she made a mental note to arrange to have some highlights done some time during the following week, while she still had most of her salary left.

3 RETAIL THERAPY

Melissa was already standing at their arranged meeting-place by the time Belinda arrived, although Belinda wasn't late. They had decided to meet at Central Station, as they would both be arriving by train, and then head for a shopping mall, so that they would have plenty of choice of shops to browse without having too much walking to do.

Melissa waved and smiled as soon as she saw Belinda, and even from a distance Belinda could see that she was wearing a casual, but very smart, woollen trouser suit. It was ivory white, with soft tailoring and a narrow gold braid around the edges of the jacket. She would have stood out in any crowd, anywhere. Belinda was glad she had made an effort with her own appearance.

"Hi, there!" Belinda said gaily. "So, where do you fancy going first then? Do you want to go to a particular store or should we just have a look round the St. Enoch Centre?"

"I like the St. Enoch Centre," Melissa replied, nodding enthusiastically. "There's a good choice of clothes shops there, not to mention shoe shops!"

"Okay, the Centre it is!" Belinda agreed, and they left the station and set off for the shopping mall. They chatted easily as they strolled along the busy streets and Belinda wondered again at the other woman's apparent lack of friends. She seemed so open and friendly.

They started to look round several of the shops quite thoroughly, and Belinda could tell from her comments about where to go next that Melissa was quite familiar with their layout and contents. She was slim and of medium height, so sizes were an easy fit for her. Belinda envied her that as she was generously built in the hip area and often had trouble finding jeans and trousers that fitted her properly.

Two hours and several purchases later, both of them were experiencing a bit of an energy gap.

"Let's go for a bite to eat, shall we?" Belinda suggested, feeling her stomach rumble at that precise moment, as though it had heard her.

"Yeah," Melissa agreed readily. "I don't know about you, Belinda, but I'm starving!"

They made their way to the Food Court, where they discussed their purchases, and fashion in general, while they waited for their food to arrive. Melissa had bought two dresses and a matching top and trousers – and Belinda had bought one top from Next. Their food order didn't take long to appear, and as Belinda munched away at her chicken salad, it didn't surprise her to see Melissa tucking into a substantial plate of lasagne and chips. Belinda tried not to feel the unfairness of it. It wasn't Melissa's fault if her metabolism was a lot faster than Belinda's. They each had a very large glass of wine along with their meal.

As they began to relax with each other a little more, Melissa started speaking about her husband and her little boy, Toby, who was nearly five and would be starting school in the autumn. Belinda watched as her face became animated while she described her little family and it was obvious that she loved them both very much and was extremely happy. She also mentioned that she enjoyed her job as an accountant and was doing well at the firm.

Beauty, brains, money and a happy home life, Belinda thought. And suddenly she realised why this woman was short of female friends – she was too perfect. She seemed to have virtually no body or personality faults and no life problems. Some women would feel envious of her for even one of the wonderful aspects of her life, but to have virtual perfection in everything was extremely unusual and was guaranteed to engender envy and resentment in others who weren't so fortunate. Belinda was glad that she had figured this out because she really liked Melissa and intended to make the woman's life even happier by becoming good friends with her. She wasn't petty-minded enough to take against her just because she seemed to have unbelievably good luck. Also, Belinda was used to feeling somewhat inferior to other women, because of the attributes of her sisters. She became aware that Melissa was beginning to gaze a little anxiously at her and that she hadn't taken in the previous comment she'd made to her.

"Are you bored, Belinda? Am I talking too much about myself?" She asked worriedly.

Belinda could almost hear the woman thinking that this friendship was going to go down the drain, too, as her previous friendships seemed to have done.

"Of course not, Melissa," Belinda reassured her, adding, "I'm really enjoying myself. And by the way, I don't have a lot of friends, either."

Melissa smiled contentedly and took another sip of her wine, then she spoke again.

"But it must be really nice to have two sisters, though. Are you good friends with them?"

"Well, most of the time, I suppose. Is it okay if I call you Mel?" Belinda asked.

"Of course it is, Belinda. You can call me anything you like!"

"Well, I was just thinking that I've really enjoyed today and we should do this again sometime soon."

Mel beamed at her and agreed that she would like that very much. When they had finished eating, they drained their glasses and headed towards the station again. As Belinda went off to find the right platform for her train, she turned and waved goodbye to Melissa, who was standing beneath an overhead light. Her hair was glowing like a halo. She seemed to radiate happiness. Belinda prayed, as she hopped onto the stationary train, that one day she would feel happiness like that and that maybe some good luck would rub off on her if the two of them continued to stay friends.

When she alighted at Yoker train station, carefully remembering to lift her solitary store bag from the seat beside her, she was still pondering on the unfairness of life, although not in a bitter way. She was in a reflective mood as she walked the few streets to her home and opened the front door absent-mindedly. She could hear, inside her own head, her mother saying, "Ah yes, the grass is always greener on the other side of the fence, isn't it? Well, it isn't, you know – it just looks that way!" As soon as she stepped inside the house, confident that April and Scott would have departed some time earlier, she realised that this was not the case. She could hear the chatting going on in the living room and Scott's deep voice was clearly audible amongst the feminine tones.

As she had already eaten, she decided to go straight upstairs to the bedroom and try on her new top. It was made of a soft, smooth material, a deep forest green colour, and had a cross-over neckline. It had really suited her in the store changing room and she was keen to put it on straight away. She hoped she wouldn't be disappointed. Sometimes clothes could look very different once you tried them on at home, she mused as she climbed the staircase.

However, she wasn't disappointed. The colour was a good contrast to her brown hair and fresh complexion. She was pleased by how she looked in the mirror, but decided not to take her hair out of its customary ponytail as she didn't want to look too dressed-up in the house. She especially didn't want Scott or anyone else to think she was dressing up for him. She tiptoed quietly downstairs again and went into the kitchen to get a glass of water. The wine she'd had earlier was beginning to dehydrate her. Her mouth went even drier, however, when Scott's voice spoke suddenly behind her. She gulped down plenty of the water and then turned round to look at him before she answered his greeting.

"Oh, hi, Scott. Didn't realise you were here," she fibbed. "Thought you'd both have gone out earlier, it being Friday night, because you usually go out then." She stopped speaking abruptly as she realised she was starting to babble.

Scott merely smiled calmly, looking extremely relaxed and comfortable. "You look very nice tonight, Belinda; that colour suits you," he told her in a friendly way, and she was really annoyed to find herself blushing furiously.

"You know, you could really look quite attractive if you took a bit more trouble with your appearance," he informed her in a matter-of-fact tone.

She was suddenly furious, which made her face go even redder, and her mouth was open to issue a sharp retort when April popped her head round the kitchen door and asked Scott to hurry up. She was keen to leave for their night out. He poured some water into a glass and drank it swiftly.

"I'll be there in a minute," he told her. Elspeth Carter came into the kitchen then and raised her eyebrows at Belinda's flushed face.

"Is that a new top, Belinda?" she asked, then rattled on without waiting for an answer. "I don't know, the clothes these days – so thin you could pat peas through them!" She sniffed and started filling the kettle to make some tea.

Scott soon joined April in the hallway and Belinda heard the two of them closing the front door behind them as they went off to visit a new club in the centre of town. She went through to the lounge and plonked herself down on the settee beside June, folding her arms tightly across her chest and staying silent. She was hopeful that watching a little television would help to settle her down before she went upstairs to bed.

"What's up with *you?*" June asked, whilst steadily munching her way through a large packet of vinegar crisps. Belinda could see both of her parents turning towards her out of the corner of her eye.

"Nothing's up with me!" Belinda snapped back at her. Then she jumped up and said goodnight to nobody in particular. She wasn't in the mood for socialising and her plan to calm down by watching television obviously wasn't working.

She tried to take deep breaths and calm herself down as she climbed the staircase once again, but she wasn't having much success. She really wished that she didn't have to go to work the next day, but it was Saturday and she couldn't take the day off. She sighed dispiritedly and got ready for bed, knowing full well that it would take hours for her annoyance to wear off.

Arrogant so-and-so, she muttered to herself as she tried ineffectually to massage the tense muscles at the back of her neck. *How dare he talk to me like that? Talk about condescending! Who does he think he is anyway – God's Gift to Women?*

She made up her mind there and then to have as little to do with him as possible from then onwards. He seemed to be able to upset her equilibrium so easily. She had no intention of allowing him, or any other man, to do that. She resolved to try to ignore him as much as possible without actually being rude, because she knew being rude would only draw attention towards her. She would be cool and polite to him; that was the way to go. Belinda had no way of knowing at that time that she was going to find it virtually impossible to stick to her resolution.

4 SPOILT FOR CHOICE

April had enjoyed herself on her date with Scott the previous evening. He was always fun to be with, had loads of money to spend and always took her to the best clubs in town. He was fond of paying her compliments, too, which pleased her. And a doctor, into the bargain. What more could a girl ask? The trouble was, he was too nice – well, too nice for her, at any rate. She'd always been a sucker for a 'bad boy'.

Her thoughts turned towards the man who was occupying her mind most of the time these days. She was meeting Max that morning and she knew they would make love again – wildly, as always. She couldn't get enough of him and he obviously felt the same way about her. But he wasn't into commitment and neither was she – normally. She sighed as she pushed the duvet aside and slid out of bed.

While she showered, she sang to herself as she compared the two men, giving them each points out of ten; but she couldn't complete the comparison because she hadn't slept with Scott yet. He must be old-fashioned or something, because he hadn't made a move on her as yet, except to kiss her passionately in the car or outside the front door each time he brought her back home. She knew that situation wouldn't last long, though, and she wondered what it would be like. One thing she did know for sure, was that it wouldn't be anything like it was with Max. It had never been like that with anyone before. She hoped that Scott wouldn't find out about Max, though, because she didn't want him to finish with her. Things would end between herself and Scott when she said so and not before. Nobody had ever ended a relationship with her and that's how she wanted things to stay. If she was very careful, she decided, Scott would never find out he had competition and she could have the best of both worlds for as long as it suited her. Having made that decision, she dried herself quickly, used almost half a bottle of body lotion on her skin and then dressed carefully in a sexy, leopard-skin outfit to go out and meet her 'bad boy'.

*

It was Saturday and June was at a loose end. She was lounging on the settee flicking through the television channels. She'd heard her sister slamming the front door and heading off out somewhere – again. She was bored, but had no money to go anywhere or do anything. She wasn't working yet because she was going to start University in the autumn. She had tried to get a part-time job doing something, even a bit of Saturday work, but there was just nothing going these days. It was a waste of time. She switched the television off and threw the remote control onto the other chair. It wasn't fair, she thought. April had everything she wanted and more. But she, June, had nothing. No job, no boyfriend, no money. Hell, even Belinda had a job. It just wasn't fair.

She stood up and looked at her reflection in the large mirror above the fireplace. It had hung in that same place for as long as she could remember. The room had been redecorated quite a number of times, but the mirror was always put back in the same place afterwards. She smiled at her own image. She was just as pretty as April, she knew, in her own way, and there was no reason why she should hang around here all the time doing nothing while everyone else was out having fun.

Her mum came into the lounge just then and June told her she was going off out for a while. "I hope it doesn't plump down while you're out," her mum replied. "That sky's not looking too good. Where are you going anyway?" she asked.

"Just out for a walk, Mum," June replied. I'm fed up and the weather's not bad. Don't worry, I won't go far. Probably just go over to Sophie's for a while or something."

"Okay, love. Just mind and let me know if you're going to be late for tea," her mother urged.

"I will, Mum. See you later. Bye."

She grabbed her jacket from one of the pegs in the hallway and pulled it on as she closed the front door behind her. She walked on a few steps and then decided she may as well go to Sophie's and see if they could think up something to pass the time. She drew her mobile phone out of her pocket and called her friend. She was at home and not doing anything special, so she told her to come over any time.

June was wearing her trainers, so she managed to walk the few streets in record time. Sophie answered the door herself and they both went straight upstairs to her room.

The two of them sat down on the bed without saying anything.

"I'm bored stiff," June complained.

When Sophie didn't reply, June turned and looked more closely at her. The girl wasn't saying a word, but it was obvious that she was harbouring a secret. Her eyes sparkled and her air of smugness was unmistakable.

"Go on then – spill!" June challenged her. "You're dying to tell me something, so don't bother trying to pretend. Come on. Which one is it? Jason or Mickey?"

Sophie kept her silence for a few more minutes, but when June stood up as if she was about to leave, she pulled at her sleeve and made her sit down again.

"It's Jason. It happened last night. He rang me after I got home from school and asked if I wanted to go out with him, so I did. Isn't it great? I can't believe it. He's well fit. Are you jealous?"

"What do *you* think?" June answered, trying not to look as despondent as she felt. "I'm pleased for you, Sophie. Honest," she fibbed.

"Don't worry, Junie, I won't be out with him all the time. I'll still hang out with you lots, as well," Sophie assured her, trying to sound as though she meant it.

"Yeah, sure," June agreed. She'd heard that one before. "Hey, ask him if his mate's looking to take anyone out, will you? Mickey's not bad either. I wouldn't say no."

"Sure I will. Maybe we can double date some time, you know? I'll ask him and see what he says," Sophie promised.

The two girls spent the rest of the afternoon playing music and discussing boys and make-up. By the time June left to go home for her tea, she felt a little happier and was mentally crossing her fingers that she would get fixed up with someone – anyone – soon. She didn't like asking boys out, in case they knocked her back, but she decided she would have to do something soon to relieve the boredom. It was doing her head in.

She could smell steak pie as she opened the front door and she was pleased to see that Scott had arrived to take April out for the evening.

"Hi, Scott," she crooned, batting her eyelashes shamelessly at him and earning a frown from her father.

"June, go upstairs and fetch your sister, will you?" he ordered. "Scott's been waiting for her for ages."

Probably not long back from seeing Max, June thought, suppressing a smirk. *Would serve her right if I told him that!*

She went off upstairs to find her sister, leaving Scott, Mr Carter and Belinda sitting in an uncomfortable silence, trying to think of something to say to each other.

"You're very quiet today, love," Mr Carter said, glancing over at Belinda.

His daughter merely smiled and nodded, then turned away to look at the television screen. Her chin was slightly tilted and her lips remained tightly closed. Mr Carter frowned again, wondering why everyone seemed so tense today. He wished his wife would announce that dinner was ready.

Deciding to take matters into his own hands, he stood up and said he was going into the kitchen to help with the tea. When he'd closed the door behind him Scott looked across at Belinda and cleared his throat.

"M – Belinda, are you mad at me or something? Have I done something wrong?" he asked. "I feel like you're blanking me today."

"I'm perfectly fine, thanks," she answered stiffly.

"I don't think you are ..."

He didn't get to finish his sentence as April chose that moment to come breezing into the lounge. She went straight over to him and kissed him on the lips.

Belinda looked away again as the two of them moved out into the hall, but she could still hear them speaking.

"You look stunning, April," Scott murmured, obviously awestruck by her glowing appearance. She was wearing a shimmering, figure-hugging gold frock with a cropped, faux-fur jacket over it. She had used a musky scent liberally. She oozed confidence and sensuality and she was well aware of it.

"I know," she answered smoothly, opening the door and skipping outside in front of him.

Scott didn't give Belinda another thought that evening, especially after he'd asked April to come back to his place with him at the end of the night and she'd said 'yes'.

He held her hand as they walked up the path together. 'His place' turned out to be a ground-floor flat in Kelvinside. It was in a traditional building and looked very up-market on the outside. It didn't disappoint on the inside, either. April was impressed.

When Scott asked her if she would like coffee or anything she giggled, wrapping her arms around him suggestively.

"Coffee?" she sneered. "That'll be right! Get into that bedroom, Mister, and show me what you got!" she ordered. She turned round and strode along the high-ceilinged hallway as though it was a catwalk, looking for his bedroom and pulling her clothes off as she went.

"I don't suppose you share with anyone, do you?" she asked him. "Now that could be interesting!"

"No, I don't," he replied, obviously taken aback.

Judging by his shocked expression, she realised the good doctor hadn't expected her to say anything like that.

"Just kidding," she purred, removing the last of her clothes and throwing aside the duvet.

Looks like I'm going to have to give this guy a few lessons if we're going to have any fun, she thought. She patted the pillow invitingly and laughed out loud when he tentatively climbed in beside her, still wearing his briefs!

5 HAPPY DAYS

The spring days lengthened and became milder as summer approached and April continued to see both of her men; Belinda continued working at the salon and building a strong friendship with Melissa; and June had started going out on double dates with Mickey, Sophie and Jason.

June was really enjoying herself now and the dating was helping to take her mind off the fact that she still hadn't managed to find a summer job. She was having a little difficulty, however, with the amount of alcohol she was having to consume in order to keep up with the others. Sophie didn't seem to have a problem with it, but June was quite prone to hangovers and found that it took her days to get over one session, and then they started another session and the whole process began all over again. Her mum and dad kept asking her why she was going out so much and she told them she was dating, but only casually, because she didn't want them inviting Mickey over to the house to vet him. He seemed to her to be a decent bloke, generally speaking, and he was really fit, but it seemed to her that he was always smoking and drinking, and she also had her suspicions that he wasn't averse to a bit of drug use. He had made various comments along those lines, but she preferred to assume that it was just talk. She didn't want to get involved in anything like that, so she told herself it was just bravado – that he said these things to impress her. He obviously didn't realise that she wasn't the type of girl to be impressed by drug-taking.

She decided, all things considered, that it was best to keep a low profile regarding Mickey for the time being. She was young, she was having some fun at last, and there was no harm in it; so it suited her well to keep the status quo. Time enough to introduce him to her parents if and when things became more serious between them. Their dates were low-key and inexpensive as none of them was working, but it was better than sitting at home while everyone else went out, and so June was casual and off-hand whenever the subject was mentioned. She still drooled over April's boyfriend whenever she saw him, but she didn't feel quite so envious any more. She had her own life now.

Belinda was happier nowadays also. She and Melissa got on very well with each other and often went shopping or lunching together, or both. As time went on, Belinda became a little anxious that perhaps Melissa's husband wouldn't be too pleased about her encroaching on their quality time together as a family, but when she said this to Melissa one day as they sat opposite one another in Costa Coffee, Melissa assured her that this wasn't the case.

"You don't know Cam, Belinda – he's a sweetie," she said, a fond smile on her face. "He just wants me to be happy. He has lots of mates himself and he goes out with them a lot while I'm home with Toby; it kind of evens things up that I've got a friend of my own now, too. He would never begrudge me that or try to keep me at home all the time. He's not like that."

Belinda was reassured and felt that she had achieved a level of contentment that had eluded her until then. It wasn't the same as having a boyfriend, but it was fun and it eased her loneliness. She tended to spend more of her salary on fashions now, too, and she had had those highlights done at last. Sometimes she even let her hair hang loosely around her face and down her back. She looked and felt better and more relaxed, and she tried not to get annoyed when she remembered Scott's condescending remark about her appearance. She now found it so much easier to be nice to him on the few occasions when she spoke to him. Perhaps 'nice' was an exaggeration, but she could converse with him without striking an obvious attitude towards him, and because of that, nobody was aware of her feelings, especially not him, or so she hoped. She kept the attraction well tamped down inside her, to the extent that she could almost convince herself that it had gone. Almost.

Whilst all these changes were taking place with her sisters, April didn't really take much notice because she was having the time of her life. She could hardly wait to finish her work each day and slope off with Max for a quickie; and a couple of times a week she would do this and then go home to get showered and changed before Scott arrived to pick her up. Sometimes she would get ready very quickly and run downstairs to the front door when she heard him knocking because it was becoming tiresome to her to sit and talk with him and her parents so often. She was starting to wish that she had a place of her own so that she could live her life on her own terms, without having her parents overseeing everything all the time. But that situation was, she knew, not very likely, as she hardly earned enough to keep herself in clothes and cosmetics. This was one of the reasons she was keeping up her relationship with Scott. He was obviously loaded and she was very keen on the idea of moving into that great flat with him. He was out most of the time, she knew, because of his work, and that would suit her perfectly.

She began planning and plotting and wondered how best to go about things with him. She was turning several different ideas around in her mind, including the notion of pretending to him that she had fallen pregnant, in order to make him consider asking her to live with him. She was sure he was the type of man who would support her in that situation. Rather than making him cool off, she was convinced it would make him move things forward with her. For the time being, however, she contented herself with sighing heavily and telling him, on regular occasions, that she wished they could be together more often. He responded by saying that his work came first and that it wasn't practical for him to go out on the town more than twice a week. He was often very tired because of the hours he put in and she was pleased that she had succeeded in making him feel a little guilty, as though he was neglecting her and not giving her the attention she deserved, and she was well aware that this could only work in her favour.

*

By the middle of May, June and Mickey had become an item and were together a great deal of the time. They still teamed up with Sophie and Jason now and again, but were more inclined to do their own thing these days; June was also gradually realising that Mickey was becoming slightly possessive in his attitude towards her. She wasn't sure if she liked this new development or not. It was very flattering, of course, but he could be quite moody at times and she had gotten into the habit of trying to soothe him and often consciously placated him when he was being 'off' with her. Ever since they had started sleeping together, she had felt that he wanted to own her. And he even watched her carefully when she and Jason were talking in case they would start to flirt with each other. It was a bit of a difficult situation because of the fact that the two men shared a flat. It wasn't easy for either couple to be alone together without wondering if the others were about to appear.

Sometimes Jason and Mickey would come to an arrangement, but at other times embarrassing situations would crop up. June and Sophie had spoken to each other about this, but they tended to simply laugh it off, whereas the males took it more seriously. June had now become accustomed to drinking much more heavily than she used to do and it was starting to cause comment with her parents and also to affect her appearance. She was paler than usual and had lost a little weight because the drinking bouts put her off her food and quite often made her physically sick. When her parents challenged her about it she simply shrugged and said "So?" This made them very annoyed, but there wasn't really anything they could do about it because she had just turned eighteen the previous month and it was therefore her decision.

One evening, after the four of them had had a heavy drinking session, Jason and Sophie fell out with each other over some triviality. As far as June could make out, they were arguing about which movie to watch. June and Mickey both tried to calm things down between them, but without success. This row escalated into a bitter slanging match, and Sophie eventually stormed out of the flat yelling that she was going to go home on her own. Jason went into his own room, banging the door hard behind him. June stood up on rather unsteady legs and said she was going to go after Sophie and talk to her, but Mickey had other ideas. He took hold of her wrist firmly.

"Just leave her, June. She won't listen to you anyway – she's too pissed. Leave it till the morning. Anyway, it's up to Jason if he wants to make things up with her or not. Come here!"

He pulled her close to him and started to kiss her. She tried to pull away, but he wouldn't let her go.

"Mickey, let me go," she gasped, turning her head away from him.

"Settle down," he said very quietly, holding her even more tightly.

"Mickey, I want to go now! Let me go!" she said, beginning to feel slightly panicky.

He let go of her reluctantly.

"Okay fine. If you're going to be as silly as Sophie, you might as well go," he told her. Then he started muttering something about women not being able to hold their drink.

"Aren't you going to walk me home?" she asked, rubbing her wrist, which was now red and a little sore.

"Course I am. Let's go then," he answered, but he was clenching his jaw and didn't look as reasonable as he sounded, June thought.

He grabbed their jackets as they walked along the narrow hallway and they put them on as they left the building.

"Lot of fuss about nothing," Mickey grumbled as they walked along the road together, a space of around a foot between them. This was unusual as they usually walked hand in hand.

"I know, Mickey, but Sophie's my mate and I don't want her to be upset," she told him.

"Oh, so it's okay if I'm upset, though, is it?" he asked petulantly.

"Of course it isn't. That's not what I meant," she answered, frowning.

"I don't want us to fall out just because those two idiots have. Do you?" he asked, stopping and turning towards her in the orange glow of the street lamps.

"No I don't. But we won't fall out. We're fine. And I'll speak to Soph tomorrow and everything will be all right again. It'll be fine," she assured him.

"Sure. You do that. But if it isn't fine with those two, it won't make any difference to us, though, will it? We'll still be okay, won't we?"

June knew she should be pleased that he was obviously so keen to keep seeing her, but something in his manner felt a little too insistent to her. She felt pressured and she wasn't sure what to do about it. She simply nodded in answer to his question, but the whole situation and Mickey's attitude had unsettled her.

Mickey walked her right to her door He pulled her towards him and kissed her lingeringly.

"We'll make up for lost time tomorrow. Okay, babe?" he asked, making sure she replied before he released her.

"Yes, we will," she assured him, nodding her head and trying to smile.

She closed the front door behind her with a strong sense of relief and ran straight upstairs to the bedroom to ring Sophie. There was no reply. She rang the number several more times before she eventually gave up. She would just have to wait till morning, she realised, hoping that her friend would have calmed down by then and would feel ready to sort everything out between herself and Jason.

Belinda was sitting in front of the dressing table mirror, brushing her hair. "Is everything okay, Junie?" she asked anxiously.

"Oh, yeah, fine. Silly Sophie's got her phone switched off, that's all," she answered.

Belinda slid into bed and switched off the lamp on her bedside table, and June followed suit, sighing and turning over onto her side. After a little while she managed to convince herself that everything would sort itself out the following day and slowly her eyelids drooped and she fell asleep.

6 NOT SO HAPPY DAYS

As it turned out, things didn't sort themselves out the following day. As soon as she'd had a cup of coffee, because she couldn't face any breakfast, June tried to contact Sophie again, but there was still no reply. She kept getting Sophie's voicemail, and although she left several messages asking her to please contact her as soon as possible, she didn't hear anything from her friend. By midday she was really worried and decided to go round and visit her instead of just calling. There were several messages on her own phone from Mickey, but she didn't want to speak to him until she'd spoken to Sophie; so she ignored them.

She pulled on her trainers and called out to her mum that she was going round to Sophie's. She could hear her mother asking her what was wrong, but she pretended not to hear and ran out of the door. She pulled her hood up because it was drizzling and hurried along the street. She was sure that Sophie would be at home because she would still be sulking and feeling sorry for herself. *Probably having a good cry by now*, she told herself.

When she knocked at Sophie's front door her mum answered the door and let her inside without even asking Sophie if she wanted to see her. They *were* best friends, after all. She inclined her head in the direction of the staircase and told her to go on up to the room. June ran up the steps and knocked quietly on the bedroom door.

"Come on in, June," Sophie replied through the closed door.

June opened the door and went straight over to the bed. Sophie was lying on it surrounded by lots of pink and purple silk cushions and half a box of used tissues. She was cuddling her favourite soft toy, a little dog she simply called 'Doggie'.

"I'm never going back out with Jason again, June. Never. He's a pig." She declared, sniffing loudly.

"Why? What did he do?" June asked.

"It's stuff about sex. I don't want to talk about it!" Sophie exclaimed, turning to study the opposite wall.

"Okay. Well, you don't have to go out with him any more if you don't want to," June assured her, putting her arms around her in a comforting hug. Sophie sniffed for a few more minutes and then blew her nose hard, gathered up all the tissues and threw them in the bin.

"There!" she declared, pouting a little. "That's Jason, too – binned!" She smiled and took a deep breath. She stood up and walked over to sit down at her dressing-table mirror. The dressing table was white and ornate and she had all sorts of creams and cosmetics spread all over it. June had always envied her this room and everything in it. Sophie was an only child and usually got whatever she wanted – and everything June wanted, too.

"Are you going to keep seeing that Mickey?" Sophie asked, watching her friend's reaction in the mirror.

"Yes, I think so. Why shouldn't I?" June asked, sounding a little defensive.

"I think those two are both as bad as each other," Sophie stated.

"Oh, Mickey's okay, really," June answered. "You just have to know how to handle him."

"Is that right?" Sophie asked in a strange tone of voice. As June looked at her, her mobile phone rang. It was Mickey.

"Is that him?" asked Sophie.

"Yes, it is."

"Better answer it then," Sophie advised sarcastically. "Best not to upset him, isn't it?"

"I'll just take it outside," June muttered, jumping off the bed and leaving the room. She ran downstairs and sat down on the second-bottom step. She opened her phone and said 'Hello?' rather uncertainly.

"I've been calling you all morning," Mickey said testily.

"I know. I was a bit busy. I've been trying to get hold of Sophie for ages. I've spoken to her now. She says she's not getting back with Mickey."

There was a short silence.

"Fair enough. Just as long as you don't go dumping me because of those two idiots," Mickey said, a pleading note coming into his voice to soften the words.

"Don't be silly, Mickey. It's got nothing to do with us, has it? Will I see you tonight then – or tomorrow?" June asked, biting her bottom lip and hoping he would say tomorrow.

"Tomorrow, I think. Give everyone time to calm down, eh?" he suggested.

"Fine. I'll see you then," she said and ended the call. She called out upstairs to Sophie and said she was going back home.

She walked home again very slowly, wondering why she felt so uneasy. She and Mickey were fine, weren't they? If Sophie and Jason had a problem, that was their business. It had nothing to do with her and Mickey. She could end things with him any time she liked, she reminded herself. They weren't joined at the hip. They were exclusive but not serious, as far as she was concerned. She would just relax and take things as they came. As soon as she wasn't having fun any more, she would end it. Simple. No problem. But as she walked along the street, Sophie's jibe kept coming back into her head. "Best not to upset him, isn't it?" she'd said, giving June a knowing look at the same time. June straightened her shoulders and walked on, dismissing Sophie's attitude as being the result of her emotional state after splitting up with Jason.

7 SET UP

Whilst all this turmoil was taking place in June's life, Belinda was happier than she had ever been before, and this was mainly due to her blossoming friendship with Melissa. She felt as though she had known her all her life and that they had always been friends. Only the other day Melissa had told her, rather shyly, that she was her best friend ever. Belinda had hugged her and said that she couldn't think of anyone she'd rather be best mates with.

She was thinking of this as she got herself ready for work on a bright, sunny day in May, shortly after Sophie had finished with Jason. As she got dressed after her shower, she glanced across at her sister, who had obviously had a restless night again as her bedclothes were in disarray. Belinda frowned slightly. June hadn't been her usual chirpy self lately, and Belinda suspected this was because of that boyfriend of hers. *Men!* she thought, rolling her eyes upwards in exasperation. Sometimes she found herself actually wishing that she was a lesbian, because males seemed to cause women nothing but trouble, as far as she could see. Then she thought about her parents' very happy marriage and decided it was just a matter of steering clear of the wrong type of man. April's boyfriend Scott came into her head then, as he often did, but she shook her head and pushed the thought away. She'd become quite adept at ignoring him, both mentally and physically. She still tried to avoid running into him as much as possible. Seeing him always unsettled her, although he never actually said or did anything to annoy her; he just managed to make her feel dissatisfied and restless, the way she imagined she would feel if she were trying to give up smoking or something.

She headed off for work, humming a little tune to herself as she went along the street. It was May, the sun was shining and it would be her birthday in a few days' time. She started thinking about what she would like as a present. She would be turning 22 and would have liked to ask for a new jacket, perhaps. But she was aware of her parents' financial limitations and would be careful not to ask for anything they would find it difficult to pay for.

When she arrived at the salon, which was only a few streets away from home, her mobile began to ring just as she was opening the door. She answered it as soon as she had let go of the door. It was Melissa, who sounded bright and cheerful as usual.

"Hi, Bel!" she said gaily. They had been calling each other 'Mel' and 'Bel' for some time now.

"Got something to ask you," Mel said, sounding excited. "How would you like to come over to ours for dinner this weekend? Whatever day suits you."

"Oh, well, I don't know ... is Cameron okay about it? Won't he want to have you to himself at the weekend?" Belinda said uncertainly.

"Oh, no – he's dying to meet you. I'm always talking about you and he's curious to see what you're like. But don't worry, he won't be interrogating you or making you feel awkward or anything. He's not like that at all. Please say you'll come. We'll both be so disappointed if you don't."

"Well, okay then. Do you want me to bring anything with me – a bottle of wine or something?"

"That's brilliant, Bel. And you can bring any kind of wine you like – red or white. Gotta go. Starting work now. See you!"

Belinda smiled as she closed her phone, and then started chewing the inside of her cheek, as she sometimes did when she was mulling something over. She felt quite excited at the prospect of going to Melissa's house and meeting her family. She was sure she would feel just as comfortable around Cameron as she did around Melissa. Melissa raved about him and was obviously as much in love with him as she had been when they'd first got married, if not more. Again, the thought passed through her mind that it's obviously just a matter of finding the right man. Nothing to it, really!

She made a mental note to remember to buy some sweets for their little boy when she was picking up the wine. He was just at the age where something simple like that would make him like her. And she wanted both he and his father to like her. Also, she knew that Scott would be coming over to the Carters' to collect April on Saturday evening, as it was their regular clubbing night; so it would be a good way of avoiding being at home and having to speak to him. Perfect.

*

When that Saturday evening arrived, Belinda took a great deal longer getting ready to go out to Melissa's than she would normally have done. She lay in a deep, scented bubble bath for ages, instead of taking her usual shower, and then she took her time getting dried and smoothing some body lotion over her skin. She spent a full half-hour deciding what to wear, heaping most of her clothes onto the bed as she decided. She finally settled on a knee-length black pencil skirt and a black-and-tan patterned top that hugged her figure. She put on more make-up than usual and then started to blow-dry and straighten her hair. Her deep, tawny highlights were still looking good and by the time she was finished, she looked – and felt – really confident. She wanted to make a good impression. First impressions were lasting ones, she knew, and these people were important to her. A little frown creased her brow as she became aware that she hadn't heard Scott arriving yet. She'd been in her room for a long time and didn't feel like hanging out there any longer.

She asked herself why she should hide out in her room, anyway, and tilting her chin defiantly, she left her bedroom and went down the staircase. Just as she arrived in the downstairs hall, the doorbell chimed and she turned and opened it. She knew it was Scott before she saw him. She always knew when it was him.

She was really pleased when he stared at her and said nothing.

"Come in, Scott! How're you doing these days?" she asked coolly, stepping back to let him come in. She knew she looked really smart, and that knowledge was boosting her confidence, even around Scott, who looked good enough to eat.

"I'm fine," he told her, looking her up and down. "And don't you look great! Got a hot date tonight then?"

The smile left her face.

"You could say that!" she prevaricated, not wanting to admit that she wasn't going on a date.

"Lucky boy!" he commented, giving her a strange, thoughtful look.

"Who's a lucky boy?" April asked as she bounded down the staircase and joined the two of them in the hall.

"Well, I think that's me!" Scott answered, turning his back on Belinda and whistling softly as April sashayed down the staircase, obviously revelling in his admiration. Belinda reached up to the peg nearest her and grabbed her coat. It was a rather worn, brown corduroy one that she'd had for years, but it would go well with the outfit, so she threw it round her shoulders and ran into the lounge to collect her shoulder bag. She waved a cheery goodbye to her parents and promised not to be too late home.

Scott called out a pleasant goodbye to her as she turned to leave, but she simply ignored him and rushed out of the front door, feeling rude when it slammed shut behind her. She bit her lip, then shrugged her shoulders and walked as fast as she could in her 4-inch heels towards the bus stop. He'd managed to ruffle her feathers again, as usual, and she sighed wistfully as she waited for the bus.

She'd timed it well and didn't have long to wait. It was a fairly short journey to Jordanhill, which was where Melissa and Cameron lived, and she flicked through a glossy magazine on the way. As she leafed through the colourful pages, she managed to convince herself that Scott had been totally patronising towards her that evening. Telling her she looked great, indeed. As if. As soon as April had appeared, looking like one of the girls that smiled out from the pages of the type of magazine she was now reading, Belinda had felt like a deflated balloon. Her sister was stunning and very sexy, and she knew that Scott was just saying the encouraging things he said to her because he felt sorry for her. She sniffed disdainfully and looked up in time to see her bus stop looming up immediately in front of the bus. She rang the bell, jumped up and leaped off the bus as soon as it stopped, her ankle bending over sharply as she landed on the pavement. Everyone on the bus was looking at her, so she straightened up and carried on walking as though she was fine.

The sprain didn't feel too bad at that point, but by the time she arrived at Melissa's house, it was throbbing wildly and she bit her lip in pain as she rang the doorbell. She gazed around her. The street was a quiet cul-de-sac, leafy and salubrious. She just had time to notice the house name, 'Haven', which was printed in fancy black lettering on a gold background, when the door was opened by a smiling Melissa, who hugged her happily until she realised that there was something wrong with her.

"Bel? What is it? You're white as a sheet! You're surely not nervous about meeting Cam?"

"I twisted my ankle getting off the bus," Belinda told her, screwing up her face in pain.

"Oh, no. You poor thing. Come on, lean on me and we'll get you into the lounge right away."

Cameron stood up as they entered the lounge. He blinked when he saw Melissa helping Belinda to walk.

"She's sprained her ankle, Cam. This is Belinda, by the way. And this is Mel, obviously", she added, turning back towards Belinda.

Belinda and Cameron shook hands and it was plain to see that they liked each other straight away. He went off into the kitchen to get an ice pack to put on her ankle.

"He's really nice, Mel," Belinda said quietly, trying to raise a smile. "Where's Toby?"

"Oh, he's in bed. Kids go to bed early, you know. We didn't tell him we were having company because he would've got all excited and it's hard enough trying to get him off to sleep as it is. I have to tell him at least three stories at bedtime these days!"

"Oh. I got him some sweets. Kinder Surprise and a packet of marshmallows. I'll leave them here for him," Belinda said, drawing them out of her large bag and laying them on the glass coffee table, which was of a more elaborate style than any coffee table she had ever seen before.

Cameron came back just then with the ice pack and laid it very gently over her ankle.

"Just hold it there for a while. It'll help the swelling to stay down. Ooh, are those marshmallows?" he asked as he sat down on the chair opposite the settee.

"Leave them alone, Cam — they're for Toby," Melissa said warningly.

"This is for you," Belinda said, pulling the bottle of rosé carefully out of her bag. She'd brought along a roomy leather bag because it was more discreet (not to mention safer) than a carrier bag when travelling on a bus. She'd spent nearly a tenner on the wine because she knew that Mel and Cameron were used to the finer things in life and a cheap one wouldn't do. She smiled ruefully now as she realised that they probably thought that *was* a cheap one. Mel was a director in a firm of Solicitors and she knew his salary was higher than she could even imagine earning.

Cameron grinned and stood up to put the wine into the fridge. As he turned to go the doorbell rang again, Mel and Cameron exchanged a sudden, rather guilty look. Belinda frowned as soon as the penny dropped and she understood the reason behind the look.

"Mel, you didn't! Look at the state of me."

"You look fine, Belinda. It'll be just fine, you'll see. Jim's nice, too. He works beside me and we get on great – and he's Cam's best mate. That speaks for itself."

"You set me up, Mel. I'm going to kill you as soon as I can stand up!" Belinda threatened lamely.

"Belinda, this is Jim," Cameron announced, introducing an attractive young man to her. He was tall, with dark hair and a rugged, friendly face. He treated her to a big grin as they shook hands and then looked concerned as he noticed the ice-pack on her ankle.

"Hi, Jim. Pleased to meet you," was all Belinda could manage at that point. She put her head back against the deep cushioning of the plush purple settee and closed her eyes. The ice-pack fell from her grasp. This was all she needed, she thought. He seemed very nice, but there was one major problem. He reminded her of someone else. She groaned as Scott's face swam before her eyes. Melissa lifted the ice-pack and held it round her ankle again. Belinda knew she was trying to make amends for her deception, but it was going to take a great deal more than that to placate her now – a great deal more.

8 COMPLICATIONS

Belinda's first evening at Melissa and Cameron's house proved to be interesting, relaxing and a lot of fun – despite the pain of her sore ankle. Both the wine and the conversation flowed freely and the meal was delicious. *I should have guessed Mel would have to be a great cook, too!* Belinda thought, smiling to herself. She also found Jim to be easy company, as well as entertaining. As the evening wore on, they all became a little merry and their talk, as well as the background music, became louder. They stood up to leave the dinner table in the large, ultra-modern dining area and trooped back into the lounge. Jim smiled at Belinda and sat down very close to her.

"A pity we can't all have a bit of a dance, as Belinda's got a bad ankle," Cameron remarked, looking wistfully at his wife.

"Don't mind me – you two go right ahead!" Belinda told him.

Just then the lounge door opened and a little boy in a cute little royal blue dressing gown stood there rubbing his eyes and clutching a very battered-looking teddy bear, which Belinda later discovered was called 'Little Ted'. His curly fair hair was tousled and he had the biggest blue eyes Belinda had ever seen. She smiled at him, but he only stared at her with sleepy eyes and stuck his thumb into his mouth.

"Toby, come and meet Belinda," Melissa said, scooping him up into her arms and walking over to the settee. But shyness overcame him and he turned his face into his mother's chest and refused to budge.

"Just leave him, Mel. He'll come round in his own time," Cam advised calmly.

Melissa nodded and sat down beside Jim, smiling indulgently at her son and handing him the Kinder Surprise. Belinda was surprised to see a sudden, intense expression of sadness pass across Jim's face. But it was gone again in an instant, making her wonder if she had simply imagined it.

"Time you were back in your bed, young man," Cameron said a few moments later. He lifted Toby gently out of his wife's arms and carted him off upstairs.

"He's lovely, Mel," Belinda said softly, and then felt herself begin to yawn. "Oh dear, I think it's past *my* bedtime, too! Best get a taxi ordered," she said, drawing her mobile phone out from the extensive interior of her now half-empty bag.

The taxi arrived just as Cameron came back downstairs, having settled Toby off to sleep again.

"I'll give you a hand to get into the taxi, Belinda," Jim told her. "Can't have you hobbling along the path in that state!"

"Oh, there's no need to do that –" Belinda started to say, but he took hold of her arm gently but firmly.

"I insist," he told her, helping her to put on her jacket and walking her towards the door with his arm about her waist.

"In fact, I'll share the taxi with you, as I don't live all that far away from you," he told her. "Didn't want to drive tonight as I knew we'd be having a few drinks."

She blinked and nodded as she leaned on him for support on the short walk out to the cab.

Cameron had joined Melissa to wave their guests off at the front door. She was beaming from ear to ear, having easily achieved the whole objective of the evening.

"Aren't we clever?" she said smugly to her husband, who stood behind her and enveloped her in his arms, shaking his head gently.

"They seemed to get on very well," he admitted cautiously.

"I just knew they would," she agreed effusively.

They waved again as the cab drove off and then closed the door very quietly so as not to wake Toby.

"I know a perfect way to round off the evening," Cameron murmured suggestively, holding his wife so close she could hardly breathe.

*

Jim was very quiet on the journey home and Belinda wondered what was troubling him. She thought that maybe he was put out at having been landed with a virtual stranger who was temporarily crippled.

"Aren't you getting out first?" she asked him as they passed by his street. He'd mentioned where he lived earlier on in the evening.

"No. I'll see you to your house, Belinda. That foot's really quite swollen now," he remarked.

She looked down and winced as she tried to move it a little. Just as well she wasn't going to have to hobble to work the next day, she thought.

When the taxi stopped outside her house, Jim stepped out onto the pavement before her. She groaned and bit down on her lip as the pain hit her again. It seemed it wasn't such a minor sprain after all. They stepped out onto the pavement, Jim paid the driver and then put one arm around Belinda's waist, lifted her off her feet and carried her the few steps between the pavement and her front door. She noticed an upstairs curtain twitching at April's window and wondered what her sister would make of the scene. She groaned as she tried to remember where in her massive bag her door key was, but Jim didn't hesitate. He used his elbow to bang on the door and when Mr Carter opened it,

Jim shoved it wide and stepped inside the hallway with Belinda still in his arms.

Mr Carter stood back in shock and began to frown as Jim carried Belinda through to the lounge and laid her down on the settee, arranging the cushions under her foot for support. His wife had gone off to bed a little while earlier with a headache. She had given him strict instructions to wait up till Belinda came home.

"Who are *you* and what's the matter with Belinda?" Pete asked sharply, now that he had recovered from his initial surprise.

"Dad, I can speak for myself, you know. It's only my ankle that's injured," Belinda informed him.

"Just a bit of a sprain," Jim told her father, giving him a pleasant smile and extending his arm to shake the older man's hand.

"He's Cameron's friend," Belinda explained, closing her eyes wearily. The pain was taking its toll now and she just wanted to go to bed and get some sleep.

"I'll be off now, Belinda," Jim told her, dropping a comforting little kiss on her forehead as he turned to leave.

"Goodnight," he said to both Belinda and her father.

They said goodnight and thanks to him in unison and Mr Carter saw him out of the house.

"Have we got any Paracetamol?" Belinda asked in a pathetic little voice, her eyes still closed.

The deep voice that answered her wasn't her father's. Scott had come downstairs and was bending over the back of the settee with a concerned look on his face.

"What's happened? How did you hurt yourself?"

Her eyes flew open and she jumped. The movement made her groan, but she became instantly silent as Scott quickly moved round to the front of the settee and bent down to examine her ankle. He was probably being extremely professional, she told herself, but it didn't feel like that to her. His touch was deeply soothing and sensual at the same time. It felt more like a caress than an examination.

"She twisted it jumping off the bus," her father supplied, as his daughter seemed to have been temporarily struck dumb.

Scott nodded when he finished examining her and said it was a simple sprain, but that she must stay off her feet for a few days otherwise there could be complications and it would take much longer to heal.

Tell me about it! Belinda thought in consternation. Her life was getting quite full of complications these days.

"You get off to your bed, Mr Carter," Scott suggested. "Don't worry, I'll see to Belinda before I leave."

"Thanks, Scott," Pete Carter replied as he smiled and patted Belinda's arm. He blew her a fatherly kiss as he left the room.

Belinda made herself take a few deep, calming breaths as she waited for Scott to re-appear from the kitchen, where he had gone to fetch some painkillers. He came back very quickly and held out a glass of water and two capsules to her. He had also dug out a support bandage from the First Aid box and proceeded to wrap it around her ankle, informing her that it would support her ankle whilst still allowing some movement.

While she was wondering and worrying about how she would get upstairs to bed, Scott screwed up his eyes and spoke.

"So, who's the Sir Galahad then?" he asked, a slight edge to his voice.

"That was Jim," she told him. "Not that it's any of your business anyway. And why are you calling him that?"

"I saw him carrying you when I looked out the window."

"It's a lot sorer than it was before. It wasn't too bad earlier on, just after I did it."

He nodded. "That's quite normal. You shouldn't walk on it tomorrow. And take things easy for a few days after that,"

"Right, doctor, I'll do that," she said sarcastically. It occurred to her that she should have been thanking him and instead she was being difficult, like a petulant child. He must think she was so immature.

Without warning, he lifted her up and carried her all the way up the staircase. He took her directly into her room and deposited her unceremoniously on top of her bed.

"How did you know where my room was?" she asked waspishly.

"I know which one's April's and I've seen your mother coming out of your parents' room before," he replied tersely. He was beginning to take umbrage at her tone now and turned away abruptly.

"Remember my instructions!" he said stiffly as he left the room.

She heard the front door bang loudly behind him a few seconds later. She was rattled. He had managed to get under her skin again. *Instructions indeed! I'll give him instructions!* she fumed. She raised her head to start pulling off her clothes when April came into the room.

"What's all the fuss about?" she asked, looking at her sister in irritation. "Scott left without even saying goodbye to me!" she complained, obviously implying that this was Belinda's fault.

"I sprained my ankle, that's all," Belinda told her quietly. "Nothing to worry about."

April flounced back off to her bedroom and grabbed her mobile. She wasn't pleased at the way Scott had abruptly left her and she was about to let him know it in no uncertain terms.

Meanwhile, Belinda hauled off her shoes and as many of her clothes as she could manage and drew her duvet tightly around her for comfort. June turned round in her bed and opened one eye.

"Belinda, what's all the racket?"

"Nothing, Junie. I've just sprained my ankle, that's all. Go back to sleep."

Belinda sighed. She felt exhausted by then and it was just as well, otherwise she might never have managed to sleep that night at all.

9 PATIENTS

The following morning, Elspeth Carter woke Belinda with little tap on her bedroom door, and then came into the room holding a tray of food in front of her. She spoke softly to her daughter.

"Belinda, I brought you up some breakfast so you don't have to come down the stairs for it. Sit up, love, so I can put the tray on your knees."

Belinda yawned and stretched and then said "aw, aw!" when her ankle reacted to the sudden movement.

"Thanks, Mum, this is great! I should twist my ankle more often, I think," she remarked, smiling when her mother began to frown.

"Don't you dare. It's no joke, you know. The novelty will wear off soon enough and you'll wish you'd been more careful," her mum warned. "I've told you about those silly high heels before ..."

Belinda smiled and took a long drink from the cup of strong tea. When she began to eat her boiled egg and toast, her mum left the room. Belinda enjoyed her meal but very soon felt she must get to the toilet before she disgraced herself. She pushed the tray towards the bottom of the bed and threw back the duvet. But as soon as she tried to stand up, the sore ankle delivered a sharp bolt of pain all the way up her leg.

"Belinda, are you okay?" June asked her when she heard the sharp intake of breath.

"I think I'm going to need a hand to get to the loo," Belinda answered.

June sprang out of bed and ran over to help her. Belinda felt silly having to lean on her younger sister just to get to the toilet and she decided to go straight back to bed as soon as she'd emptied her bladder, instead of trying to get dressed, as she'd originally intended. She was still wearing her underwear from the previous night, so when they returned from the bathroom June brought her a nightie and then went off downstairs.

Belinda sighed as she lay back down after getting changed and gazed out of the window at the spring sunshine. It was going to be a long day, she realised, and she wasn't even sure if she would be able to get to her work the next day. She'd never had a sprained ankle before and wasn't used to being anything other than very active during the day.

Her mother put her head round the door a couple of hours later and asked her if there was anything she could get for her.

"Maybe a book to read, Mum. I'm getting really bored doing nothing," she replied.

Her mother fetched her one of her own books, as Belinda didn't have any unread novels of her own at that time. It was lightweight romantic fiction and Belinda had to stop herself from pouting as she wasn't fond of that type of story.

"Thanks, Mum," she said half-heartedly.

She lay back down and stared at the ceiling for a while and then sat up again and opened the book, as she felt it would be preferable to doing nothing at all.

She listened enviously as she heard April stirring and then running swiftly downstairs. Shortly afterwards, she heard the front door opening and closing and June's voice saying goodbye, so she assumed that was her leaving to go and see Mickey or

Sophie. She sighed again. She was beginning to think her mother was right – this arrangement was becoming very tedious already.

Just then her mother reappeared, holding the house phone in her hand.

"It's a young man for you," she told her, holding the phone out to her. "I think he said his name was Jim," she added, with a little smile.

Belinda took the phone and was pleased to hear Jim's voice on the other end of the line. He told her Melissa had given him her number and asked her how she was doing. She told him she was going to be staying in bed for the day as her foot was really sore when she put any weight on it.

"I'm thinking of coming over to see you, if that's okay with you?" he asked tentatively.

"Of course it's okay!" she told him. "That would be really nice, but don't feel obliged to."

"Great. I'll head over now, then. See you shortly."

"Bye," Belinda said, pressing the button to end the call. At least she would have someone to talk to for a while, she thought.

Some time later, when her mum came back upstairs to retrieve the phone handset, Belinda asked her to give her a cardigan to put round her shoulders, as her nightie wasn't quite enough cover when she was having men visiting her. Her mum had just finished putting the lightweight cardigan over her daughter's shoulders when there was a light tap on the bedroom door.

"Is it okay to come in?" Jim asked through the door.

Mrs Carter crossed over and opened the door for him. She introduced herself to the young man and then closed the door behind her as she went downstairs again.

Jim held out a bunch of daffodils to her and Belinda reached up to take them happily.

"Oh, that was so nice of you. You didn't have to do that. Honestly, I'm just fine!" she protested.

"Yeah, I know, but it's no fun being stuck in bed with something like that. I know – I had enough football injuries when I was younger. I remember that frustrated feeling very well. So I just thought I'd come by and try and cheer you up a bit," he said, drawing a wooden chair over beside the bed.

"You've cheered me up already!" she assured him. "Now, tell me about all these injuries you got playing football."

She settled down to listen to him recalling his childhood and adolescent mishaps and soon forgot that they were practically strangers. He was very easy company and quickly had her laughing at the pictures he was painting of him lying in bed with a glum face and a plaster cast on his leg while his mates were all outdoors having fun.

They were suddenly interrupted by a now-familiar, deep voice. "Your Mum told me just to come on up," Scott announced from the open doorway.

Belinda froze and looked annoyed. Scott looked round to see who this man was who felt comfortable with coming into Belinda's bedroom and sitting chatting to her.

"Hope you don't mind," Scott said. "Just checking in to see how you're doing,"

Belinda looked as if she did mind, Jim thought. She wasn't saying anything and certainly didn't seem inclined to introduce them, so he stood up and held out his hand.

"Jim Doyle. Pleased to meet you!"

"Hi, Jim. I'm Doctor Walker," Scott replied, shaking his hand.

Jim raised his eyebrows.

"Don't think there's anything seriously amiss, doc," Jim said, a little smile twitching at the corners of his mouth.

"Let's have a look then, Belinda," Scott said, completely ignoring Jim's comment and using his best business-like tone.

"It's fine. It's getting better," Belinda told him grumpily, then said "Ouch" deliberately when he very gently held her ankle.

"Will I be able to go to work tomorrow?" she asked, beginning to feel anxious.

"No way. You need to stay off that foot and keep it elevated for a few days," he told her.

"What! A few days! I can't be doing with that," she complained.

"You'll just have to, unless you want to make it worse and stay off work for weeks," he said firmly.

"But it's so boring lying down all the time."

"That's tough. You don't look too bored at the moment anyway," he commented, glancing at Jim as he did so.

She frowned, wondering why Jim being there should annoy him.

"You'll just have to be patient," Scott told her, standing up again and heading towards the door. "That's what people have to do when they need time to recuperate. That's why they're called patients – because they have to be patient," he added unnecessarily as he left the room, glaring a little at Jim as he did so.

"He's such an asshole!" Belinda affirmed, blowing out a deep breath after he'd closed the door.

"He didn't seem very cool and professional, did he? No bedside manner. In fact, he was a bit tetchy, really," Jim remarked.

"He's not my doctor – he's April's boyfriend," she told him.

He raised an eyebrow but said nothing. The tension hadn't escaped him and he wondered what was causing the undercurrent.

After Jim had left, Belinda lay and thought about him and about how nice he was and she also thought about Scott. She knew he was still angry with her because she had been rude and ungrateful when he was trying to look after her. She closed her eyes as she remembered how it had felt when he'd examined her foot. She was really worried now. Her feelings for him weren't going away; in fact, they were getting worse. And she was behaving like an idiot. What she needed to do was to keep away from him as much as possible and she decided the best way to do that was to start seeing Jim. He couldn't be any nicer and they already had something in common – they were both stuck on someone else, someone who didn't belong to them and never would. Her decision made, she smiled as her mother came through the door with the tray again.

"Well, you look much happier, love. Has that young man cheered you up then?" she asked hopefully.

"Yes, Mum, he has," was her reply.

"And will we be seeing him again soon?" her mum enquired.

"You bet," Belinda said, taking the tray onto her lap and tucking into homemade soup and cheese sandwiches.

*

Later that evening, as Scott and April arrived back at his flat after their date, she asked him what was bothering him as soon as they got inside.

"You've been quiet all night," April accused him. "Come on, spit it out."

He shrugged. "Sorry, April. It's just your sister – Belinda, I mean. I've always tried to be nice to her and she's just always 'off' with me, you know? Last night I was trying to help her because she'd hurt her foot and she spoke to me like it was my fault or something. What gives with her anyway?"

"Oh, don't worry about her. She's always been a stroppy mare. She's probably just jealous," April replied, snuggling in against him and nuzzling his ear.

"Jealous? What do you mean? She's got her own boyfriend – Sir Galahad. Why would she be jealous of you?"

"Well, he's not in the same league as you, Scott, is he? And I'm fed up talking about my sister now. Why don't we slip into something more comfortable, eh – like that big bed of yours?"

They went off into the bedroom together. The conversation was over as far as April was concerned, but Scott still seemed to be brooding. She frowned as she began to wonder if he was cooling off towards her. He didn't seem to be in much of a hurry to get her into bed.

Then, a few minutes later, he surprised her by leaping up into a sitting position and asking her if she'd consider moving in with him.

She grabbed hold of him and started kissing him passionately. He pulled away for a second, looking at her in amusement.

"I'll take that as a 'yes' then!" he said, laughing, and drew the duvet up over their heads.

10 CHANGES

Belinda stayed off her work for nearly a week. Her ankle felt much better when she was lying down or sitting up in bed, but as soon as she put any weight on it, she was in pain and couldn't imagine herself jumping on and off buses or walking to the salon just yet. She could just about manage to haul herself down the staircase and lie on the settee. Her mum was wonderful, as always, and Belinda didn't have to lift a finger, but it was very frustrating wanting to get back to work and not being able to. If she could have helped around the house it would have passed the time a little better for her, but as it was, she was doing a lot of reading and watching television. She had never realised before just how boring daytime TV could become in a very short space of time. A day or two was a novelty, but any longer than that and it only made her long to be out of doors again.

Luckily, Jim had been coming to see her every day since she had been off work, and she had begun to look forward to his visits. The more they talked the more she liked him and enjoyed his company. He was a helpful, dependable type of person with a quick sense of humour and she was very glad of his company during her brief confinement at home.

Scott hadn't been to see her again since he had examined her and given her advice on her ankle. She knew he was still angry with her for being so rude to him and it bothered her that he was annoyed with her. She kept telling herself that it was better that way, given her infatuation with him, but she was finding it difficult to convince herself that it was for the best. She was thinking about this when Jim came to the door on Friday evening. Her mum answered it and went discreetly back into the kitchen while he came through to the lounge to see her. She smiled at him and dragged her thoughts away from Scott. She felt twinges of guilt towards Jim because he was being so kind and attentive and she was thinking of someone else. Because of this she gave him a very warm, welcoming smile when he sat down in the armchair.

"Well, someone's feeling better, I see!" he said, smiling back at her and handing her a box of Belgian chocolates.

"Oh, thanks, Jim. And yes, I am feeling better now. In fact, I think I might go back to work on Monday," Belinda told him brightly.

"That's great. Well then, I hope you'll be well enough to go out for a meal with me next weekend, seeing as you're having to spend your birthday cooped up indoors!"

"Thanks, Jim. That would be really nice," Belinda replied. "Where were you thinking of?"

"Um, what kind of food do you like best? Indian, Chinese, Italian ..."

"Oh, Chinese, I think. Love their curries – and the sweet & sour!"

"Chinese it is then. It's a date. And I'll come and pick you up. Don't want you hobbling about trying to get into the centre of town on your own."

"I'm sure I'll be just fine by that time," she assured him.

"Well, we won't take any chances anyway," he said.

He was always so kind to her and she was very hopeful that she would start thinking about him more often and would become emotionally involved with him. He was just the sort of man she'd always wanted to meet. She smiled up at him as he bent over her to adjust her cushions and then there was a polite cough behind them. Predictably, It was Scott.

"Ah, Dr Walker! The patient's doing much better now. She's been following your advice and resting most of the time," Jim told him.

Belinda looked at the fireplace so that she wouldn't have to see his face.

"I'm going back to work on Monday," she told him belligerently, her chin coming up in case he would try to argue with her.

"That's good. I'm glad you're feeling better," he said politely, giving her ankle a cursory inspection. "It's looking much better," he added, but he sounded crisp and professional and she knew he was still annoyed with her. She refused to meet his eyes and looked at Jim again instead.

April came breezing through the lounge door at that point and moved up close to Scott.

"Did he tell you our news?" she asked, well aware that he had done no such thing.

Belinda's stomach dropped and she held her breath as she looked at April enquiringly and waited for her next words.

"Scott's asked me move in with him and I've said yes!" April announced, sliding her arm through Scott's and smiling contentedly. It pleased her to see Belinda struggling to raise a smile herself. She liked to make people envious of her and Belinda was so obviously smitten.

Mrs Carter had come into the room just as April made her announcement and she stopped in her tracks and gasped.

"April, you never said a word! You should have told me before," she chided. However, she looked extremely pleased with the news.

"We only decided the other day," Scott said quietly. He still wasn't exactly sure why he had asked April to live with him, but it wasn't a lifelong commitment, he reminded himself; it was just a temporary measure and nothing had been decided yet about the future.

April drew Scott away towards the door and Mrs Carter went to the front door to wave them off.

"Well, I wasn't expecting that!" Elspeth said to both Belinda and Jim when she came back into the lounge.

"No, neither was I," Belinda murmured.

"I don't know what your dad'll say, though," Elspeth muttered. "He's not a fan of the modern way of doing things back to front, so to speak. I think he'd have preferred them to wait and then get engaged in a few months' time."

Belinda closed her eyes.

"Are you okay, Belinda?" Jim asked her. He was frowning and there was a thoughtful look on his face.

"Yes, of course. Just a bit tired, that's all," she answered quietly.

"I'll be going then and let you get some peace to rest," he said, standing up and blowing her a kiss as he left.

When Mrs Carter came back into the lounge she started to speak to Belinda about the new turn of events, but then her husband arrived home and she went into the kitchen to put out his evening meal. Belinda hauled herself up off the settee and said goodnight to her father. She didn't want to go back to her bedroom just yet, but she also didn't want to sit and listen to her mother and father discussing Scott and April's news.

"It's a bit early for bed, love, is it not?" Mr Carter asked.

"I've got some reading I want to do," she told him, looking away from him. "Jim brought me a new book and it looks really good," she fibbed. "See you in the morning."

"Night then, love. See you tomorrow," her parents called as she went slowly off up the staircase.

*

Belinda lay on top of her bed for a long time, just staring at the ceiling. She watched a large spider making its way across the white space. Normally she would have jumped off the bed in case it landed on her, but instead she simply followed it with her eyes until it disappeared from view.

When she started to feel chilled, she got undressed and went inside the bed, drawing the duvet up around her for warmth and comfort. When she heard June climbing the staircase, she turned her face towards the window wall and closed her eyes, pretending to be asleep. The last thing she wanted was an animated conversation about Scott and April. She gave herself a good mental shake and promised herself that she would pull herself together in the morning and try to face the facts without feeling jealous or resentful. Scott was her sister's man and Jim was hers. That was the way it was and she would just have to get used to it.

She was glad that June didn't speak to her and didn't seem to have any intention of talking at all. June was always quiet these days compared to her usual self, Belinda mused, and wondered if there was any particular reason for that. She made up her mind to ask her the next morning if everything was all right with her. That would help to take her mind off her other sister, too, she reasoned. She fell asleep trying to think ahead to her date with Jim and look forward to it as much as she could. However, she wasn't very successful. Instead, she found herself thinking that it was time she apologised to Scott for always being so unpleasant to him. She didn't like the bad feeling between them and she decided that she wanted to make things right with him. If he was serious about her sister, then it was up to her to let him see that she didn't have a problem with them as an item and that she was pleased that April was moving in with him.

11 I KNOW WHERE YOU LIVE

The following morning, June was already downstairs before Belinda had even woken up, and she went outside for a walk before she could even think about breakfast. The weather was cloudy but dry and she put her hands in her jacket pockets and walked with her head down for some time. Her head was muggy and she felt tired. These evenings with Mickey were really beginning to take their toll on her. He drank a lot and expected her to keep up with him. Also, she suspected he had begun spiking her drinks with something. She wasn't happy about these things and had wanted to finish with him for some time. *So what's stopping you?* she asked herself. For some reason she just couldn't bring herself to do it. She knew that he would be really upset when she told him and she was conscious that she was putting off the confrontation instead of facing up to it and following her very strong inclination to end the relationship.

As she retraced her steps and walked back towards home, she at last arrived at a decision. She had decided that she would end things with him that very night. There was no reason to put it off any longer. She was going to have to do it some time, so it might as well be now. She lifted her head and took a deep breath. She felt a little better for having made her decision, but she still had to go through with it and tell him. She bit her lip apprehensively. She knew that he could be quite unpleasant when thwarted.

When she went back into the house, Belinda was sitting on the settee and wasn't really looking much happier than June was feeling.

"Junie, is everything okay with you?" Belinda asked.

There was no one else in the room, so June decided to confide in her. She sighed heavily.

"I've decided to finish things with Mickey tonight," she answered.

"Oh, I see. I thought you weren't looking very happy lately," Belinda said.

June shrugged. "I'll either do it tonight or tomorrow – whatever."

"Best to get it over with if you've made up your mind," Belinda advised.

"Yeah, I suppose," June agreed.

She took herself off upstairs and Belinda frowned. She wondered why June looked so worried and she also thought her sister didn't look very well either. She wondered if perhaps there was more to this relationship with Mickey than met the eye. Was he putting some kind of pressure on her or something? She didn't know if they were sleeping together or not, and she made up her mind to keep a closer eye on her little sister in future.

*

Later that day, after a poor attempt at eating the food her mother put out at teatime, June threw her jacket on and left the house to go round to Mickey's. She became steadily more nervous as she approached his flat. She hoped Jason was out and she decided that she would only finish things with Mickey if Jason wasn't there. She didn't want them ganging up on her. Jason answered the door when she knocked, but he was wearing a scruffy-looking, faded denim jacket and he left the house as she went in. He shouted to Mickey that she was here and she moved past him into the hallway. The front door slammed behind him and June went into the lounge to look for Mickey.

She found him sitting on the sofa smoking, drinking and watching TV. She was feeling tense and it annoyed her that he hadn't even got up off the sofa to come and meet her when she arrived.

"What's up with *your* face?" he asked her as she sat down heavily beside him.

She glared at him. Her temper was roused now and she decided to simply get it over with.

"We need to talk, Mickey. I've had enough of this," she began, watching his face to see his reaction.

He said nothing but drew slowly and thoughtfully on his cigarette.

"This isn't working!" she said irritably. "I'm fed up of it and I think it's time to call it a day."

He stubbed out his cigarette and turned towards her.

"I told you before – it's over when I say it's over."

"Don't be stupid, Mickey; you can't make me stay with you!" she yelled at him, standing up to leave.

"You just watch me!" he yelled back. He stood up and grabbed her arm. She tried to pull it away, but he held her even tighter. He was really hurting her arm and she tried again to get away from him. He balled his hand into a fist and punched her in the stomach. When she doubled up he yanked her back down onto the sofa and put his arm tightly around her shoulders.

"Do we understand each other a little better now?" he asked quietly, whispering directly into her ear.

She was too winded and too afraid to speak, so she simply nodded.

"Good," he said. He let go of her and got up to pour two glasses of cider for them. This time he didn't even bother to hide the fact that he was putting something into hers.

She didn't even consider arguing with him again that evening. She knew there was no point. She was an intelligent girl and she knew what he was doing. He was trying to intimidate her so that he could control her. She kept still and quietly drank what he gave her. She had decided to simply pretend she was co-operating with him and would tell her parents what he was doing to her as soon as she got home. There was no way she was going to let him get away with treating her like this. And as the evening wore on, anger was, slowly but surely, beginning to take the place of fear.

*

June went through the remainder of that evening like an automaton. She said very little and Mickey said even less. At eleven o'clock she said tentatively that she should be getting off home, and he turned towards her and asked her why she didn't just go then. She stood up unsteadily and pulled her jacket off the back of the sofa. She was surprised when Mickey also stood up and walked to the front door. He opened it, but then he turned to face her directly, his eyes narrowing as he spoke.

"Remember what I told you, June. You're my girl and I say when it's over. And remember this as well – I know where you – and your lovely family – live."

The threat in his voice was unmistakable and she stared at him in horror. He had the nerve to threaten her family now! She was beginning to feel sick and she ducked past him and stepped outside into the cold night air.

"Bye now!" he called out, laughing as he watched her run out into the street.

"I'll ring you," he added sneeringly when she turned round to glare at him. She walked as fast as her unsteady legs would take her. When she was round the corner and out of sight she bent over and threw up into some long grass. A man and woman who were walking along the pavement looked disapprovingly at her and shook their heads in disgust as they passed her. She closed her eyes and carried on with her miserable journey home.

*

Mr Carter had gone to bed earlier in the evening, but June's mum was still waiting up for her to come back home. When she quietly opened the front door, Elspeth ran into the hallway.

"June, where on earth have you been till this hour?" she asked, anxiety making her sound angrier than she actually was.

"Just over at Mickey's place," June answered, looking away from her mum's searching gaze. "I'm off to bed. I'm knackered."

"Just a minute, love. Are you all right? You look awful," Elspeth said, frowning.

"I'm fine, Mum. Don't fuss. It's late and I just want to go to bed."

"Well, we'll talk in the morning then," her mother said firmly.

"Okay. See you in the morning," June said, climbing the staircase carefully on her still-shaky legs.

Her mother watched her with anxious eyes. She sighed heavily and switched off the lights. She had been very tired and ready to go to bed herself for quite some time.

Upstairs, in the bedroom, Belinda sat up in bed and switched the bedside lamp on when her sister came into the room.

"June, is everything okay? You're awful late." Belinda mumbled, rubbing her eyes sleepily.

"Yeah, fine, Belinda. I'm going to bed now," June told her, trying to sound as normal as possible.

"Oh, all right then. See you tomorrow," Belinda replied. She felt relieved that June was home safely, but she also felt quite sure that all was not well with her sister, and she had no intention of being fobbed off quite so easily in the morning.

12 MOVING ON

In the morning, however, Belinda found it very difficult to pin June down long enough to quiz her about what had happened with Mickey. She had the distinct feeling her sister was deliberately avoiding her. During the week that followed, June seemed to have to go out a lot during the day and was still going round to Mickey's place of an evening.

Belinda kept telling herself it was just teenage relationship stuff and it would probably sort itself out, but still she couldn't help worrying. When Friday arrived, her sore ankle was almost back to normal again and by late afternoon she was busying herself getting ready to go out with Jim. She had decided to wear her new green top over black trousers, but unfortunately the sight of it instantly reminded her of Scott's reaction when she'd first worn it, and so she opened her wardrobe door again to choose something else. She sighed and drew out a cobalt blue fine woollen top instead. It was a long-line top with a cowl neckline and she always felt good when she wore it. As she drew it over her head, she heard Scott arriving at the house to pick up April. She frowned and muttered to herself whilst she rummaged about in her jewellery box for a silver pendant and silver hoop earrings to go with her outfit. She could hear her mother speaking to Scott in the hallway.

"Scott, love, I don't think April's quite ready for you yet, but I'll give her a shout," she was saying. "You know, I'll soon just be making dinner for two in the evenings at this rate!" she added.

"Oh, how come?" Scott asked.

"Well, both April and Belinda are going out tonight, and I think June will probably go out as well. She usually does."

Scott nodded in reply and Mrs Carter went into the hallway to call up the staircase to April. Scott sat down on the three-seater sofa and drummed his fingers impatiently on the arm while he considered what Mrs Carter had said. He assumed Belinda was still seeing that Jim guy, because she couldn't have met anyone new while she'd been at home recovering from her sprained ankle. He shrugged his shoulders. It was none of his business and Jim seemed to be a decent bloke. April was constantly asking him now when she could move in with him and he was running out of excuses to ward off the actual event, even though it had been his suggestion in the first place. He frowned to himself as he wondered, not for the first time, why he was putting it off.

Belinda appeared in the lounge at that moment and his eyebrows shot up as she walked round to the front of the sofa and sat down beside him. He had intended asking her how her ankle was now, but instead he commented on her appearance – again.

"Hey, you look great!" he told her. "That colour really suits you."

"You said that about the green," she reminded him.

"I think it's your hair colour – it goes with everything," he concluded, tilting his head to the side so that he could consider her more carefully.

She took a deep breath and licked her lips.

"I wanted to speak to you actually, Scott," she began, feeling her face flushing a little. "I know I've been a bit short with you a couple of times, and I wanted to apologise and to wish you and April the best of luck for living together and all that."

She was a little breathless by the time she had finished her little speech and neither of them had noticed April coming into the room. They were looking at each other intently and April didn't like that. However, she decided it would be best to ignore it. It's not as if Belinda was any real competition, she reminded herself.

"Hi, Scott, honey!" she said cheerily, bending over the back of the settee and kissing him lingeringly on the lips.

Belinda looked away and was relieved to hear her mother announcing that she could see Jim arriving outside. She went into the hall cupboard to get her black jacket with the fur trim. They were going out for a meal, so she didn't want to look too casual.

"Belinda, don't run off straight away. Invite Jim in for a wee blether —" her mother began, but Belinda cut her off.

"Mum, I don't want to hang about. We've booked the table for 6 o'clock, so we'd best be off."

"But it's only 5.15," her mother pointed out.

"Won't be late back, Mum — bye!"

Belinda stuck her bag on her shoulder and walked down the outside stairs carefully. She was wearing low-heeled, black patent pumps she had bought the day before on her first expedition out of the house since her sprain. She didn't want to risk hurting her ankle again — and they would be comfortable for wearing all day at work, too.

Jim stepped out of the car, a dark blue Toyota Celica, and opened the passenger door for her. He said "Hi!" quite casually, but gave her an appreciative look and smiled warmly. She breathed a sigh of relief and sank back into the car seat. She felt conflicted about Scott and April. She didn't want her sister to move in with him, especially if their living together led eventually to marriage, but neither did she relish the thought of too many more run-ins with him. It was becoming impossible for her to behave normally around him and he wouldn't have to come to the house any more if April was staying with him. Belinda bit her lip thoughtfully and squared her shoulders. She turned towards

Jim and began to chat to him about the La Lanterna Italian restaurant they were going to in Hope Street, as she hadn't been there before.

The two of them ate an enjoyable meal together in the very pleasant atmosphere of the restaurant and chatted easily and comfortably with each other during the evening. It was the best first date she'd ever had, except for the fact that her mind would insist on wandering from time to time as vivid pictures of Scott came, unbidden, into her head.

Later in the evening, when they arrived back at her house they sat together for a while in his car and she thanked him for a lovely evening. He promptly asked her to come out with him again soon.

"I'd like that," she told him honestly. She had really enjoyed their time together.

He leaned across and kissed her warmly and firmly on the lips and she responded to his kiss, sliding her arms around his neck. He was a very nice young man and she wished once again that she could feel about him the way she felt about Scott. *Why does life have to be so complicated?* she asked herself as she walked back into the house, turning to wave to him as he drove off. She wondered why she couldn't fall for Jim the way she'd fallen for Scott. She shook her head impatiently and made up her mind to try harder in future. She also hoped it would help when April moved in with Scott. Out of sight – out of mind, as her mother would have said. However, Belinda strongly suspected that absence would only make her heart grow fonder.

*

Belinda went back to work the following Monday morning. It was great to get back into her usual routine again and during her lunch break, Melissa rang her on her mobile.

"How's your first day back at work going?" she asked excitedly, "and more to the point, how did the first date with Jim go?"

Belinda laughed and told her they had both gone well.

"You *are* seeing him again, aren't you?" Melissa asked.

"Yes, he's going to ring me soon," Belinda replied. She could almost hear Melissa mentally clapping her hands in delight.

"I knew you'd like each other!"

"Well, you were right, weren't you?" Belinda replied, feeling guilty because she knew that there was no future in it and that she wasn't really being fair to either Jim or Melissa in continuing to see him. But at the same time, she had no real reason for ending things with him so soon. He was good company and she didn't want to sit at home alone while everyone else went out on dates.

"Cam and I are going to a dinner dance in a couple of weeks," Melissa told her. "We were wondering if you and Jim would come with us. It would be more fun that way. What do you think?"

"Um – I haven't anything to wear," Belinda answered lamely.

"It'll be on the Saturday, end of the month, so it's just after your payday. Please say you'll come, Bel – it'll be great fun with the four of us there."

"Okay. I'll ask Jim what he thinks when he rings me."

Melissa gave a little squeal of delight and rang off. Belinda bit her lip. She wasn't sure how she felt about double-dating; things could get complicated that way. She was beginning to worry that she might lose Mel's friendship if things fell through with Jim. That made her think about June again as she stood up to go back through to the front of the salon. June never seemed to see much of Sophie nowadays, since the double dates had stopped, she realised. And June was looking quite unwell, too. The thought struck Belinda forcibly that perhaps her sister was pregnant and that was why she hadn't finished it with Mickey. She was horrified by that thought. She would tackle her about it that very night, she decided, as soon as she arrived home.

She did just that, as soon as she's hung up her jacket in the hallway. She called out to her mother that she was home and then went upstairs to find her sister. She went into the bedroom and stopped in her tracks. June was asleep in bed! She looked pasty-faced and had dark circles beneath her eyes. Belinda went across the room and bent over her, shaking her shoulder gently to rouse her.

June opened her eyes slowly and groaned.

"What's the matter, Junie? Are you sick?" Belinda asked.

"No, I'm okay," June answered.

"You're obviously not okay, June," Belinda said worriedly. She sat down on the side of the bed and asked her quietly if she was pregnant.

"God no, I'm not. Are you kidding?" June answered heatedly, screwing up her face and shivering at the very thought.

"Well, what is it then?" Belinda asked again, exasperation making her tone tetchy. "I thought you were going to finish with that Mickey?" she added.

"I'm just tired, that's all. Leave me alone, Belinda. Just leave me alone," June begged her, turning round to face the wall.

At a loss to know what more to say, Belinda stood up to go.

"You know you can tell me if anything's wrong, June? You do know that, don't you?" she asked.

She received a grunt in reply and she left the room, going slowly downstairs to the kitchen, where her mother was serving out the dinners.

"Did you tell June to come down?" Mrs Carter asked.

"She's a bit tired right now," Belinda replied, avoiding her mother's eyes.

"She's always tired these days!" her mother commented, muttering under her breath as she put her husband's and her daughter's plates into the oven on a low heat. She wondered if she should put June's meal into the fridge for her to reheat later, I case she didn't come down for it for a while. She tut-tutted to herself and went into the hall to shout upstairs to her. There was no response. She went back into the kitchen and sat down across from Belinda to eat her own meal.

"Well, it's lamb hotpot," she said pragmatically, "so I suppose it will reheat okay later on, if needs be. I wonder where your dad's got to. He's not usually late."

"Oh, here he is now," she said, rolling her eyes heavenwards. "But I'm going to finish my own dinner before I put his out!"

Belinda merely nodded, barely tasting the excellent casserole. She was preoccupied with wondering about June's behaviour and puzzled by a series of bumps and thumps she could hear going on upstairs.

"What on earth is all that racket?" she asked.

But when her mother spoke in reply, she had Belinda's full attention.

"Oh, that's just April, love," she told her breezily. She's packing her things. She's moving in with Scott this evening."

Belinda put down her knife and fork, her appetite suddenly deserting her altogether.

13 UNLUCKY FOR SOME

Elspeth sighed and shook her head, and her tone of voice held a note of foreboding.

"I just wish she hadn't decided on today to be moving in with Scott."

"Oh, why is that?" Belinda replied automatically. She laid her knife and fork down on her plate, sending her mum an apologetic look.

"Well, it's Friday the 13th, isn't it? Unlucky for some!"

Belinda nodded understandingly. *It certainly is,* she thought, an ache that wasn't caused by indigestion beginning to settle in her chest.

"Something wrong with your hotpot, love?" Pete Carter asked as he sat down beside Belinda at the table.

"Just a wee touch of indigestion, Dad," she lied. Standing up, she took her plate over to the bucket and scraped the leftover food into it.

She heard someone at the front door just as she was leaving the kitchen and she knew it would be Scott. She intended to skip upstairs without answering it, but her mother shouted to her to get it, so she opened the door and stood back to let him come inside.

"Is she ready?" he asked without preamble.

"Don't know. I'll go and see," she replied curtly, running upstairs and disappearing into her sister's room.

Belinda helped April to finish her packing rather than go back downstairs and get into conversation with Scott. Then she began to lug some of the bags out into the hallway.

"Oh, don't bother with that," April said gaily, shrugging her shoulders, "Scott can get those for me!"

Belinda rolled her eyes and privately thought Scott would rue the day, but she said nothing. It was his decision and, technically, it was nothing to do with her.

Her mother stood at the front door with Belinda when it was time to see the couple off, and they both waved goodbye to them. Elspeth was a little tearful when they came back indoors, so her husband gave her a hug and Belinda went into the kitchen to make a fresh pot of tea, so that she wouldn't think too much about the tangle of emotions bubbling up inside her.

*

April chattered all the way to Scott's apartment. She was in high spirits, as she always was when she was getting what she wanted. She sighed contentedly as she looked forward to twisting Scott round her little finger and not having to run everything by her mum and dad all the time. She could see Max any time she wanted now, she mused, as soon as she got used to the ins and outs of Scott's daily routine. She would have to be very careful, though. It would be a shame to upset the applecart by being careless and getting caught with her lover. She was sure it was just a matter of time before Scott would propose to her and then she could have her cake and eat it, too!

Scott drew up outside his building and started to unload the suitcases and holdalls onto the pavement.

"Jeez, April, how much stuff does one woman need?" he asked. "Did you remember to bring the kitchen sink as well?"

"As if!" April replied, sniffing disdainfully. "I need lots of accessories to complete my outfits and I need my blow drier, straighteners and crimper for my hair," she informed him, smiling as she walked up to the front door and held out her hand for the keys.

"I hope you've had a spare set made for me?" she asked.

"Haven't had time," he replied. He handed her his own keys and went back out to the pavement to collect the rest of the cases.

"I suppose I'll have to do it myself tomorrow then," she said, pouting a little. She opened the door and walked straight inside, leaving him to bring all her luggage in for her.

When he was finished he slammed the front door closed with his foot and went into the lounge to sit down for a few minutes and get his breath back. It was early days, he told himself. She was probably just feeling a bit nervous; that's why she was behaving like this.

"I got a bottle of champagne for us, to celebrate," he told her. "I'll open it in a minute. Have you had your dinner yet?"

"Yeah, I have, but a glass of bubbly would be nice," she said.

"I'll see to it while you do your unpacking," he said, standing up to go and fetch it.

"Oh, I'll maybe unpack tomorrow," she said, checking her fingernails for any little chips on her varnish. "I've already broken a nail today doing all that packing."

Scott went into the kitchen, a little frown creasing his forehead as he lifted the champagne out of the fridge and unscrewed the metal cage around the cap. It popped open with a loud bang and he was glad he had put a tea towel over the bottle to catch the cork. He could hear April laughing and he tried to smile, but he couldn't help worrying if he had done the right thing in inviting her to share his flat. They were very different from each other and he knew there would be a great deal of adjusting to be done on both sides. He filled the two glasses and walked back into the lounge, handing one of them to April, who had already switched on the television. He sat down beside her and they clinked their glasses together.

"I thought you'd maybe want to talk for a wee while, April. We've got a lot to discuss," he said.

"Like what?" she asked.

He raised his eyebrows.

"Like how things are going to be with us living together, sharing the same space. It's a lot different than dating, you know."

"Oh, I'm sure we'll be fine," she answered, turning back to the screen and flicking through the channels. "You'll hardly know I'm here," she added.

Scott very much doubted that this would be the case. He screwed his eyes up as he gulped down his drink rather more quickly than he would normally have done.

It's not permanent, he kept telling himself. *It's not permanent.*

*

Belinda was sitting in the lounge with her mum and dad, trying to focus on what her mum was saying to her.

"What?" she asked for the second time.

"Belinda, what's the matter with you?" her mum asked. "I'm saying that now that April's moved out, you can move into her room if you like. Do you want to do that?"

"Um, I'll have a think about it," Belinda replied distractedly.

"Well, I'm surprised. I thought you'd jump at the chance. It's what you've wanted for years, isn't it – to have your own room to yourself?"

Belinda didn't reply. She had been sitting nursing the same mug of half-cold tea for a long time and staring into space. Her brain seemed to be on a go-slow. She told herself she was just tired and that she really should go off to bed, but then she heard June coming through the front door.

"Is that you, Junie?" her mum called out.

"Yes," June replied. "I'm just going straight up to bed, mum. See you in the morning."

"Okay, love. Night-night."

Belinda could hear June's footsteps going slowly and heavily up the staircase.

"I worry about that girl," Elspeth said to her husband.

"The teenage years," Pete replied, shrugging. "I'm sure she's just fine."

Belinda wasn't quite so sure about that and it galvanised her into action. She hauled herself off the sofa and took her mug into the kitchen, calling out a vague "goodnight" to her parents as she did so.

When she went into the bedroom, she wasn't surprised to see her sister already lying in bed, even though she was fully clothed.

Belinda switched the light on and June groaned and turned towards the wall.

"Okay, I want to know what's going on with you, June, and don't tell me fibs because I'll know you're lying and I'll just keep asking till you tell me the truth," Belinda warned.

She sat down on the edge of June's bed and leaned over her.

June said nothing and showed no sign of turning to look at her, so Belinda laid her hand on her shoulder to pull her round to face her. June jumped and moaned, drawing away from her. She rubbed her shoulder, still keeping her face averted. Belinda's eyes rounded. She knew something was very wrong.

"Leave me alone, will you? I'm fine," June muttered irritably.

"Not till you tell me what's wrong," Belinda replied. She took hold of her shoulder again.

"Aw!" June moaned, on a sharp gasp.

Belinda pulled her sister's cardigan back from her shoulder and stared. June quickly pulled it back again, but Belinda had seen the bruises.

"It's that Mickey, isn't it? I knew something was wrong."

"I banged it on a cupboard door, that's all. It's nothing to do with Mickey," June lied, doing her best to sound convincing. She longed to confide in her sister, but was too afraid of what he would do to her family if she did. He was capable of turning very nasty. She had no doubt about that now.

Belinda pursed her lips and said nothing. She walked back over to her own bed. She knew she wasn't going to get anything out of her sister tonight, but she was determined to get to the bottom of what was going on. The whole situation puzzled her. If Mickey was treating her sister badly, why didn't she just stay away from him? What was the problem? Did he have some kind of hold over her? And if he knew that June didn't want to be with him, why was he trying to make her stay with him? It didn't make any sense.

Belinda lay a long time in the dark, considering what to do for the best. Should she tell her parents, or should she go round to see Mickey herself and have it out with him? Doing nothing was not an option. She was very angry on her little sister's behalf and had to keep taking long, deep breaths to try to steady herself. She didn't close her eyes until she had made her decision. She was going to tackle him herself. She didn't want her parents upset. Then, if she couldn't resolve the situation, she would tell her mum and dad – and the police, too, if need be. If that Mickey was bullying her sister, he couldn't be allowed to get away with it.

14 FAMILY TIES

Belinda ate her breakfast very quickly the following morning and set off early for Mickey's house. She knew roughly how to get there and vaguely remembered what the number of the house was, having been told that information some months previously. She had been careful not to ask June for those details again because she didn't want her to realise what she intended to do. She knew June was still sleeping, so there was no risk of her turning up while she was speaking to her boyfriend. Belinda wondered if she herself was simply imagining things and getting everything out of proportion; but she had to know one way or the other, so that she could stop worrying about her sister. She was quite sure that June wouldn't thank her for interfering in the relationship, but her own anxiety was getting the better of her and she just knew, deep down, that June was unhappy and was being bullied in some way by this boy.

When she turned into the street where he lived, she stopped and frowned in concentration as she struggled to remember which house number was his. She decided to pick one she thought was close to the right one and simply knock on the door and ask if they knew where he lived. She knocked tentatively and the door was soon opened by a heavy-set, scruffy man, who looked at her irritably.

"Yeah? What d'you want?" he asked.

"Sorry to bother you," Belinda replied. "Is this where Mickey Soames stays?" Belinda enquired.

"Nah. Three doors down, hen," the man answered, closing the door so fast she blinked and took a step backwards.

Very helpful neighbours, she muttered to herself.

He hadn't said in which direction, and his house was mid-terrace, so she took a guess at which way to go, telling herself that if it wasn't the right door, then she would try the other direction. Just as she reached the third door along, she saw Jason coming out of it. He glared at her and strode past her without acknowledging her, although she was aware, from the way he looked at her, that he knew who she was. She pursed her lips and took a deep breath, telling herself to be calm and take things as they came. She knew she might well be making a mountain out of molehill, as her mother would say.

She knocked on the door and waited. After a few moments Mickey opened the door and just stood there looking at her.

"Yeah?" he asked lazily, folding his arms across his chest.

"Hi, Mickey. I'm Belinda, June's sister. I wondered if we could have a wee chat," she suggested, licking her lips nervously.

He raised his eyebrows and stood to the side to let her go past him. She walked inside and then he followed her into the lounge. He indicated that she should sit down and she was glad to do so.

"What's this about?" he asked. She noticed he didn't ask if June was all right. In fact, he didn't seem to be at all anxious about anything.

"I'm just a bit concerned about June," she told him. He didn't reply, so she pressed on, noting the fact that he didn't seem surprised by her visit. "She seems a bit down lately, and she won't talk to me, and I just wondered if there's anything wrong," Belinda said, not liking the way he made her feel uncomfortable without actually doing anything to achieve that.

"No, everything's fine," he said evenly, with a careless shrug of his shoulders.

"Well, she's got some bruises on her shoulder, and I wondered if you knew how she got them," Belinda said, beginning to tremble a little.

"Nope. No idea," he stated calmly. He certainly wasn't going to make this easy for her, she realised.

"Well, I think you do know," she stated boldly, sitting up straighter and tilting her chin. Her anger was beginning to surface as June's pale little face floated to the front of her mind.

He screwed his eyes up but didn't reply.

"In fact, I think you gave her those bruises," she asserted, her heart beginning to beat faster as she watched his reaction.

"And I think you should mind your own business," he answered, "unless you'd like some bruises of your own."

Her jaw dropped in shock and she stood up indignantly.

"If you think you're going to get away with hurting my sister, you've got another think coming!" she told him, but she was beginning to shake with a potent combination of anger and fear.

He grabbed hold of her arm and frog-marched her to the front door.

"Get out and don't come back here, you stupid little girl!" he sneered as he shoved her outside and banged the door shut behind her.

She stood for a moment on the doorstep, trying to gather her wits before making her way home. All the way back she thought about him and about how scared June must be feeling. Her anger grew with every step and she made up her mind to speak to her parents about this the minute she arrived home, whether June was there or not. She walked at a steady pace, taking long, deep breaths to settle her nerves. She soon arrived at her own street, but was surprised to see her father's car parked outside. He never came home for lunch, as his work at the other side of town was too far away for that. She frowned, quickening her steps as she drew nearer. By the time she walked through the front door she was sure that something must be wrong. She went straight into the lounge, and was taken aback to find her father lying on the settee and her mother fussing around him.

"Dad, what's wrong? Are you sick or something? You don't look too good."

"I'll be just fine, love. I came home from work because I'm feeling a bit under the weather, but I'll be right as rain in no time, don't you worry. Just a touch of indigestion, you know."

Belinda looked at her mother, who scooted away into the kitchen to fetch an antacid and another cup of tea for her husband.

Belinda sat down in the chair next to the sofa.

"Dad, there's something ..." she began, but stopped when she saw him wince and rub his chest. He was very pale, not his normal colour at all, and she began to feel quite worried about him. He wouldn't normally come home from his work in the middle of the day, no matter how unwell he felt. She swallowed and bit back the words she'd been about to say, deciding to leave things for the time being. Her father didn't look as though he could handle that kind of aggravation at that moment and her mother was obviously anxious about him and very busy trying to look after him. She stood up and took her coat off. Dealing with Mickey, she decided, would just have to wait till another day.

By the evening, her father was still no better and Mrs Carter had now called for the doctor, who arrived around 9 o'clock. Mr Carter had earlier insisted that it was only indigestion that was wrong with him, but his face was now ashen and he was obviously in pain. As soon as the G.P. arrived, she said he would need to go into hospital and she called for the ambulance herself. She told Mrs Carter, Belinda and June that she suspected he might be having a heart attack.

The ambulance arrived quite promptly, at the same time as April and Scott. They walked up the path just as he was being lifted into the ambulance. Belinda had rung her sister a little earlier. As Elspeth climbed into the ambulance to be with her husband on the way to the hospital, Belinda explained to Scott what their G.P. suspected, and he immediately offered to drive them all to the hospital. They set off straight away and arrived at The Royal Infirmary very soon after the ambulance. When Scott enquired at the A & E reception desk about Mr Carter, they were told he was currently being examined by a doctor.

"Please take a seat in the waiting area," the receptionist advised them, adding, "it could be some time before there's any news."

Scott nodded and ushered the three sisters along to the family waiting room.

"It's more comfortable and private than the general waiting area," he told them, then asked if any of them would like tea or coffee. They all nodded and he turned to go along to the dispensing machine to get it.

"I'll come with you," Belinda said, falling into step beside him. "You won't manage four cups by yourself."

They didn't speak as they walked along the corridor and round the corner to the machine. There was someone else already using it, so they had to stand and wait for a few minutes.

Belinda began to sniffle and turned her face away to hide the unexpected tears.

"I'm sure he'll be just fine," Scott assured her, putting a comforting arm around her shoulders.

"I know, I know he will," she replied. "It's just been such an awful day."

"Yes, I'm sure it has," he agreed.

"No, it's not just about Dad ..." she began, but broke off as the woman using the coffee machine moved away.

Scott moved forward and busied himself getting the teas and coffees. He handed two of them to Belinda and held the other two himself as they walked back along the corridors to join the others.

"Why, what else happened today?" he asked.

"Oh, nothing. It's not important now," Belinda replied.

He frowned but didn't press her for an answer. He decided it was best to wait till they knew what was happening with Mr Carter before trying to find out what else was upsetting Belinda so much. They were all fairly quiet as they waited anxiously for news. After a little while, Scott said he was going along to the vending machine to get a cup of tea for Elspeth, who hadn't wanted anything previously; but his main intention was also to see if he could find out what was going on with regard to Mr Carter's condition before his wife and daughters were told. If it was bad news, he felt it would be a little easier for the family if it came from him rather than a doctor who was a stranger to them.

15 IT NEVER RAINS

Scott took the cup of tea back to Elspeth, and then went off again to see if he could locate Mr Carter's doctor. A little while later he was able to come back to Mrs Carter and tell her that they were conducting tests but that her husband was not in any danger and that he was expected to make a full recovery. Elspeth thanked him tearfully and said she would stay for a while until he had had his tests and she would be allowed in to see him.

"You girls can get away off home," she told them. There's no point in you all hanging around here for hours, is there?" she pointed out thoughtfully. I can get a taxi home later on, once I've seen your dad."

"That's true," Scott agreed. "Just give me a call at any time if you need any help with anything," he told her, giving her arm a comforting squeeze.

She smiled her thanks and he rounded the girls up and shepherded them out towards the car park. Whilst he'd been gone, Belinda had said nothing to June about Mickey, as they were all too worried about their father to focus on anything else. The last thing she wanted to do was add to their troubles.

"Scott, are you sure it's okay for us to go home? Is Dad really going to be all right, do you think?" Belinda asked, looking at him anxiously as they all piled into the car,

"Your mum's right," he replied, nodding his head firmly. "It's best if you go home just now because it will be hours before you would be able to get in to see him. And it's important for him to rest at the moment. You can come back in the morning for a visit."

They all nodded and Scott drove them back home. April stayed in the car while the other two girls got out and walked up the path to their door. She was surprised when Scott also climbed out of the car.

"What are you doing, Scott?" she asked.

"I just want to say to them that they can call me any time they need to," he answered, striding off down the path before she could reply. June went inside first and he caught up with Belinda just as she stepped into the hallway. He held her by the arm to make her stop, and then asked her if there was something wrong with June.

"She doesn't look well at all," he commented, frowning.

Belinda didn't answer and turned her head away from him while she debated with herself whether or not to tell him what was going on. She certainly couldn't tell her parents now. Eventually, she decided to trust him.

"Scott, there *is* something wrong, but I can't speak about it to you with June sitting in the lounge. I'd have to see you alone," she whispered.

He took out his mobile phone and swiftly moved it to the section for entering a new number, then handed it over to her.

"Put your mobile number in there and I'll text you later and we'll arrange something," he replied, smiling reassuringly.

She had her own number memorised and quickly tapped it into his phone, then said goodbye and went indoors.

"What was all that about?" April asked when he climbed back inside the car.

"Just offering my help," Scott told her, "and I got her to give me her number, just in case it's needed," he added. He frowned a little as he wondered why he didn't want to tell April there was something amiss. He told himself it was because he wanted to wait until he found out exactly what the problem was before he said anything to anyone. She had enough on her mind at that time, he reasoned.

Scott sent Belinda a text an hour later offering to pick up both her and June and take them to the hospital at visiting time the next day, and suggesting that he and Belinda could try to get some time alone where they wouldn't be overheard.

She replied that that would be best. And she was hopeful that it would give her time to calm down a little. Too many things seemed to be happening and changing all at the one time, and she needed to settle down and come to terms with what action she should take on June's behalf.

When her mum came home late in the evening, looking extremely weary but very relieved, they gave each other a big hug. June was already upstairs in bed.

"How is he now?" Belinda asked.

"Much better. He seemed quite settled and ready to sleep when I left," her mother answered, sniffing sadly. "Won't get his test results till tomorrow. Oh, it never rains but it pours!"

"Tell me about it!" Belinda agreed, smiling wryly. Her mother seemed to have a ready-made expression for every situation.

*

The next day was Saturday, so that meant they could all go to see their father without taking time off work. Except for Belinda. She had to ring the salon and explain what was happening, but Janine, her supervisor, very kindly told her not to worry, that she could make up the time later. She also rang Jim to put him in the picture. He said he was very sorry to hear it and immediately offered to drive her to the hospital for afternoon visiting.

"Oh, that's okay," she told him, "Scott's offered to take us all there."

"It's no bother, Belinda," he assured her, "and I'd like to see your dad for a minute or two as well, if that's all right with you."

"Well, I don't know if the nurses will let us all in ..."

"I'd like to take you over there anyway, Belinda. It's the least I can do. Poor Pete. And anyway, it would be a bit of a squeeze for Scott to get you girls and your mum into the car at the same time."

"Yeah, that's true. Okay, I'll see you later then, about 1.30," she said, putting down the phone.

This was probably going to make it difficult for her and Scott to have their little pow-wow, she realised, but there was nothing she could do about it. Jim would have wondered what was wrong with her if she'd insisted on his not picking her up. She sighed and sent Scott a little text to let him know the situation.

Scott arrived at the house at 1.30, the same time as Jim, and they strode up to the front door together. Mrs Carter and the girls were all ready and waiting and they piled into Scott's car, while Belinda climbed into Jim's car.

When they walked into the ward their father had been transferred to, the nurse informed them that there was a maximum of four visitors allowed at each bed. Scott immediately said he would wait behind. Belinda wanted to wait behind, too, to speak to him, but she knew it would look strange if she held back and told Jim to go in before her, so she said nothing. Jim stood back beside Scott and the women all went in to sit by Mr Carter's bedside. Belinda was quite shocked at her dad's appearance. He had always been such a large man and now he seemed to have shrunk and his cheeks looked pale and sunken. He smiled bravely at them, however, and was quite cheerful when he told them that he would probably be allowed home the next morning, once the doctors had done their rounds, as his tests had shown that the mild cardiac event was over and that his heart was returning to normal.

They stayed with him for half an hour and then came out to let the men go in to see him.

On the journey home, Jim asked Belinda if she felt up to going out with him in the evening, but she shook her head.

"Maybe next week," she replied. He looked so disappointed that she felt guilty, but there was too much on her mind just then for her to go on a date. And besides, she knew her mum would be grateful for some help around the house.

Jim drove off home, promising to ring her later, and Scott and April went home, too.

Scott sent Belinda a text message as soon as he and April arrived back at his flat. He asked her to meet him in the park the following morning at about 11 o'clock. She said 'yes' right away. Her anxieties about June were beginning to weigh on her mind now that she knew her father was going to be all right, and there was no way she was going to add to her parents' trials and tribulations at that point in time. She knew it was important for her father not to get agitated or upset about anything until he was fully recovered.

She found it difficult to get off to sleep that night and there were dark shadows under her eyes when she rose in the morning. She put on a little light make-up after giving her mother breakfast in bed and then said she was just off to the shops to get the papers and some rolls. Her mum nodded and smiled at her.

"You're a good girl, our Belinda," she told her gratefully.

Belinda said goodbye and headed off to meet Scott. She was trying very hard not to feel excited about meeting him like this, but it was very difficult not to. It did feel exciting, especially as no one knew about it except the two of them.

It was a beautiful, fresh sunny morning and she walked briskly along to the local park, reminding herself why she was going there. The memory of her encounter with Mickey and the knowledge of her sister's predicament were enough to put a damper on her nervousness, which was just as well, otherwise she would have blushed furiously as soon as she saw him. She had just sat down on the bench when he arrived and he looked a little agitated, too. She reminded herself that he didn't as yet know what the problem was and was probably imagining all sorts of things.

He was the first to speak.

"Hi, Belinda. Lovely morning, isn't it?"

"Yes, it is. And hopefully Dad will get home today, too."

"Yes, I'm quite sure he will. Of course, he'll need to take things easy for a while, till he's fully recovered." He waited a moment before he spoke again.

"Belinda, do you know what's wrong with June? Has she told you what's the matter?"

Belinda took a deep breath.

"No, she wouldn't tell me anything. But I saw the bruises – and I knew."

"Bruises! Where? Did she hurt herself? I had been thinking that maybe she was pregnant because she's looking so pale and thin!"

"No, it's not that – well, not as far as I know, anyway."

Belinda shivered at the thought of her sister being pregnant to that violent creep.

"She's ... it's difficult ... her boyfriend – Mickey – he's been hurting her."

Scott stared at her intently and she swallowed and looked away from him. She gazed across to the other side of the park at the people who were walking their dogs. The sun shone on her freshly-washed hair and brought out its coppery tones, and anxiety gave a pallor to her face that made her brown eyes look larger and sadder. Scott had a sudden, very strong desire to take her in his arms and hold her very tightly. He coughed to ease the tension.

"Are you sure?" he asked quietly.

"Yes, I'm sure. I went round there to ask him what was going on and he said if I told anyone he'd give me some bruises, too. And he's threatened my family as well. I think – I got the feeling he's on some kind of drugs. He's very aggressive."

Tears filled her eyes now and he moved beside her and put his arm around her shoulders. She leaned against him and a little sob escaped her lips.

"I don't know what to do, Scott, I don't know what to do. April won't listen to me and I can't say anything to my mum and dad, not the way things are right now."

"Don't worry, Belinda, we'll think of something," he said firmly. He clenched his teeth together to keep his anger tamped down till later. The thought of that man hurting June and intimidating Belinda made his blood boil, but he could give vent to that later, he told himself. For the moment, he contented himself with holding her closer and she leaned into him, finally saying goodbye to the self-delusion that she wasn't head over heels in love with him. Her heart belonged to him and she couldn't deny it to herself any longer.

She looked up into his face and then wished she hadn't. He was looking at her very intently again and this time she couldn't look away from him. Her heart began to race. Was she just imagining things, she wondered? Then Scott bent his head and kissed her lightly on the lips. She gasped in surprise and drew back a little; then she put her arms up around his neck and they kissed deeply for what seemed to both of them a long time. When they drew apart, Scott stood up immediately.

"I'm so sorry, Belinda. I didn't mean to do that. That should never have happened. I don't know what came over me. I have to get back now. Do you want a lift home?"

"No, I'll just walk, Scott. It isn't far," she answered shakily, still reeling from the after-effects of their kiss.

"Are you sure?" he asked.

She nodded silently and watched him as he turned and walked quickly away from her towards the car park.

16 SCOTT'S SOLUTION

Scott knew he had a lot of thinking to do. As soon as he got home that day he went into the bedroom, leaving April watching television in the lounge. He paced up and down, trying to calm himself so that he could formulate a plan of action. The one thing he couldn't do was give vent to his anger and frustration. He knew he must calm down completely before he could tackle the situation. If he was all worked up, he would only end up making things much worse. He wanted to go round to Mickey's place and thump him, but then he would just be sinking to his level. Violence wasn't the answer. It never solved anything. But it was so difficult to restrain the impetus to go round there and give the cowardly little bully a couple of black eyes. Scott made a fist with his right hand and thumped it into the palm of his left. Every time he thought about how June must be feeling right now, and also when he remembered how distressed Belinda was, it made him furious.

But as a doctor, he knew that a violent response would destroy his career and his credibility as a caring professional. No, he decided, he must find a way to resolve this situation without ruining his own life – or involving April's parents. He also felt, for a reason he couldn't quite fathom, that it would be counter-productive to tell April herself what was going on. It would only upset her, he reasoned, and there was nothing positive she could do to help her sister. He didn't want to admit to himself that he wanted to share this burden with Belinda, not April. He told himself that if he told her, April might try to tackle Mickey herself, as Belinda had done, and simply make things a great deal worse, and he knew that would make it almost impossible for him to contain his own temper.

He eventually made up his mind about the best course of action. First, he would try to speak to June so that he could assess the full situation and then he would tackle her boyfriend. He would make sure that the young man was left in no doubt that his liaison with June and his ill-treatment of her were over; and then he would make some attempt to persuade him to try to get clean, to wean himself off whatever drugs he was taking. Scott wasn't very hopeful of achieving much success with that aim, if his previous experiences with addicts were anything to go by, but he intended to try anyway. It could be that the violent tendencies were as much a product of the drugs as they were of Mickey's personality or upbringing.

Scott sighed deeply and ran his hand through his hair distractedly. He had made his decision now and felt a little calmer. He would go and see June later that day and then pay Mickey a visit in the evening. He went into the living room and sat down beside April, putting his arm around her shoulders. She turned and looked at him but didn't say anything. She simply turned away and looked at the screen again. He was glad of that because he was feeling guilty about what had happened with Belinda; and he was feeling really confused about it, too. It wasn't the sort of thing he would normally have even considered doing when he was seeing someone else. So why had it happened, he wondered? He came to the conclusion that his feelings of pity for Belinda had got the better of him and she had given him such a sad, pathetic look that he hadn't been able to stop the kiss happening. It felt to him as though it had been almost inevitable. He wasn't worried about Belinda saying anything to anyone. He knew she wouldn't. It wasn't her style. She had a lot of integrity and he knew she would keep it to herself. But he was determined that it wouldn't ever happen again.

*

Belinda was in a state of emotional turmoil also. She wasn't even sure if she had done the right thing by telling Scott about Mickey. She spent the afternoon helping her mother prepare the Sunday dinner and all the time she was silent, chewing on her bottom lip and mulling over the situation. She was also completely bemused by what had happened between her and Scott that morning. It had been totally unexpected and she didn't know what to make of it. She knew he wasn't the kind of man who would normally behave like that, especially given the fact that he was actually living with her sister. She didn't feel as though she was any further forward in her deliberations by the time they sat down to eat their meal.

"You're very quiet today, love," her mother remarked.

Belinda smiled and shrugged, trying to make light of it all, but she didn't entirely succeed.

"Oh, I'm just a bit tired today, Mum, and thinking about Dad, too," she prevaricated. "A pity the weekend hasn't got three days instead of just two, isn't it?" she joked.

Her mother pursed her lips and frowned a little. She hadn't failed to notice that June was very quiet also. She sensed that something was going on with her daughters and if she hadn't been so preoccupied with her husband's problems, she would have sat the two of them down by now and made sure she got to the bottom of the problem. She sighed and promised herself that she would speak to them both during the next day or two and coax it out of them, whether they wanted to confide in her or not.

While they were clearing away the dishes after the meal, the doorbell rang and Belinda tensed. She knew it would be Scott. Her heart started to beat a little faster and she swallowed nervously as she helped to load the dishwasher and clear the table. June went to answer the door, and Belinda wasn't surprised when she didn't come back.

"Who was it, June?" her mother called out as she and Belinda sat down in front of the television.

There was no answer, but they could hear two sets of footsteps going up the staircase.

"Probably Sophie coming to make things up with June," Belinda suggested, knowing full well that it wasn't.

Her mum nodded and shrugged. She got up to ring the hospital to make sure that Pete was still doing all right, even though she had just seen him at visiting time that evening, and then she sat back down to watch a Sunday evening film, hoping to take her mind off her husband's illness for a little while.

Belinda chewed on her lip again and fell to wondering what Scott would decide to do. She really wanted to go upstairs and join in the discussion between Scott and her sister, but she knew that would only arouse her mother's suspicions. She fervently hoped she and Scott could fix things without upsetting her parents. They had enough to deal with as it was.

Some time later, she heard the same footsteps coming back downstairs, then someone going out of the house. June went back upstairs then.

"I'll just pop upstairs and speak to June, make sure she isn't upset," she told her mum.

"Okay, love," Elspeth replied. "Just give me a shout if she needs a shoulder or anything," she said.

"Righto," Belinda answered, relieved to be able to slip away. She was anxious to know what Scott had said to her sister.

When she went into their bedroom, June was sitting on the edge of her bed. She looked worried. Her brows were drawn into a frown and her arms were crossed tightly over her chest.

"Why did you have to go poking your nose in, Belinda?" she demanded. "You've just gone and made things a hundred times worse. He's going to go and speak to Mickey and then Mickey'll take it out on me for telling on him!"

"We have to do something, June. You can't go on like this –"

"That's up to me, Belinda. It's got nothing to do with you. You shouldn't have interfered. I'm never going to trust you ever again!"

So saying, she turned her back on her sister and slid beneath her duvet, drawing it up over her head.

Belinda sighed and went out into the hallway, closing the bedroom door carefully. She took her mobile out of her pocket and sent Scott a message to ask what was happening.

He replied straight away and said that he was on his way to see Mickey and try to sort him out and make sure he didn't bother June again.

Belinda texted 'good luck' to him and closed her phone. She went back downstairs and tried to relax, to pretend that everything was all right. She could see her mum looking at her anxiously from time to time and she hoped and prayed that Scott would have more success with Mickey than she'd had herself. She would probably not know how it all went until the next day and it was so difficult to have to wait and wonder.

*

Scott felt anxious also as he drove towards Mickey and Jason's flat. He knew he would have to be careful to handle the situation delicately to begin with, because it could potentially become unpleasant or even violent if he pushed too hard or came across as being belligerent. Tact and diplomacy and a firm hand were what was needed. He knew that from past experience. But he hadn't been personally involved before, as he was this time, and his self-control was going to be tested to the limit.

He drew up outside the house and sat for a few moments to settle his anxieties and gather his thoughts. He kept reminding himself that what he actually said to Mickey, and how he said it, would carry more weight than anything else. He clenched his teeth as he tried to tamp down his instinctive desire to thump the nasty little thug as soon as he opened the front door. When he felt he was sufficiently in control, he got out of the car, shutting the door hard and striding purposefully towards the house. He rapped on the door like a policeman and his face and jaw were hard and set by the time the door opened.

"Who're you? What do you want?" Mickey asked aggressively, his eyes narrowing into slits of suspicion.

"I'm Dr Walker, April's boyfriend. I just need a word or two," Scott replied, his tone steady and as mild as he could manage.

"What about?" Mickey asked, barring Scott's way with his arm as he tried to step inside.

"I've got something I want to ask you," Scott said quietly. "It's private stuff, but I can do it here on the doorstep if you want all the neighbours to hear."

Mickey said nothing. He stood back reluctantly to let Scott inside and then kicked the door shut and followed him into the living room.

"Well, what's it about?" he asked as he plonked himself down on the settee.

Scott didn't sit down.

"Jason here?" he asked innocently.

"No, he's out. Not that it's got anything to do with you," was the reply.

Scott moved across swiftly towards Mickey and grabbed him by the front of his tee-shirt. He hauled him off the settee and pinned him against the nearest wall, well away from the window. He was careful not to harm him, but he was a great deal heavier and stronger than Mickey and he was able to keep him pinned against the wall easily. It would be his word against Mickey's if the lout tried to complain about it officially.

"Just a wee message for you from me, Mickey, on behalf of June," Scott ground out through clenched teeth.

"Fuck off!" Mickey spat out.

"You don't go near her again, or any of her family, do you hear me?" Scott said, pressing harder so that Mickey couldn't move at all.

"Or what?" Mickey asked, sneeringly. "What d'you think you're gonna do, big man? You can't touch me or I'll finish you. Doctors can't go about thumping people. You know that as well as I do."

"You go anywhere near any of the Walkers again and I'll be paying a little visit to the police station, Mickey. And from what I hear you won't be coming out of that one too well, will you? Don't make the mistake of thinking I'm bluffing, either, because you will be very sorry if I have to prove you wrong. Are we clear on that?"

"Fuck off," Mickey said again, but with less conviction in his tone.

"Have I made myself clear to you?" Scott asked again, grudgingly letting go of him but standing directly in front of him, his face very near to Mickey's.

Mickey pushed past him without answering and walked out into the hallway to the front door. He opened it and held it open until Scott approached him.

"Mickey," Scott persisted, "I can help you with the drug problem. Whatever you're on, you can kick it, with a bit of help."

Mickey gave Scott a shove and banged the door closed immediately afterward. Scott straightened himself up on the front doorstep and stalked off towards his car. He didn't really care if he never saw or heard from Mickey again, but he was determined to keep that boy away from June and the rest of her family. If he had to go to the police he would. He would do anything to protect the Carters from him and his like. He just hoped no lasting damage had been done to June and that Mickey would do as he'd been told and stay away.

He decided he would call Belinda that night, as soon as he got back home, and tell her it had been dealt with. He hoped and prayed that it *was* dealt with, because he didn't know what else he could do if it wasn't. Also, if he had to tell the Police about Mickey, there could be repercussions for his career, because he was sure that Mickey would embellish the facts of his little visit to him. He hoped and prayed that this would be an end to it all. Cowards usually back down when someone stands up to them, and Mickey had nothing to gain by ignoring Scott's warnings. He would know he had bitten off more than he could chew. Mickey had banked on the fact that June would be too scared to say anything to anyone. The little coward would always look after number one, Scott was sure – and he was quite prepared to deal with him much more harshly if he didn't.

17 THE DUST SETTLES

Belinda ran upstairs when her mobile started ringing. She mumbled to her parents that it was Jim so that they wouldn't wonder why she was running off upstairs. As soon as she heard Scott's voice telling her that he'd been to see Mickey she could feel the tension draining away from her. She closed her eyes and breathed a sigh of relief.

"I can't say for sure that it's worked, but I don't think he will bother June again," he told her quietly. "Too much hassle for him. He's a coward at heart and cowards always take the easy option. Fingers crossed that it works."

"Oh, thanks, Scott. And I'm sure you're right – I'm sure he'll back off now. After all, what would he have to gain by pestering her again? He thought she was an easy target and now it's obvious she isn't, that should be enough to make him steer clear. Here's hoping. I'm going straight upstairs to tell June. Or do you want to speak to her yourself?"

"No, I'm happy for you to do that, Belinda. Speak to you again soon."

"Yes. And thanks again, Scott, from both of us!"

She smiled as she closed her phone and went across the hallway to tell June the good news. However, her sister was fast asleep and she didn't want to disturb her, so she decided to leave it till the next morning. She was extremely relieved and was sure that it was the end of the problem. She didn't know what they would have done without Scott's help and she felt deeply grateful to him. She bit her lip as she realised that these dramatic events were making her fall even more under his spell and she sighed dreamily as she climbed into bed and closed her eyes. His face swam into her vision and she supposed she would always visualise his face now when she was relaxed and alone. She was glad that the previous animosity between them had gone. And now she could dream about the lovely kiss they had shared, even though she knew it would never happen again. But she knew also that she would have to be extra vigilant when her sisters or parents were around. She didn't want them to guess her feelings. She would have to keep them tightly wrapped up and be careful to only indulge her fantasies when she was alone.

*

The rain battering down onto the bedroom window woke Belinda quite early the following morning and she yawned and stretched, smiling as she remembered what Scott had told her the night before. She slid out of bed and crossed the room to June's bed. She spoke to her and when she heard her sister's muffled response, she sat down on the end of the bed. June groaned and rubbed her eyes.

"What do you want at this time of day, Belinda?" she asked sleepily.

"Scott rang me last night, June," Belinda replied. "He's been to see Mickey and has told him to stay away from you," she added breathlessly, her eyes shining.

June came instantly awake and sat straight up in bed, staring wide-eyed at her sister.

"He did? Really? Why?"

"To make him leave you alone, of course. We know what he's doing to you, June. But he's not going to get away with it. I don't think he'll bother you again now."

"Hmm, I'm not so sure. He doesn't like people telling him what to do, Belinda. And he'll probably think I put Scott up to it. He might try to get his own back now."

June sounded scared and was obviously unconvinced that Scott's intervention would work. But Belinda shook her head.

"I don't think Mickey will do that, you know. It's too much bother. He knows we won't give up till he leaves you alone. He doesn't need the aggro. I think it's sorted. I hope so. And I need you to promise me that you won't get in touch with Mickey. That would undermine Scott's authority. Promise me you won't, June. I know it's hard to just wait and see, but it's important that you stay away from him. Do you promise?"

She took June's hand and squeezed it encouragingly.

June nodded slowly. "Okay, I promise," she said, adding, "You've got an awful lot of faith in Scott's powers of persuasion, Belinda."

"Yes I have and you will, too, when you see that it's worked," Belinda assured her. She stood up and went off into the bathroom to get showered and changed. She hummed a little tune to herself as she did so, feeling as though a tremendous weight had been lifted from her shoulders.

June lay back down in her bed and drew the duvet up over her head. She wasn't so sure that this was going to work, but at least they had done something – at least they had stood up to Mickey. She was beginning to hate him and she had been worrying that she was never going to be free of him. She hadn't slept well for some time and she was very tired. Her eyelids began to feel heavy and she knew she would soon fall back to sleep. She was having a recurring bad dream these days – in which she was pregnant with Mickey's child and when she gave birth to it, it turned out to be a little demon with horns on its head! As she dropped off again, she felt better than she had done in a long time and she promised herself that she would go out and buy a pregnancy testing kit as soon as she woke up. She would have to do that if she was ever going to have any true peace of mind and start to get over this horrible relationship so that she could move on with her life.

*

Belinda's buoyant mood continued throughout the day and her parents were pleased to see that she was behaving more like her old self again, because she had seemed so quiet and withdrawn of late. Now she was cheerful and helpful and chatty. So much so that they didn't even notice when their youngest daughter slipped out of the front door very quietly and went off down the street in the direction of the bus stop. There was a chemist and a Spar shop next door to each other just a couple of streets away, but she had no intention of buying the kit there. Too close to home. This was private and personal and she didn't want anyone to know, not even Belinda. June was beginning to feel very nervous and was glad when the bus arrived on time and she jumped on board. As soon as it arrived at the town centre, she jumped off and headed straight for Boots. As she approached the glass doors, she caught sight of her own reflection and was shocked at how thin and pale she looked. Her stomach flipped as she reached up and lifted the little box from the shelf. This was all beginning to feel a little bit too real now that she was actually buying a testing kit. She paid for it hurriedly and almost ran out of the shop in case anyone she knew would see her.

She went straight to the bus stop and waited anxiously. She had to wait for ten minutes or so and was feeling quite unwell by the time the bus arrived. It was very busy and she had to stand because there were no seats. The interior of the bus was stuffy and clammy and she hadn't eaten anything for almost a full day. She began to sway a little. She felt sick. Please don't let it be morning sickness, she prayed, sending up a heartfelt prayer to a God she didn't even believe in!

She dashed upstairs when she arrived home and locked herself instantly inside the bathroom. She did the test and then went back into her room to wait for the result. Her heart was thumping in her chest. Her period was a full month late and she felt dreadful. As the seconds ticked away, she began to cry softly. She was sure she was pregnant. And if she was, she told herself, she would just want to die. Then she told herself it wasn't the end of the world, even if she *was* pregnant. She would get rid of it. She could go to Scott and he would help her. She knew he would, even if he was reluctant or disapproving. She was shaking by the time she lifted the stick to check the result. It was blurred because her eyes were so full of tears. She dashed them away and looked down. It was negative. It was negative! She wasn't pregnant. If she had been, it would definitely have shown up by then.

She wasn't pregnant. She kept telling herself that over and over and she sat right down on the floor of her room, glad that Belinda had moved into her own room now. She didn't want her sister to see the state she was in. She felt weak with relief. She dried her eyes with a tissue and blew her nose. Then she began to take deep breaths and tell herself to get a grip. It wasn't morning sickness – it was simply withdrawal symptoms. She had stopped taking the pills Mickey had been forcing on her. He had stopped bothering to drop them into her drinks and had begun to hand her a pill and watch while she swallowed it. She didn't even know what he'd been giving her. She'd been putting them into her mouth and then taking them out again as soon as he wasn't looking. A little of the drugs had dissolved in her mouth, of course, but she had usually managed to go to the loo and spit most of it out into a tissue. She had been doing that for some time, so she knew there was a good chance she would be able to just simply come off them and get back to normal, without going through a long process of withdrawal or having to take substitutes or anything. She didn't want to take anything like that ever again. She didn't even want to drink alcohol any more. With a bit of luck, she promised herself, she would be clean and clear and she could start University in the autumn with some chance of making a career and a life for herself. And it was all thanks to April's man!

18 APRIL'S OTHER MAN

It was Monday morning and April was feeling very pleased with herself. As far as she was concerned, everything had been going very well for her since she had moved in with Scott. He was very easy-going and agreed with almost everything she said to him. His job kept him extremely busy, also, so that she was able to do as she pleased a great deal of the time. She was out at work most days, but sometimes she and Max would leave early and go back to Scott's flat together. It was so much easier than the brief, hurried sessions they had been able to snatch when she had been living at home, she reflected as she put the finishing touches to her make-up and hair. She was sure Max was coming round to her suggestion that he should ditch Sylvie, his current girlfriend, and she was hatching a plan to convince Scott that getting married would be a good idea. He was loaded and she intended to eventually relieve him of at least half of what he had (through the divorce courts) so that she could live in the style to which she was becoming accustomed. And then she and Max would be able to do whatever they liked. And in the meantime, she was having fun with both of them. She felt a tiny bit guilty when she thought of what she was intending doing to Scott, but she knew there was no chance she would ever have any serious cash if she didn't do it, so she had no choice, really, she told herself. *And I'm well worth it,* she concluded.

She sighed contentedly as she slung her bag over her shoulder and sauntered out of the flat to go to the studio. She twirled her house keys around her finger as she headed off down the street. She knew she would need to put the next phase of her plan into action soon before Scott started to cool off towards her. She was going to pretend to feel unwell and make out that her period was late. He was a doctor. He would suspect a pregnancy instantly!

Max was very attentive towards her that day and she looked straight at him as he took endless shots of her in lots of different skimpy outfits. Her eyes sent him a message, that he would be welcome to come back home with her, as Scott would be busy doing his duties at the hospital that afternoon. He smiled at her and her knees went weak. He was really the dishiest man she had ever known and he always had that effect on her.

"That's it, honey," he crooned, his voice silken and sexy. "You're the best. None of the other girls are a patch on you, you know. You say so much with those big blue eyes."

"You know what my eyes are saying, Max. How about it?" she asked in her best husky tone.

"Where's the doc going to be?" he wanted to know.

"Very busy healing the sick and making pots of money!"

"Well, let's go for it then. A couple more angles and we're done here. Just face the side wall, then turn your head round towards me," he instructed.

She smiled in triumph and licked her lips in anticipation.

They left the studio together after the photo session and he drove at a ridiculous speed all the way to the flat. April threw her head back and laughed. Everything he did excited her.

He parked the car in the next street, just in case. As he'd said to April the first time they'd come back to the flat, there was no point in sneaking out the back door in an emergency if his car was parked out front for everyone to see, was there? And you never knew when nosey neighbours were watching you.

They were careful not to touch each other as they walked down the driveway and went inside the building. This was just the sort of neighbourhood for twitching curtains, so it was best not to be behaving like a couple.

Their 'afternoon delight' was the best ever that day, April thought as she sighed happily while they sat in bed and smoked together afterwards, as they always did. She had been pretending to Scott that she had given up the cigarettes; so she would just have to admit to having had a little slip when he noticed the smell of smoke later on.

Just as she was saying that to Max she heard Scott slam the front door and they both scrambled out of the rumpled bed at the same time and stubbed their cigarettes out in the ashtray April usually kept hidden in a cupboard. She slipped hurriedly into her cream silk dressing gown and whispered to Max that she would try to distract Scott long enough to give him time to slip out through the back door. He nodded silently as he fumbled with the fastenings of his jeans. April opened the bedroom door and closed it hurriedly behind her. She tiptoed along to the lounge and tried to look sleepy when Scott turned round and saw her.

"April, what are you doing home? I thought you'd be back much later," he commented, frowning at her dishevelled appearance.

"Oh, I came home from work early, Scott. Not feeling too well, actually," she said, trying to look and sound pitiful. "Anyway, I didn't expect you'd be back this early either!"

"Not as many patients to see as I'd thought. Hmm, you do look a bit flushed, actually. Not coming down with that 'flu that's going round, are you?" he asked in a concerned voice.

"I hope not! I was just having a wee rest when you came in."

"Well, maybe you should just go back to bed, April. Do you want a drink of water or anything? You need lots of fluids and bed rest if it *is* 'flu, you know."

"I'll bear that in mind," she muttered to herself.

"What?"

"I said I will, if you don't mind – go back to bed, that is."

"Okay. I'll make the tea tonight. You go and get some rest."

April turned and sloped back into the bedroom. She heard the soft click of the back door closing and smiled to herself. But that was a bit close for comfort today, she thought. They would have to be more careful in future. It was all very exciting, of course, but getting caught would be the pits. No point in making big plans and then screwing it up by being careless. But she consoled herself with the thought that she had at least started to put her plan into action. Scott had it in his mind now that she was feeling unwell and she would play that card as gradually and as subtly as she could for the next few weeks.

She jumped into the rumpled bed again and lifted her mobile from the bedside table. She sent Max lots of kisses in a text message and then slid down under the duvet as she heard Scott padding towards the bedroom with a glass of water in one hand and Paracetamol in the other.

Meanwhile, Max opened her text message at the same time as he opened his car door. All in all, it had been a pleasant afternoon and his getaway had been easier than he'd anticipated. He was thinking the same thing as April, though, that they would have to be more careful in future. He thought her plan to fleece Scott was a bit ridiculous but typical of her. He suspected Scott wasn't as gullible as he seemed and that she would have her work cut out to convince him that getting hitched to her was a good idea.

Max himself was happy to go along with things, though, while it was all going smoothly and he was enjoying being with her. If it paid off, fine. But if it didn't, he wasn't really bothered. Plenty more fish in his sea, after all. Girls like her were ten-a-penny to a good-looking photographer like himself. He put on his shades and zoomed off. He'd stop off somewhere for a meal and then give a couple of the lads a ring to see if they fancied a drink. It was only Monday, but so what? His session with April had given him a bit of a thirst. Women were hard work and she certainly wasn't low maintenance on the physical side of things. And, he reminded himself, he always had Sylvie to fall back on if things didn't go according to plan with April.

19 A DECENT PROPOSAL

Belinda's buoyant mood continued during the following few weeks. She was pleased that everything seemed to have settled down with June. She didn't even mention Mickey any more and she and Sophie were best friends again. Belinda did her work happily and always had a smile on her face. She and Melissa had become even more friendly. Melissa was always inviting her over to the house – sometimes just her and sometimes Jim, too. Belinda and Jim were getting on very well with each other, but she hoped he wasn't getting too attached to her because of her feelings for Scott. He never pressured her or made her feel that she was obliged to be with him. However, Belinda had noticed, several times, that he looked at Melissa in a particular way and she was beginning to suspect he still had deep feelings for his best mate's wife.

Towards the end of a particularly busy Saturday at the salon, Belinda received a call from Melissa asking her if she and Jim would like to come over and have dinner with them that evening.

"I'd love to, Mel, but I'm bushed," Belinda told her. "I can't wait to get finished and get home and put my feet up."

"Oh, well, if you change your mind, I'm making plenty of food, so just drop by if you feel more energetic later on."

"I might just do that!" Belinda said, wishing she had a job where she didn't have to work on Saturdays. She rang off and put her mobile away in her pocket before Janine saw it. She wasn't supposed to have it switched on while she was dealing with clients.

She made her way home and had a long soak in a warm, scented bath. She enjoyed showering sometimes, but a bath was best for tired legs and feet. When she was finished she got dressed, dried her hair and spritzed herself with perfume. She felt tired but relaxed, and she was coming round to the idea of spending the evening over at Mel's. It was Saturday night, after all, and Jim was going there, too. She ran downstairs and told her mum to put her dinner in the fridge and she would reheat it the next day. Slipping on a light beige, casual jacket over her black jeans and tee-shirt, she grabbed her bag and set off.

As she hurried down the path, she almost collided with Scott striding along towards the front door.

He laughed and put out a hand to steady her.

"Don't want you turning that ankle over again, do we?" he pointed out, treating her to a very warm smile that made her feel weak and seemed to wipe every coherent thought out of her mind at the same time.

"No, I s'pose not," she said stupidly and felt like an idiot.

"You look very nice. Going somewhere special?" he asked.

"Just over to Mel's again."

With the White Knight?"

"I think Jim will probably be there, too," she agreed.

The smile seemed to freeze on his face and he spoke again rather stiffly.

"Well, have a good time, won't you?"

He was looking at her oddly and she began to feel rather uncomfortable. Memories of the kiss they had shared hung heavily between them. She quickly glanced over at his car to see if April was inside and was relieved to find she wasn't.

"April not with you?"

"She's not feeling too well at the moment, actually," he said quietly.

"Oh, why's that?"

"Not sure. A bit run-down probably,"

"Well, give her my love and tell her to get some rest, will you?"

"Yeah, sure. She gets plenty of rest, I can assure you,"

Belinda frowned. There was an odd note in his voice and she was beginning to feel quite awkward with him. She decided it was time to go and took a couple of steps away from him.

"I'd better go," she said.

"Right. Don't want to keep Sir Galahad waiting, do you?"

She blinked and was frowning by the time she reached the gate and went out into the street.

"Do you want a lift over to Mel's?" Scott called out.

"No, it's fine. There's a bus due now if I run," she replied, setting off at a trot.

Scott seemed to glare at her departing figure and as she turned the corner, out of sight, she drew in a deep breath. What on earth was all that about, she wondered? The way he'd looked at her and the way he'd spoken about Jim – it was almost as if he was – jealous! But he couldn't be, she told herself, because he was living with her sister. She was just imagining things because of her own feelings for him.

She was still feeling a little distracted by her awkward meeting with Scott when she arrived at Mel's house. As she was a little late, they were all already sitting around the table and Mel was just about to serve the meal. They were eating in the conservatory and there was a relaxed atmosphere and a lovely golden glow over the whole scene. The overhead lighting was soft and subtle and Belinda felt herself relaxing immediately. She hoped that one day she would have a home like this, with such a wonderfully happy atmosphere. She sat down and smiled over at Jim, who looked extremely pleased to see her. He stood up and leaned across the table, planting a little kiss on the tip of her nose.

"Hi there," he said. "Glad you could make it. Mel said you've been really busy today."

"Yeah, I have. Saturdays are always busy, but today was hectic. End of the month rush, I suppose. I was going to stay in, but then I decided to get off my backside and make the effort. I always enjoy coming over here."

She smiled as Mel brought in the serving dishes and they all began to help themselves to southern fried chicken, roast potatoes and Caesar salad.

"You know you're always welcome here any time," Cam assured her, looking at Mel for confirmation.

Belinda sighed as she began to eat her meal. Her mind kept drifting back to the way Scott had looked and sounded earlier on, with the result that she jumped guiltily when Jim said her name loudly.

"You're miles away, Belinda. What's up?"

"Oh, it's nothing. Just me being silly. I'm glad I chose this wine – it's excellent. I hope I don't fall asleep after I drink it, though!"

"Oh, that's okay – as long as you don't snore!" Cam answered flippantly.

Everyone laughed and the moment passed. Belinda was aware of Jim looking at her keenly several times during the evening and she also saw the look that passed between Cam and Mel when he did so. She knew what they were thinking, what they were hoping for – that the foursomes would go on indefinitely.

As the evening wore on, Belinda's eyes began to droop as the tiredness caught up with her.

"Are you ready to go off home now, Bel?" Jim asked when they were alone for a moment.

"Yeah, I'm falling asleep. Do you mind, Jim? Can't keep going much longer.

"Don't mind at all," he assured her.

"We're going to get off home now, Mel," he said as she came back into the room, with Cam following behind.

"Okay, you two. Now don't you be keeping this girl up too late, Jim," she ordered, wagging her finger at him. "She's dead on her feet, poor lass."

"I promise to take her straight home," Jim said softly.

They took their leave and Belinda's eyes closed immediately they drove off.

But Jim didn't drive straight to her house. He pulled over and stopped a couple of streets from Mel and Cam's house.

"Jim? What are you doing?" she asked, her eyes flying open.

"I wanted to ask you something, Belinda," he said, licking his bottom lip nervously.

"Okay, make it quick, will you, before I doze off."

"Will you marry me, Belinda?" he asked suddenly, releasing a whoosh of breath immediately afterwards.

"What? Marry you? Where did that come from?" she asked, frowning. "Did you have more to drink than I thought or something?"

"I know who you're thinking about and it's never going to happen, Belinda, so why don't you think about my idea. I won't rush you. Take all the time you need."

"Jim …" she stuttered. "You know who I'm thinking about? What do you mean?"

She was wide awake now and her heart was racing.

"That doctor guy, Scott, who's shacking up with your sister. I see the way you look at him. But they're living together and will probably get married. Anyway, think about what I've said, will you? I'll get you home now."

"Well, if you know I'm thinking about him, why are you proposing to me?" she demanded.

"Because I think you're great and we're good together."

"Oh, really? Well, I know who you're thinking about, too, and that's definitely not going to happen, is it?"

He went a little pale.

"I don't know what you –"

"Mel, that's who – and don't deny it because I've seen it from the beginning!"

He thought about that for a moment.

"And yet you're still going with me, so that means something, doesn't it?"

"It means I should have faced facts and ended it with you a long time ago, Jim. That's what it means."

"Well, why didn't you then?"

She thought about that for a moment or two.

"Because you're Cam's best mate and Mel's mine, that's why. It's – difficult. It would make things quite awkward if we finished with each other. We'd probably lose our good friends."

Jim drummed his fingers on the steering wheel in silence for a moment, and then he spoke again quietly.

"Look, it's late and we're both tired. Let's talk about all this later – tomorrow maybe?"

"Okay," she agreed, and he started up the car again and headed for her street.

They said nothing to each other during the remainder of the journey and Belinda was glad to jump out of the car and say goodbye once they arrived. She ran into the house and closed the door behind her, leaning against it for support. Her mind was spinning after her conversation with Jim. What a day it had been! Exhausted though she was, she knew falling asleep quickly was likely to be a tall order.

20 DECISIONS, DECISIONS

The following morning, Belinda started her Sunday by pacing up and down her bedroom in her pyjamas. She had eventually slept fairly well, but now that she was awake her brain was fairly buzzing with the whole idea of getting married to Jim. She was compiling a list of pros and cons in her head. He was a very nice man, a steady, hard-working man, and he was, obviously, very fond of her. She was quite sure he would make an excellent husband and father. But on the other hand, she wasn't in love with him. She was in love with someone else and so was he. She continued thinking about these things as she drew her gown around her and ran downstairs to have some breakfast. She wasn't sure of what to do; she wasn't sure of anything. She couldn't even make up her mind whether to tell anyone else about the proposal or simply be content to mull it over by herself.

Unknown to Belinda, her sister April was taking decisions about marriage also. She was standing in the kitchen of Scott's flat filling the kettle and daydreaming about her wedding day. What she'd wear, how she'd have her hair done and where she'd like to go on honeymoon. The Maldives, probably, she was thinking – or maybe the Seychelles.

"Well, you're looking a lot better this morning!" Scott said, coming up behind her and putting his arms around her waist.

"What? Oh, yes, not bad. Still a bit queasy, though, you know."

"Well, you look fantastic. I'll have a coffee if you're making some. I'll do some scrambled eggs if you fancy that?"

She fancied it a lot, but she shook her head.

"No, don't think I could manage that, Scott."

"Okay. Eggs for one then," he said, looking out the eggs and a non-stick pot to do them in.

April tried to squash down her annoyance. He just wasn't taking the bait so far and he seemed a little bit preoccupied lately. Maybe he was going off the boil. She would just have to up the ante a little. It was time to get this show on the road, but she didn't want to overdo things. He was a doctor, after all, and he would know if she went too far with her faking. She would have to be subtle. As she put their coffees down on the table, she made sure he was looking in her direction and then grabbed hold of the corner of the table, drawing in a little gasp of air as she did so.

"April? Are you okay? What's up?" Scott asked. He sounded concerned, and that was exactly what she wanted. He put down the eggs he was whisking and walked over to her.

"I'm fine, really. Just felt a bit faint for a minute, that's all. I'll be all right in a minute." She said softly, trying to sound brave and pathetic at the same time.

"Don't be silly. You go through and sit down and I'll finish breakfast. No point in struggling on if you're not feeling right."

She gave a tired little smile and walked off slowly into the lounge.

"Oh, would you bring my coffee in for me, please, Scott?" she called out over her shoulder, wishing she could wolf down some of those eggs and a slice of buttery toast at the same time. Even though she was a model, she'd always had a very fast metabolism and never went on diets or worried about what she ate or anything like that. But it would be worth it in the end, the pretences she was obliged to go through with now, she told herself. She had a lot to gain and she intended to do just that.

*

Belinda was glad it was the weekend. She couldn't stop thinking about Jim's proposal. She kept telling herself that it was crazy to marry someone you didn't love, but then, she knew she would never love anyone other than Scott, and he was with her sister. So her only real alternative to marrying Jim was to stay single, and she just couldn't see herself doing that. She still had her whole life in front of her, and she would have to watch April and Scott getting married and having a family together while she spent her days lonely and unloved. And the thought of never having children was not something she could live with. She knew her own nature. She wanted a home, a husband and a family. But could she love one man and live her life with someone else? She just didn't know the answer to that question. She chewed on the inside of her cheek so much as she dwelt on these questions that it was quite sore by the time the afternoon arrived.

Belinda tried to keep busy by helping her mother with the housework and looking after her dad. She was aware of her mother looking at her thoughtfully a few times and she looked back at her and smiled so that she wouldn't worry about her or ask awkward questions.

Suddenly the doorbell rang and Belinda froze. If it was Jim she would have no idea what to say to him. Her mum went to the door and Belinda could hear a male voice speaking to her in the hallway. She cringed and tried to concentrate on polishing the lounge furniture very hard.

Jim came into the room and her mum asked him if he would like a cup of tea.

"Actually, I thought maybe Belinda would like to come out to a cafe or something and get a bit of lunch," he answered, glancing at Belinda while he waited for her to respond.

"Well, that sounds nice, but I'm helping Mum right now," she prevaricated.

"Oh, don't be silly, Belinda," Mrs Carter protested. "The tidying up's nearly done. You get off with Jim while the weather holds. Looks like it'll plump down later on."

Belinda smiled weakly and went to get her jacket. She and Jim left the house and jumped into his car.

"There's a wee place I know just ten minutes or so away, Belinda. It's nice and quiet. We can have something to eat and talk things over," he told her, glancing over at her to gauge her mood.

She simply nodded and fell to gazing out of the car window at the people walking along the street. She didn't know if this talk was going to help her state of mind or not, but she was getting nowhere thinking about it on her own, so she decided that it couldn't hurt.

A few minutes later, Jim drew up outside a very cosy-looking pub, which had an advertisement for all-day food on a billboard outside. Belinda could hear quite a bit of noise coming from inside.

"Thought it was somewhere quiet, Jim," she said, with a puzzled frown.

"It's always busy downstairs, but there's an upstairs restaurant where they do a very nice lunch menu and it's usually quiet enough to talk," he assured her.

They stepped inside and went straight upstairs. A very pleasant, middle-aged woman with short blonde hair ushered them over towards a small table for two against the far wall and handed them each a menu.

"What would you like to drink?" she asked.

Belinda ordered a Martini and Jim ordered a bottle of Becks Blue. They looked at the menu while they waited for their drinks.

"Jim –" Belinda began, but he held up his hand.

"It's okay. I'm not going to pressure you, Belinda. I just thought it might help if we talked about this so that we can iron out a few things so we both know what to expect."

Belinda sat back in her seat and let herself relax a little.

"Yes, it all tends to go round and round in your head, doesn't it?" she said.

"I know. And we have to discuss what we'd do if circumstances changed for one or both of us while we were engaged. And what we'd like to aim for if we do get married. The kind of house and lifestyle we'd each like; how many kids we'd want, etcetera. It's best if we both know the score about these things before we commit to each other, if that's what you decide you'd like to do."

Their drinks arrived and Belinda took a long draught of her very refreshing vermouth. She felt much better already and decided she'd like to have a toasted sandwich and salad. She just wished the other decisions she had to make could be achieved as easily as that, and she said so to Jim.

"I know, I know. It's a big decision," Jim agreed. "But first things first. I think I should say that I'd like to stay somewhere in Glasgow. I don't really want to move away anywhere. I'm not bothered about the type of house. I'll let you have your preference there, if you say 'yes' to getting married. And I don't think I'd like any more than two children. What about yourself?"

"I ... well, like you, I want to stay in Glasgow and I really like Mel and Cam's house, so maybe a house like that would be nice. I'd like children, but I've never actually thought about how many before," she replied, feeling quite shy about discussing these matters with him.

The waitress arrived with their meals then and they sat eating quietly for a while.

"Well, there's no hurry for a decision – on anything," Jim reassured her.

"I won't keep you hanging around waiting for an answer for long, Jim," she told him. "That wouldn't be fair to you."

They fell silent and Belinda watched his face while he ate his lunch. He was a lovely man – kind and considerate and caring – and she knew she wouldn't get another chance like this again in a hurry – if ever. But she'd seen him flinch a little when she'd mentioned Mel and Cam's house, and that made her undecided all over again. What if they ended up resenting each other? Could this really work or were they just kidding themselves, settling for something that was never going to work out? She felt torn all over again and no nearer to reaching a decision than she'd been when they'd set out earlier.

She gazed out of the large bay window and noted the very heavy sky. It seemed her mum had been right. She could see the first large drops of rain on the window pane already. It was only the month of May behaving more like April, but it felt like an omen to her. She told herself not to be silly, but she couldn't help wondering about what Jim had said earlier about changes. Life circumstances can change just as suddenly as the weather. What if circumstances changed during their engagement? That would be fair enough, she mused, because they could release each other from their understanding if they weren't married yet. But a much worse scenario would arise if they got married and things changed then, either with Mel's marriage or with Scott's relationship with April. Belinda remembered the way he had kissed her in the park just a few days ago and she knew she would never forget it. But that couldn't sustain her through a lifetime of loneliness and she was quite sure that it would never happen again. Scott wouldn't let it happen again. And even if it did, Belinda would never get involved with the man who was living with her sister. It was unthinkable to her! An idea began to form in her mind. Melissa was well and truly married, but Scott wasn't. And she made a promise to herself that if Scott became engaged to April, she would get engaged to Jim. She didn't say anything to Jim about her decision. She knew she couldn't marry him while Scott was still free; so she made up her mind that if he pressed her for a decision while Scott and her sister were still together, her answer would be 'no'.

She felt a little happier once she had come to that conclusion, but as they finished eating their meal, the rain began to pour down very heavily, battering angrily against the window panes, and she was sure she could hear the ominous rumble of thunder in the distance.

21 THE LAST STRAW

One week later, Scott drew into the driveway at his flat, gathered up his mobile and his doctor's bag and jumped out of the car. He walked briskly towards the front door and went inside. He had a whole day off to himself the following day and he was really looking forward to it. He was very tired, having been up half of the previous night with a very ill patient, who had eventually been admitted to hospital in the early hours of the morning. All he wanted to do was pour himself a drink, have something to eat and chill out in front of the television. He hoped April had made some dinner for them because he was too bushed to cook anything.

However, there was no appetising smell of cooking as he entered the hallway and his heart sank. They would just have to order takeaway again, he decided as he went into the lounge. Not very healthy to be doing that on a regular basis, though, he thought, sighing. There was no sign of April, so he walked back along the hallway towards the bedroom.

When he opened the door, he was puzzled to find April lying in bed.

"April?" he asked. "Are you sick again?"

"I don't feel good at all, Scott. I've been feeling sick all day. And tired. I just want to go to sleep all the time," she answered, sighing pathetically.

Scott frowned and bent over her, looking intently at her face.

"Let me take a look at you. You do look a bit peaky, actually," he commented.

"Scott, I don't want to worry you, but I think I might be pregnant," April said softly, watching his face carefully to see his initial reaction.

Scott stood up straight.

"What!" he gasped. But you can't be. You've been taking your pill, haven't you?"

"Yes, of course I have," she answered, looking hurt.

"Sorry, April, but I don't know how you could be pregnant then. It must be something else."

Suddenly it hit him.

"April, when you went to see your G.P. a few weeks ago, did he prescribe any tablets for you?"

She nodded, trying not to smile.

"Antibiotics," she replied innocently. She'd done her homework and she knew that a course of antibiotics could sometimes cause hormonal changes, which can at times result in a lowered protection against pregnancy.

"Oh my God, I don't believe this. I didn't even ask you. I should have thought. I'm so sorry, April," he said, bending down to take her in his arms.

"It's okay, it's not your fault, Scott," she told him in a soothing voice. "Maybe it's not that anyway. We'll just have to wait and see."

"We don't need to wait. I'll get you a test first thing tomorrow. Let me bring you a cup of tea and something to eat," he told her, leaving the room quickly so that he could hide his reaction from her. He was horrified. This was the last thing he wanted. If she was pregnant there was nothing else for it – he would just have to marry her. He felt sick. And for some reason he couldn't quite understand, a vision of Belinda's face swam before his eyes. He put his head in his hands, trying to cope with the sudden shock of the situation and trying to calm himself down. He went into the kitchen and began to make some sandwiches and drinks for them both. He couldn't concentrate properly and managed to scald his hand on the boiling water as he poured out their drinks. He sat down at the breakfast bar for a moment and made a valiant effort to pull himself together before taking the food through to April. He made sure she was okay and then went through to the lounge again to have his own meal.

He sat down and ate mechanically, shovelling the bread into his mouth without really tasting the cheese and pickle. This couldn't be happening. Maybe it would be all right, he told himself; maybe she wouldn't be pregnant after all. But the sinking feeling in his gut told him otherwise. He should have been more careful. He was a doctor. He asked himself wretchedly how he could have been so careless.

By the time he had finished eating and drinking he felt a little calmer and told himself that he would just have to go with the flow. There was no way he wanted her to have a termination, so if they were in that situation, they would be married – as soon as possible. He would never leave her to cope with something like that on her own. He felt sad at the very thought of it and wondered why that was. They were living together and she was a perfectly nice companion and they were fine in the bed department. Why shouldn't they get married? He sighed heavily and went through to the bedroom to collect April's plate and cup. She had managed to eat half a sandwich and had taken a few sips of the tea.

"Sorry, Scott. My stomach just isn't up to it," she said apologetically. She crossed her fingers under the duvet, hoping he wouldn't notice that the food she'd eaten earlier that day was missing from the fridge. She hoped he'd be too upset to think about things like that. Anyway, if he did notice, she could just say that she'd felt hungry at the time but had brought it all back up again afterwards. Having made that decision, she closed her eyes and turned her face into the pillow. After a minute or two she heard him closing the door behind him and she relaxed. Well, she'd done it. She'd actually done it. She knew instinctively that he would stand by her and propose to her and she was all ready with her answer. She lifted her mobile from the bedside table and sent Max a little text to keep him up to date. They would have to be more careful than ever now, she told him. He sent her back a couple of kisses and said he'd see her the next day. She smiled and put the phone down again. She dozed off, wondering how long it would be before Scott proposed to her.

*

Scott didn't get very much sleep that night, even though he was exhausted. He tossed and turned restlessly and eventually rose very early and set off for the nearest chemist. He picked up a pregnancy test and paid for it at the desk. He could have asked April for a urine sample and sent it off to the lab, but it was much quicker to use the kit. Then they would know right away. He slipped it into his inside pocket and left the shop. As soon as he arrived home he took it into the bedroom and left it on the bedside table for April to find when she woke up. Then he tiptoed out of the room because it was still very early and he didn't want to disturb her sleep.

He had some All-Bran for breakfast and then put his track suit on and went for a jog. He hoped it would clear his head and help him to relax. He found himself going in the direction of the park and he was soon sitting on the bench where he and Belinda had kissed that Sunday morning while he had comforted her when she was so upset about June and Mickey. He had never felt sadder in his life and he was beginning to have some inkling about why he felt so upset. It wasn't just the feeling of being trapped, which was bad enough in itself. He was slowly coming to realise that he had serious feelings for Belinda. He had tried to pretend to her and to himself that he didn't because he was living with her sister, but this shock to his system had brought him directly up against the truth. He had to face it. He was going to have to marry April, but he was in love with Belinda. '*God, what a mess!*' he muttered to himself. He couldn't believe that this had happened. It was like some sort of unlikely soap opera plot. He had always felt superior to the type of person who let their life get into an emotional mess. He was used to taking charge, to being in control and knowing exactly what to do in a crisis. Well, this time he knew exactly what he *ought* to do, but every atom of his being cried out against it. He stood up slowly and walked even more slowly back home. It started to rain as he walked, but he barely noticed it.

As soon as he got back home, he took a shower and changed into jeans and a sweatshirt. He went to sit in the lounge and watch television. It could still be some time before April got up, so he flicked through lots of channels and then switched the television off. He went into the kitchen and started to prepare lunch. He thought he might as well. There was nothing else to do and it would keep him from dwelling on his situation. As he peeled and chopped mushrooms and onions, the thought occurred to him that maybe April wouldn't want to marry him, even if she was pregnant. This thought cheered him up for a little while, but eventually he had to face the fact that that scenario was very unlikely. Suddenly there was blood all over the onion he was slicing. He had sliced into his finger. He swore and ran it under the tap to clean it. Then he dried it with a paper towel and rummaged in the drawer for a sticking plaster. Just as he finished applying it, April came into the kitchen. She stood quietly at the door with a tragic look on her face.

"Scott, I did the test. It was positive. I'm pregnant," she wailed, hurling herself forward into his arms. He held her close, wincing as his cut finger continued to throb.

"Don't cry, April, don't cry. It's not the end of the world. How do you feel about it? Do you want to keep it?" he asked.

She drew back from him instantly, staring at him in horror.

"I don't believe you just said that! I can't believe you would think that I –" she broke off dramatically. She burst into tears and he put his arms around her again.

"I didn't mean it like that, April. I just needed to know how you felt. Don't worry, I won't let you down. I'm here for you. We'll get married as soon as possible – if that's what you want to do."

"Oh, Scott, do you mean it?" she asked, tears welling up in her eyes. He wasn't to know they were tears of joy. And he tried to tell himself that the onion he'd been slicing onion was making his own eyes water.

"Of course I mean it, silly." He went down on one knee and forced himself to ask her properly.

"Will you marry me, April?" he said, his voice shaking with emotion.

"Of course I will, Scott. Of course I will," she answered, hugging him tightly.

"Right then, that's settled," he said, clearing his throat. "We'll get it arranged as soon as possible." He was glad she couldn't see his face because *his* eyes were filled with tears also, and they certainly weren't tears of joy.

22 RULES OF ENGAGEMENT

The following evening, Belinda and her family were just finishing their evening meal when April rushed noisily through the front door and burst into the kitchen, banging the door against the wall as she did so.

"We're getting married. Mum, Dad – we're getting married!" she announced proudly, as if she had just passed an important exam. Scott had asked her to wait a little while before delivering their news to the family, but she had told him she just couldn't wait and he had eventually given in and said she could tell them.

Belinda froze, experiencing a confusing combination of disbelief and shock. Her parents and June all got up immediately to hug and congratulate April.

"Belinda, come and give your sister a hug. Isn't this wonderful? We're delighted for you, love!" her mother said sincerely, and Belinda reluctantly stood up and hugged April, but couldn't quite bring herself to congratulate her. She sat back down on her seat at the kitchen table while the others trooped noisily through to the lounge to pour celebratory drinks. She sat very still, staring straight ahead of her as the news sank into her brain. There was no room for hope now, she realised. He was marrying her sister. The kiss they'd shared must simply have been a moment of madness for him, a result of his compassionate nature, and he probably deeply regretted it now. She took a slow, deep breath and forced herself to go into the lounge and join her family. She didn't want anyone to suspect what her feelings were for Scott or to realise how horrified she was that he and April were engaged. She sat down and smiled woodenly, trying to join in the general euphoria, but her heart wasn't in it, and she soon bade them all goodnight and went off upstairs to her room, her footsteps on the staircase feeling nearly as heavy as her heart.

She was glad she no longer shared her room with June because she knew when the numbness wore off there would be many tears on her pillow that night.

*

The following morning Belinda rose reluctantly and began to get ready for work. She had cried herself to sleep the night before and was sure she was all cried out; but as soon as the warm water of the shower slid over her head the tears started again. Slow, hot tears that burned her eyes. She wished she could wash away her misery as easily as she could wash her body.

During the rest of that day, as she did her work like an automaton, she tortured herself with visions of Scott's happiness and excitement, his elation at the thought of marrying April. He had to be in love with April, she concluded, otherwise why would he have proposed? Belinda was trying very hard to come to terms with the news, and that was why she was being ruthless with herself every time she felt that little niggling feeling that maybe he wasn't as excited about it as April – that maybe he had proposed for another reason. Maybe April was pregnant! But that thought was even worse, Belinda decided. It made her feel physically ill. She couldn't bear for April to carry Scott's children. It just didn't feel right to her.

A dull ache had started in her head by the time she left work and was still throbbing by the time she eventually arrived back home in the evening. As soon as she had finished picking at her plate of chicken and chips, she complained loudly about the headache and went off upstairs. She decided if she was going to get any sleep that night, she needed some peace of mind. She would never be able to relax without some help. Her nerves were shattered with the effort of trying to hold her feelings inside. She swallowed a herbal sleep remedy and got ready for bed. As she slid between the cool, smooth sheets she hoped that sleep would not elude her and that she would feel the effects of the tablet soon. But a tiny part of her couldn't help wondering why Scott hadn't come with April to break the news of their engagement. Belinda told herself sternly to stop that nonsense immediately. She needed some respite from the emotional turmoil she felt and she desperately needed to not even think about the decision she had to make regarding Jim's proposal. It was all becoming too much for her.

*

Belinda felt more rested the following day, but was still in a state of unease and indecision. She spent the morning trying to sort out her situation in her own head. She was feeling calmer now, but still hadn't decided what to do about the future. She kept thinking about Jim and how he felt about Melissa. She was now much more aware of how awkward and difficult his situation must be for him and she felt sorry for him. As if in response to her thoughts about him, Jim rang her during her lunch break.

"Belinda, can I come and see you tonight?" he asked. "We could go out for a drink somewhere if you want."

"Of course you can come and see me," she answered, his kind and pleasant tone acting as a soothing balm on her raw emotions. "But I don't know if I'm going to be feeling like going out anywhere. I'm not very good company right now," she added apologetically.

"That's okay. I'll try and cheer you up,"

She smiled and sighed into her phone. "Thanks, Jim. I do need cheering up," she admitted.

He rang off and she went back to work. After a while, she realised that she would probably be glad to get out of the house for a while that evening, even though it was only Monday night. She would need to escape from all the marriage and wedding talk she knew would go on between her mum and June. They were very excited about it, particularly so because it would be happening very soon, and they were bound to notice, sooner or later, that *she* wasn't excited about it at all.

Jim and Belinda were just leaving the house that evening when they ran into Scott and April, who were just arriving.

"I believe congratulations are in order," Jim said, shaking Scott's hand and bending to kiss April's cheek.

"Thanks, Jim. We're very excited about it all, aren't we, Scott?" April said, looking to Scott to confirm this.

"Yes, of course," he agreed.

"Got a date yet?" Jim asked, trying to cover the fact that Belinda had gone very silent.

"Oh, quite soon, I think," April said smugly, glancing up at Scott, who merely nodded.

"Well, we'd better get off," Jim said quietly.

"Okay, see you later then!" April chirped, smiling as she pulled Scott by the arm and guided him towards the front door of the house.

"If you ask me, the poor guy doesn't look too rapturous about it, does he?" Jim commented as he opened the car door for her.

Belinda didn't answer him and he shot her a look as he sat down in the driver's seat.

"Do you think she's up the duff?" he asked.

Belinda winced and closed her eyes. Jim put his arm around her shoulders and just held her. After a moment he spoke to her gently.

"I know it's hard, Belinda, but it's happening, so you just have to accept it. I had to, as well, when Mel and Cam got together; so I do know how you feel. And to make matters worse, it was me who introduced them to each other!"

"I know you understand how I feel, Jim," she told him, "but that doesn't make it any easier. In fact, it makes it worse in a way. We're both settling for second best – and marriage is difficult enough when two people are madly in love with each other, never mind just making do!"

He drew back from her and started the car. They didn't speak again until they'd reached the Chinese Restaurant.

They were ushered to their seats and Jim ordered a soft drink for himself and a large glass of wine for Belinda. After a few moments, he leaned across the table and took her hands in his.

"Can I take it, then, that you've decided not to go ahead with our own engagement?" he asked, disappointment evident in his expression.

"Oh, Jim, I couldn't make a decision like that right now if my life depended on it," she answered, shaking her head in despair.

He sighed in relief and let her hands go.

"Okay then. Let's just play it by ear and not rush into anything," he suggested.

She smiled gratefully.

"Thanks, Jim. I hope you don't think I'm leading you up the garden path. I really am trying to decide what to do for the best, but it's not easy. I want to say 'yes', but what if we go ahead with getting married and then things change with either Melissa's marriage or April and Scott's? What then?"

"Okay, what about this for an idea?" he suggested. "How about we get engaged soon, but don't set the date until after April and Scott's wedding? That way we're aiming towards something but aren't fully committed yet. That's what engagements are for, after all, isn't it?"

"And if things change with the others after we're married – what do we do then? Soldier on or let each other go?" she asked, needing to know exactly where she stood, both now and in the future.

"Hmm. Maybe we both need to give that some thought for a while. I think maybe if we didn't have any kids to consider, we could make a pact to let each other go if either Scott of Melissa became free unexpectedly. How would you feel about that?"

"I don't know, Jim. It sounds fine in theory, but would it be that easy if it actually happened? As you say, I think we both need to think about this some more."

The waiter arrived with their starters at that moment and Belinda sat back in her seat to consider what they'd discussed. Maybe that would be a good way to go about things, she thought. And she knew if she had to choose anyone for her 'second option', it would be Jim. He was a lovely man – and he had integrity, too. She could trust him. She knew he would always keep his word to her. She smiled thoughtfully as she lifted her spoon to start her soup. It wasn't a bad idea at all to get engaged but still keep their options open. And she knew that he wouldn't make life difficult for her if Scott and April split up and Belinda decided to call things off with him.

By the time they had finished their meal and Jim had paid the bill, she had made up her mind. She was going to go for it. She had nothing to lose and everything to gain. As soon as they got into the car she turned towards him and told him that she wanted to get engaged and that she would happily marry him once Scott and April were settled together.

"Yes!" I was hoping you would say that!" he exclaimed, gathering her up in his arms and squeezing her tightly. He kissed her firmly on the lips and hugged her again. She smiled happily as she leaned against his shoulder and relaxed. She knew she was so very lucky to have him. He always calmed her fears and made her feel loved and wanted.

"So, when do you want to announce it?" he asked.

"Well, why wait?" she replied. "No time like the present, is there? Poor Mum and Dad are going to have their work cut out coping with all of this happening at the one time, but we'll tell them straight away that it's not going to happen for a while yet."

"Sure. No problem. Would you be mad at me if I said I've already bought a ring for you?" he asked, glancing at her uncertainly.

"Jim, you haven't!" she gasped.

"I wasn't being presumptuous, you know," he added hastily. "I just wanted to be prepared in case you did decide to accept. You don't mind, do you?"

"Well, that depends on whether I like it or not!" she said cheekily.

He slowly drew a black velvet ring box from his jacket pocket and handed it to her.

"If you don't like it we can easily change it, the jeweller said, so don't worry about that," he assured her.

She opened the little box, her heart beginning to beat quickly in her chest. It was a square solitaire on a white gold band. Tears came unexpectedly into her eyes as she lifted it from its silky blue setting.

"It's lovely, Jim," she said softly. "I love it."

"Phew, that's a relief. Go on, try it on. We can get it resized if it's too big or anything."

He took hold of the ring and slid it onto her left hand. It fitted well. She looked up at him and sighed tearfully.

"It fits just fine," she told him.

"Good. That's great. Let's get you home now – you've got work in the morning. And so do I. As to announcing it, well I'll leave that up to you," he told her, sounding calm and satisfied. He started the engine and drove off. Belinda said very little on the way home, but she kept looking down at her engagement ring, trying to get used to how it felt and what it symbolized.

When they arrived back at Belinda's house, they both noticed that Scott's car was still parked outside.

Jim looked across at her, knowing how uncertain she must be feeling.

"I'll come in with you, Belinda, to say goodnight to your parents. And if you want to say something now, that's fine. And if you decide to wait, well that's fine, too. It's up to you."

She nodded gratefully and they entered the front door together. Belinda hung up her coat in the hallway and then she took hold of Jim's hand and opened the lounge door. Everyone was sitting around chatting and drinking cups of tea and coffee. They all turned and looked at the two of them as they came into the room.

"Hi, Mum, Dad," Belinda said, excitement building with every moment. "Jim and I have got something to announce, so we might as well do it while everyone's here," she said nervously.

Jim smiled. "We've just got engaged!" he announced proudly, lifting Belinda's hand to kiss it.

There was total silence and shock for a moment and then everyone gathered around them, exchanging hugs, kisses and handshakes. The women all wanted to see her ring immediately and Belinda's eyes sparkled as she showed it off to them. She was taken aback at how delighted April seemed to be for her, especially since she herself had received April's wedding news in such a lukewarm way. She was careful not to look too closely at Scott, who had gone very quiet. She had made her decision and she intended to do right by Jim and not to hurt him, if she could possibly help it. Only time would tell if she had in fact made the right decision.

23 THE WEDDING PLANNER

The Carter household was fairly buzzing the following evening. April had appeared unexpectedly after dinnertime and was sitting chatting with her mother, father and sisters, when she suddenly said she had something to tell them.

"Oh, no. I don't think I can take any more excitement!" Mr Carter said, clutching at his chest melodramatically.

"Don't worry, Dad. It's nothing bad. It's very good news, in fact," April assured him.

She felt a little nervous because she was deceiving them, but it had to be done, so she took a deep breath and told them she was expecting a baby.

Belinda's jaw dropped open. She didn't know what to think now. She had suspected that this was the case, but now that April had confirmed her suspicions, she felt suddenly deflated. There was no way Scott would back out of his commitments now, that was for sure. That knowledge should have made her feel even more certain of her decision to accept Jim, but instead it only made her feel sad.

They all said "Congratulations!" together and Elspeth excitedly asked when she was due. April had worked it all out and said it was due at the beginning of December.

"So the wedding will be as soon as possible, obviously," she added. "Otherwise, I'd have suggested a double wedding, Belinda!" she said excitedly.

Belinda tried to hide her absolute horror at the very idea of that and simply nodded understandingly.

"Oh, ours won't be for some time yet," she said hurriedly.

"Thank goodness for that," her mum said. She looked absolutely delighted with this fresh news and she and her husband smiled contentedly at each other. She was so relieved because she didn't have to worry about her daughters any more and she was sure that everything would be just fine now.

However, Pete Carter wasn't quite so convinced of that. He felt that all of these changes were happening just a little too quickly for his liking, and Belinda still had some sadness in her eyes from time to time. He frowned a little as he tried to remember when he had first noticed it, and he wondered if he should ask her in private if everything was all right with her. He decided to do this sooner rather than later. They had always been close and he was sure she would tell him if anything was amiss. He decided he would tackle her as soon as an opportunity arose. He looked over at her and there it was again – those shadows in her eyes, and a troubled frown between her brows.

*

A little while later, as Belinda was heading into the kitchen to rinse her cup out before going to bed, her father appeared behind her. He touched her elbow and she turned to face him. He had closed the door, she noticed, and she became a little tense, wondering what he was going to say to her.

"Belinda, love, is everything all right with you? Sometimes you look a bit sad. There's nothing wrong, is there?"

"No, of course not, Dad. Everything's fine. Couldn't be better, in fact" she fibbed, chewing on her lower lip. Her dad was no fool and if he persisted in quizzing her, she knew she would eventually give in and tell him all her troubles.

But thankfully he didn't pursue it.

"That's okay then, love. Just wanted to make sure," he said. "Night then."

"Night, Dad," she replied, relieved when she was able to run off upstairs to the safety of her own room. As she undressed she hoped that her dad would be content to let it go and not question her again. She would have to be on her guard now. He wouldn't like the arrangement she and Jim had entered into at all, she knew that much. She would have to warn Jim, also, to be on his guard against anyone asking too many questions about their relationship. She tried hard to focus on herself and Jim and their situation, so that she wouldn't have to think about April and Scott and the child they were about to have together.

*

A couple of miles away, in his own house, Scott was having a similar problem. He couldn't seem to focus on his current situation with April and the pregnancy. All he could think about was Belinda and the announcement of her engagement to Jim. He had tried to catch her eye the previous night so that he could be sure that she was happy, but there had been too many other people around, and she had refused to look directly at him. That in itself was preying on his mind. Surely, she wasn't doing this to get back at him for kissing her that morning in the park? He had begun to realise that he had feelings for her then and he was almost certain she had feelings for him, too. He wasn't an arrogant man and didn't imagine that every woman he met was lusting after him, but he couldn't get that day out of his head and he strongly suspected that Belinda felt the same way. But even if she did, he reminded himself, they couldn't do anything about it now. They were both with other partners and there was a baby on the way. He ran his fingers distractedly through the front of his hair. There was nothing else to be done – he had responsibilities now and couldn't just act on any feelings of attraction that might exist. Quite apart from anything else, Belinda was April's sister. The situation seemed to be turning into more and more of a mess as time went on.

He eventually came to the conclusion that he would just have to try to forget his feelings for Belinda and also try to see as little as possible of her from now on. But the trouble was that he didn't want to do that. He thought about her constantly and was always wondering if she was thinking about him, too. He wondered if there was any point in talking to her and asking her if he was simply imagining things. Maybe he was just dreaming up this attraction because he felt trapped and saw it as a possible way out. That possibility made him feel like a heel, on several levels. And what if he spoke to her and she gave him a horrified look and then told the rest of the family what he'd said to her? No, it was no good. He would just have to bite the bullet and make sure he looked after April and the baby as best he could. He also wondered why he didn't feel any excitement about the baby, either. He'd wanted to become a father for some time, but he didn't feel anything at all. He frowned and sighed heavily as he heard April calling to him from the lounge. He stood up reluctantly and walked into the other room.

"Scott, can you bring me something to eat now? I haven't managed to eat anything at all today and I'm a bit peckish now," she explained as he stood uncertainly in the doorway. "Oh, and I need to discuss some arrangements for the wedding with you, too," she added.

"Sure, love," he said, turning his back on her and going into the kitchen again. He knew what she was going to suggest and he had his excuse ready.

When he returned to the lounge with her ham salad, she wrinkled up her nose and told him that it wouldn't feed a bird.

"It's nutritious," he replied. "So, eat up. What did you want to talk to me about?"

"Well, I thought the end of the month for the wedding. I don't want to be all fat and heavy-looking in my wedding outfit," she told him.

"I'm sorry, love, but that's out of the question," he answered quickly.

"Well, it's going to have to be sometime soon, Scott. I'm feeling quite bloated already."

"Well, my parents are on a Caribbean cruise right now and I'm not getting married without them at the ceremony," he told her.

"But Scott – can't you ask them to come home early or something?" she wailed.

"No, I can't, April. They've been saving up and looking forward to this holiday for years, and I've no intention of cutting it short for them."

April pouted and looked aggrieved, but Scott remained adamant. He wasn't ready to tie the knot yet. He knew he was simply putting off the inevitable, but he couldn't face a ceremony in a mere couple of weeks. It was too soon. He needed time to get his head round the idea first and come to terms with it properly. He spoke to himself sternly. This was going to be his life from now on and he would just have to get on with it. As Mrs Carter would have said, "Whatever way you make your bed, that's the way you have to lie in it!"

24 DEAD END

Three weeks later, towards 12 noon on a sunny Saturday morning in early June, Melissa was at home alone. She had closed the blinds and was lying on the sofa with a cold cloth across her forehead, trying to sleep off a really bad migraine. She was propped up by cushions and had brought her duvet downstairs to snuggle into. She was glad it was the weekend because she didn't like taking time off her work. She was dozing fitfully and having a rather unpleasant dream when she heard someone ringing the front doorbell. She groaned and tried to ignore it. She felt really unwell and extremely tired and she couldn't seem to make herself get up to answer the door. She stayed where she was and told herself that they would go away if she didn't answer it, and if it was important they would come back later.

However, she heard the bell ring yet again, rather insistently. Someone seemed determined to force her to come to the door. She swore, threw back the duvet and hauled herself up from the sofa.

The bell rang again as she walked along the hallway.

"Oh, all right, all right, I'm coming. For goodness sake stop making that racket!" she muttered angrily, her head aching even more now.

She drew the door open and squinted against the strong sunshine. She could see two people standing there against the light, but she couldn't make out any more than that.

"Well, what's all the hurry?" she demanded. "I'm trying to rest."

"Are you Mrs Bancroft – Mrs Melissa Bancroft?" one of them asked her.

She put her hand over her forehead to shield her eyes and realised with a jolt that they were police officers. They both flashed their ID badges at her and told her their names.

"Yes, I am," she answered, her heart beginning to beat faster. "What is it? What's happened?" she asked, needing to know but desperately not wanting to know, all at the same time.

They asked if they could come in and she stood back to let them pass. The three of them walked into the lounge and they suggested that she sit down.

Melissa felt as though she was going to faint. She began to sway. She couldn't speak now. One of the men took hold of her arm and led her over to the sofa she had been resting on.

They began to speak, but Melissa somehow knew what they were going to tell her and she put her hands over her ears and kept saying "No, no, no," over and over again. Eventually she stopped speaking and looked at them, taking her hands down from her ears. One of the officers cleared his throat nervously and spoke to her directly.

"Mrs Bancroft, I'm afraid your husband and son have been involved in an accident – a car crash. Your husband's car was hit by a truck which went through a red light. I'm sorry to have to tell you that your husband didn't make it. He died in the ambulance on the way to hospital."

Melissa closed her eyes and shook her head in denial.

"This isn't happening. It's just a dream – a very nasty one. It's not real. It can't be." She looked at the officers for reassurance, but the man who had told her about Cam simply carried on speaking in the same flat tone of voice, obviously intent on getting this unpleasant duty over with.

"I'm afraid your son has sustained head injuries and we've been told he's in a coma. He's at the Southern General Hospital. Do you want us to take you there or is there somebody you would like us to phone for you?"

Melissa was now rocking herself back and forward and didn't reply.

"She's in shock," the older officer said. He went over to sit beside her and asked her if she would come with them to the hospital.

She simply nodded. The younger officer lifted her handbag from the table and handed it to her. On the way out, the older man retrieved her jacket from the hall cupboard and put it around her shoulders. They drove in silence to the hospital. Melissa had begun to shake now and she drew her coat more tightly round her. She felt very cold. As soon as the fresh air had hit her, she had had to face the fact that this wasn't a bad dream – it was terribly, horribly real. She couldn't cope with it and so she simply sat staring straight ahead and trying not to think about what they had told her.

When they arrived, the older officer took charge. He went to the desk and informed the receptionist that they had come to see Toby Bancroft. She gave him the room number and he guided Melissa along the corridor and into the lift to go up one floor. He tightened his hold on her arm as they approached the room and opened the door of the single room. Melissa gasped at the sight of her little boy lying so still on the bed and she put a hand over her mouth in distress. She rushed towards the bed and leaned over him anxiously. He was connected to several monitoring machines and a ventilator. Tears flowed from her eyes as she sat down in the chair next to the bed and lifted his little hand to hold it. She couldn't speak to him. She couldn't take all of this in. She was trying to concentrate on Toby, but she kept hearing those words again, telling her that Cam was dead. He couldn't be, not her Cam. He just couldn't be. Someone had made a dreadful mistake.

The younger officer asked her again if there was anyone he could ring to come and be with her. She thought suddenly of Belinda and nodded.

"Belinda. My phone's in my bag," she told him shakily.

"Is she your friend?" he asked. She nodded.

He took the mobile out and called up the Contacts list. He connected to the number and when the woman answered he gave her a brief account of what had happened to her friend's family and asked if she could possibly come to the hospital. She said, in a very shocked voice, that she would do that straight away, and he hung up.

"She's on her way, Mrs Bancroft. Hopefully she won't be long. We have to go now, but here is my card if you want to contact us again," he told her, slipping the card into her bag for her. He turned and left the room. He had a baby girl himself and couldn't imagine what it would feel like to have something like this happen. It was a living nightmare.

*

At the other end of the line, Belinda ended the call, but didn't put the phone down; she simply stood, staring into space. She didn't know what to do. This dreadful thing had happened to Melissa's lovely little family and she had no idea how to help her. Poor Cam – and poor, poor little Toby! It was unthinkable. And how was she even going to get to the hospital? It would take ages on the bus – and she had no idea what to say to Melissa when she got there.

"What is it, love? You're white as a sheet!" her mother said in alarm as she turned and saw her daughter standing looking shocked, the phone handset still in her hand. Belinda explained what had happened and her mother was as horrified as she was. Pete was still unwell and in no fit state to help her, so Mrs Carter tried to think of anyone else who could fill the breach. The only one she could think of was April's fiancé, Scott. She lifted the phone out of Belinda's hand and pressed the speed dial for his number. It was April who answered.

"Oh, hi, Mum. How's things?" she asked cheerfully. Her mother explained the situation and she gasped.

"That's absolutely dreadful, Mum," she replied.

"April, is Scott there?" Mrs Carter asked.

"No, but he's due home any minute," April told her.

"Love, I know it's a bit of a cheek, but I don't want to ask your dad to help, for obvious reasons, and I don't know who else to ask. Do you think you could tell Scott what's happened and ask if he wouldn't mind coming over and maybe drive Belinda to the hospital? She's in too much of a state to go clambering on and off buses."

"Of course I will, Mum," April said reassuringly. "In fact, I'll text him right now," she added. She put the phone down and lifted her mobile to send the text.

Scott replied to her within a few minutes that he was just leaving the surgery and would head straight over to the Carters' house.

He was as good as his word and arrived to find Mrs Carter handing out cups of tea to her husband and Belinda, who both looked pale and shocked. Belinda didn't stand up when Scott arrived; she merely sat and sipped her tea, to which her mother had added sugar to help with the shock, although she didn't normally take any sugar in it.

Elspeth poured out a cup of tea for Scott and he swallowed it in a couple of gulps. He kept looking over at Belinda, but her head was lowered and she wouldn't look up at him.

"Belinda, just let me know when you're ready to leave and we'll go," he told her. She simply nodded, still avoiding his eyes.

A few moments later she stood up shakily and went into the hallway to get her coat. Scott stood up to follow her.

"I'm sorry we had to bother you with this, Scott," Elspeth said apologetically. "I didn't know what else to do."

"That's okay, Mrs Carter. I'm really glad you let me know about it. I can't even imagine what Melissa must be going through. I hope the little boy recovers. It will be hard enough for her to cope if he does, but if he doesn't ..."

"I know, I know," Elspeth replied, shaking her head in deep sympathy.

Scott heard Belinda leaving the house and turned to follow her. He didn't like the look of her and wanted to keep a close eye on her. He just hoped that he would be of some help to both her and her friend when they reached the hospital, and he sent up a silent prayer that Fate wasn't about to deal Melissa a second cruel blow that day.

25 NIGHTMARE

Scott reached across to fasten Belinda's seatbelt for her, as she had forgotten to do it up herself.

"Are you going to be okay, Belinda?" he asked, concern giving his voice a rough edge.

She swallowed. "I'll be fine. I'm just struggling to take all this in. Poor Cam. I can't believe it. How is Melissa going to cope with this? She adored him. They were so happy –"

Tears began to well up in her eyes and Scott resisted the urge to put his arm around her shoulders and hold her. He knew they would never get to the hospital if he started to comfort her because the floodgates would open and it could take a long time for her to calm down enough to speak to Melissa when they got there. Instead, he squeezed her hand sympathetically and turned on the ignition. They drove in silent apprehension until they arrived at the car park. They both got out of the car and Belinda took a deep, steadying breath. She kept picturing little Toby lying in a bed and Melissa sitting beside him, willing him to wake up. She fervently hoped she would be able to be strong for her and offer her some comfort. The entire day was developing a feeling of unreality, like a dreadful nightmare that you can't wake up from.

The two of them walked slowly and reluctantly into the building.

"Thank you for doing this, Scott," Belinda said gratefully.

He smiled grimly at her.

"I just hope there isn't worse news to come," he said, his brow furrowing anxiously. When he saw the dismay on her face, he swiftly added, "I'm sure there won't be. Toby's being looked after now. He's in the best place. And it will give Melissa time to recover a little from the shock of Cam's death before her son wakes up."

Belinda nodded and they went upstairs to the first floor together, to the ward which they'd been told Toby was in. He was in a single room and Belinda was glad of that. Scott pushed the door open for her and she steadied herself and walked through it and past him. The scene inside the room was just as she had pictured it – Melissa was sitting as close to Toby's bed as she could and she was holding his hand. She wasn't saying anything; she simply sat and looked at him with dazed eyes. Belinda walked over towards them and laid her hand gently on Melissa's shoulder. Melissa turned round slowly and looked at her as if she didn't know who she was.

"Mel, it's me. I've come to sit with you," Belinda said, feeling useless and feeble.

Scott pulled up a chair for her to sit on and she sat down on it gratefully.

"I'm going to go and get a cup of coffee. I'll get three, shall I? Either of you want something to eat?" Scott asked.

Belinda looked at Melissa, but she shook her head.

"If you could get three coffees and a couple of muffins or packs of crisps or something, Scott?" Belinda said, adding, "I'll pay you back later."

But Scott frowned at her and said there was no need. He went off to find the nearest coffee machine and to see if he could find a snack machine, too. As he wandered back off down the corridor, he noticed there was a coffee machine and the sign beside it reminded him that there was a cafeteria and a small shop on the ground floor. He went downstairs to get crisps for them and then went back up to the first floor to get the coffees. He was reminded of the last time he had been at the hospital with the Carters when Mr Carter had been taken ill. He stuffed the snacks into his pockets and had to carry the coffees very carefully to avoid spilling any of them and when he arrived back at Toby's room, he called through the door and Belinda opened it for him. He laid their coffees down on the bedside trolley and handed each of them a cup. Melissa looked at him for the first time then.

"Who are you?" she asked.

"Mel, this is Scott, April's fiancé," Belinda informed her, adding, "He's a doctor."

"I'm very sorry about your husband, Melissa," Scott told her. He could see she was still feeling numb and he didn't want to trigger a landslide of emotion. It was best if she focused on her little boy for the time being, as there was still hope for him.

"Have they said anything to you about Toby's progress?" he enquired, wondering what the prognosis was.

She shook her head.

"I'll go off and try and find his doctor when my coffee's done," he promised.

"Thanks, Scott," Belinda said, giving him a rather tearful smile.

They all sat in silence for a few moments and nobody seemed interested in the crisps and muffins he'd bought. He finished his drink and perused the medical notes at the foot of Toby's bed.

"Okay, I'm off to find the Consultant, if I can," he announced. It was a relief to leave the room again and he went along to the nurses' station to ask if Toby's doctor was available. A very pretty, red-haired nurse advised him pleasantly that the doctor would be visiting Toby again in half an hour or so. He thanked her without even noticing the encouraging smile she gave him, and went downstairs and outside for a few moments to get a breath of fresh air. He waited for ten minutes or so, giving the girls time to speak privately if they needed to, and then headed back upstairs to the ward again.

He went back into Toby's room and sat down beside Belinda.

"The doctor will be here in about twenty minutes," he told them.

"Thanks, Scott," Belinda said gratefully.

"I'll stay with Melissa if you want to take a breather," he told her.

She smiled and said she would and she got up and turned to leave the room.

"I'll be back in a wee while, Mel," she said, still feeling rather useless. Melissa just nodded and continued looking down at her son.

Belinda went downstairs and took a stroll round the outside areas. The air was fresh and breezy and she was glad of the respite. A heavy cloud of sadness had settled inside her mind. She was so glad that Scott was here to help her. She had been worried about what to say to Melissa, but as soon as she'd seen her, she'd known that no words would reach her friend anyway. She was in a deep, dark place of suffering that Belinda could only imagine. She had a little weep to herself as she thought about Cam and thought about his lifeless body lying in this same hospital, in the Morgue. She sent up a fervent prayer to the heavens that little Toby would survive, because she was sure that Melissa wouldn't be able to handle it if she lost both of them. She started shivering and decided to go back indoors.

When she returned to Toby's room the Consultant had just arrived and was speaking to Melissa. She didn't seem to be really taking in what he was telling her; so he turned towards Scott, who was well known to him personally, and began to tell him the details of Toby's condition. He said that, as far as their preliminary tests could establish, Toby was not in any immediate danger, but that there was no way of knowing how long he was likely to be unconscious. He said that they would do further tests the following day and that they would hopefully know more then. Scott thanked him and the doctor left the room.

"That didn't sound too bad," Belinda commented, keeping her voice low so as not to upset Melissa.

Scott nodded. "He seems to be holding his own at the moment," he said reassuringly. "Do you want to get off home now, Belinda? I can run Melissa home, too, if she's ready to go. No point in hanging around. He could be like this for a while."

"Mel, are you ready to go home yet?" she asked.

Melissa looked round but shook her head. "I want to stay another wee while. I'll just get a taxi when I'm ready to go home," she told them.

Belinda and Scott stood up then and Belinda bent towards Melissa and gave her a little kiss on the forehead.

"Don't sit there too long, Melissa," she advised. "You'll need to get some sleep tonight so that you can be here for Toby tomorrow. You know the nurses will ring you right away if anything changes."

Melissa nodded distractedly and Scott and Belinda left. They made their way down to the car park and both of them sighed when they were settled into the car and had fastened their seatbelts. Belinda felt guilty at the relief she was experiencing at the thought of getting away from the hospital; she also felt guilty for being relieved that Melissa hadn't been with the others when they had gone out earlier that day. All her emotions were tumbling around inside her and conflicting with each other. She could feel a headache coming on and she closed her eyes and rubbed her forehead.

"Do you want to go somewhere for a bite to eat?" Scott asked.

"I've kept you away from April long enough," Belinda replied.

"I think I'll give April a ring and tell her we're going to get a meal somewhere," he said. "I don't want her to prepare one for us as she's not feeling great at the moment," he explained.

"Well, that's fine with me, Scott, as long as April's okay with it," she told him.

He rang April and spoke to her rather brusquely, explaining the situation. He ended the call and started the car, heading towards the city centre, where there were plenty of eating places.

He took her to a McDonald's, and they ordered burgers and chips. As they ate, neither of them enjoying the food much because they were both feeling upset, Belinda felt the urge to confide in him. He always seemed to have that effect on her, she reflected wryly.

"I feel guilty about everything I'm doing and everything I'm thinking today," she told him, shaking her head in an effort to straighten out her thoughts.

"That's only natural, Belinda. You're very close to Melissa – and you were close to Cam, too. And Toby ..."

His kind words brought tears to her eyes and she wiped them away with a rather inadequate serviette.

"If it makes you feel any better, I've thought and felt a lot of things today that have made me feel guilty, too," he confessed unexpectedly.

She frowned.

"Why should *you* feel guilty?" she asked.

"It's really best if we don't go into that," he said quietly, glancing at her and wishing he hadn't mentioned his feelings.

"No. Go on. You've helped me so much today – again – that I want to return the favour, if I can," she told him, looking into his eyes and willing him to open up to her.

He looked right at her.

"I'm feeling guilty because I'm enjoying being with you today – and I shouldn't be enjoying being with you," he admitted.

She gave him a puzzled look.

"They're my friends, not yours, Scott. Obviously, you're not going to be affected by all of this the same way as me." She pointed out. "And I don't know what I'd have done without you today," she added.

He couldn't seem to stop himself now. He shouldn't have started, he knew that. Now he just wanted to tell her everything.

"I want to stay here with you and not go back home to April," he told her very softly, and then wished he hadn't said anything because of the look of total shock on her face. He cursed himself for being selfish. She had enough on her plate right now without him adding to her troubles, he told himself. He bit his lip and fell silent.

Belinda's mouth was full of chewed chips, which she was now having difficulty in swallowing. She lifted her Coke and took a large gulp of it. She managed to somehow swallow the food, but put her fork back down onto her plate. She looked at him in amazement.

"I'm sorry, Belinda. You don't need this right now. You don't need this at all. I shouldn't have said anything. Let's get back to the car and I'll drive you back home."

They stood up and went over to the food disposal container, tipping their half-eaten meals into it. He took her arm and guided her back out of the door and over towards his car. She stopped before they reached it.

"Scott, are you saying what I think you're saying?" she asked, desperate for his answer.

There was no point in back-pedalling now. The cat was out of the proverbial bag. He looked at her miserably and nodded, then opened the car door and got inside. After a moment she did the same and they made their way home, each of them wrapped up in their own private thoughts.

When they arrived at the Carters' house, Scott stopped the car and said "Goodnight, Belinda," to her without looking at her.

"Goodnight, Scott," she replied. She turned at the end of the driveway and watched him drive away into the night.

Later, as she lay in bed, she was assailed by guilt again. She should be thinking of Melissa and her awful situation. It had been a dreadful, seemingly endless day and nothing else should be occupying her mind at that time. The cruelty of Melissa's loss made hot tears run down her cheeks, but she couldn't prevent her thoughts from eventually straying back to Scott and his amazing announcement. She knew exactly what he had meant that evening and she realised she had known, deep down inside herself, since the first day. But she had no idea what to do about it, or how she was going to be able to give Melissa the support she would need in the coming days. She closed her eyes and gave up trying to make any decisions. All she knew now was that she and Scott were in an impossible situation; not as harrowing and devastating as Melissa's, but dreadful nonetheless. She was almost asleep when she realised that she had completely forgotten about Jim! She sat bolt upright, unable to believe that he had gone out of her mind altogether. He was Cam's best friend and he didn't even know what had happened to Cam and his son yet. She threw back the duvet and switched on the light, retrieving her mobile phone from her bag and dialling his number. Her hands shook as she waited for him to pick up and as soon as he answered she burst into tears again.

26 IT'S COMPLICATED

Belinda had told Scott that she didn't know what she would have done without him on the day of Cam's death. Little had she known then that she would come to depend on him even more during the days that followed. He was there every day to take her in to the hospital. Sometimes he did this at rather odd hours, as he had to fit it into his very busy working schedule.

Jim was driving Melissa back and forward from the hospital now, and she stayed there during every day, from morning till night. Then Jim would arrive to drive her home and as soon as he had left she would take a sleeping pill so that she could get some rest. There was still no change in Toby's condition, for better or for worse. She had been to see Cam's battered and bruised body lying in the Morgue, and Jim was the one who had had to make most of the arrangements for his funeral. She would always be grateful to him for that. She was still having difficulty in grieving properly for Cam because she was so taken up with waiting for Toby to wake and despondently wondering if he ever would.

Jim and Belinda saw very little of each other during that time. When the day of Cam's funeral arrived at the end of that week,

Jim arrived at the crematorium with Melissa, and Scott and Belinda arrived together. Belinda was somewhat calmer now and was becoming heavily dependent on Scott's support to give her strength. She dreaded the time when he would tell her that he'd had enough of taking her to and from the hospital. Being in his calming company was the only thing that was keeping her sane and her engagement to Jim seemed to have faded into the background. As she stood and listened tearfully to the eulogies for Cam, she looked at Melissa and Jim standing side by side and she knew she should speak to Jim soon. It was time to face the truth. She couldn't marry him. She saw him glancing over at her and Scott and wondered if he was thinking the same thing.

There were a great many people attending Cam's funeral service, and Melissa had asked Jim to arrange for a meal for all of them at the Hotel Du Vin. The morning had seemed interminably long to Belinda and she didn't intend to stay very long at the hotel, unless Melissa asked her to. She looked around as everyone began to sip their drinks, but she couldn't see her friend. As soon as Melissa and Cam's immediate family had said hello to everyone when they arrived, Melissa had slipped outside to use her mobile phone to ring the hospital and ask about Toby. She wasn't surprised to be advised that there was still no change. She ended the call and stood up straight. She squared her shoulders and took a deep breath. She knew she had to do this for Cam; she had to be there for him this one last time.

She walked back inside the hotel and went over to Cam's mum and dad to ask her how they were holding up. As she did so, Melissa was struck by how much Cam's father resembled him. She'd never really noticed it before because he was considerably older than Cam. But today he looked so much like him that it hurt Melissa to look at him. She could only imagine what these two wonderful people must be feeling at the loss of their son. She suspected they were still in shock, as she was herself. Mary Bancroft's eyes filled with tears again and she pulled out a handkerchief from her bag to blow her nose. Melissa didn't know what to say to her. She knew the woman's grief would never leave her, just as she herself would never stop missing her beloved husband. And she still had the rest of her life to get through. The only thing that was keeping her feet on the ground was the faint hope that Toby would come out of his coma. She squeezed Mary's arm and turned to go and speak to some of the others, to thank them for coming. Cam had a wide circle of friends and they were all there, talking quietly amongst themselves. Melissa looked across at Jim and Belinda, and as soon as she did so, Jim looked back at her and walked over to her. She sometimes thought that he could read her mind.

"Mel, are you coping all right?" he asked. "You know, everyone would understand if you felt you wanted to be alone," he assured her.

"No," she answered, shaking her head. "I've got the rest of my life to be alone, Jim. I have to do this for Cam."

He smiled understandingly and put one arm around her shoulders.

"Thank you for everything you've done since it happened, Jim," she told him sincerely. "I honestly don't know what I would have done without you through all this." It was obvious to her as she looked at him that he was finding it difficult to cope with his emotions, too.

"You know I'm always here for you, Mel, and I always will be," he told her, swallowing the lump in his throat. She smiled gratefully up at him and then saw Belinda coming over to them. Belinda took both her hands and asked if Melissa would like her to call the hospital for her.

"No need. I've already done it, Belinda. No change."

Belinda's parents came over to say goodbye then. Mr Carter still hadn't got his full strength back and was feeling in need of a rest. Belinda felt very alone after they had left. At that point the staff asked them all to be seated so that they could serve the meal and they all took their seats. Belinda managed to get through the next couple of hours with difficulty and couldn't help wishing that Scott was there with her. He'd had to go straight back to work after the service. She seemed to think about him more and more these days. Her love and respect for him deepened with every passing day. It was depressing going to see little Toby lying so still in the hospital bed every day, but this was softened by the fact that Scott was still driving her there each evening after they had both finished work. His company was always soothing to her.

Melissa had started driving herself back and forward to the hospital see her son now, so Scott and Belinda just left each evening whenever they were both ready to go. She hadn't seen April for weeks and she was glad about that. She couldn't bear to think about her sister's pregnancy beginning to show. She felt guilty for feeling that way and tried to remind herself of the tragedies unfolding in her friend's life, so that she could put her own heartache into some sort of perspective. That helped a little and she promised herself she would support Melissa as much as she could in the difficult weeks to come. She was sure she would need all the help and support she could get. If only little Toby would wake up, she thought hopefully, then Melissa could focus on looking after him and they could be a comfort to each other to some extent.

When the afternoon was finally over and everyone had gone home, Jim drove Melissa and Belinda to the hospital. Belinda rang Scott to let him know that she didn't need a lift that night. But the events of the day had taken their toll on them all and Jim drove the two of them home about an hour after they'd arrived at the hospital. They were all feeling shattered. After he had dropped Melissa off, Jim took Belinda home and said goodnight to her before she left the car. She knew there must be a million thoughts and feelings chasing themselves around in his head and so she didn't mention the fact that they really needed to talk, to straighten out what was going to happen about their engagement. There was plenty of time to sort things out. They both needed to get some rest first.

The next day was Saturday and Jim rang her during the first hour of her shift at the salon.

"Belinda, I think we really need to talk," he began hesitantly.

"I know, Jim," she replied. "Pick me up later and we can go somewhere quiet and talk things through."

"Okay. I'll see you later then," he said unhappily. It was obvious to her that he was dreading the discussion they needed to have.

*

When he picked her up in the early evening, he took her to a little restaurant they had never visited before. She was glad it wasn't the same one they'd gone to when he'd proposed to her, just a few short weeks ago. It seemed like a lifetime ago to her now.

They were seated in a little booth against the far wall. The lighting was subdued and as it was still early, the restaurant was fairly quiet. They ordered very light meals and made trivial conversation while they ate their food. As they sipped their coffees afterwards, Jim started to speak, but Belinda held up her hand.

"Jim, I know. I do understand. None of us knew this was going to happen. I realise that everything's changed now and we have to call it off –" she began, but Jim broke in.

"Belinda, that's not what I wanted to say at all," he said anxiously, and she gazed at him in surprise.

"It's not?"

"No, no. You couldn't be more wrong. I'm devastated about Cam and I can't stop thinking about it, but being with you means so much to me now. I feel so dreadfully sorry for Mel, but I feel guilty, too. I feel so terribly guilty, and it makes it very hard to be near her just now. She adored him with all her heart and she always will. I realise that now. I was so stupid before. Cam was my best mate and I wanted to take his wife away from him. What kind of person does that make me? I feel sick just thinking about it. It's almost like Fate took a hand and decided to take him from her because of what I was thinking and feeling. I can hardly bear the guilt and I miss Cam like hell. But I couldn't bear it if we split up as well, Belinda. I need you now more than ever."

Belinda stared at him in amazement and consternation. She couldn't believe what he was saying. She had been so sure he would want to extricate himself from their arrangement now that things had changed. But she couldn't say that to him; he was too distressed. The burden of his guilt was weighing on him heavily. She had to force herself to focus as he began to speak again.

"Obviously, if Toby wakes up and Melissa needs my help to cope, I'll be there for her. I always will be. But I can't think about her the way I used to. It's just not right. She would be horrified if she knew how I used to feel about her. If I said anything to her now, she would probably push me away for good. And I wouldn't blame her. Please say you're not going to dump me, Belinda. Please," he begged in a pathetic voice.

He put his hand over hers and gazed at her pleadingly. She would have had to have a heart made of stone to tell him it was over at that moment. She gave him a little smile and reassured him that nothing had changed. As they left the restaurant and headed for home that night, she was sure she must be feeling even guiltier than Jim. She had got herself into this situation and she was certainly not going to kick him when he was down. She would have to be patient, she told herself. The time would come when things would be easier and she could try to let him down gently. Things were so bad they could only get better, she promised herself, and she was sure that her life couldn't possibly get any more complicated than it already was. Things had to improve; they just had to.

27 IT'S EVEN MORE COMPLICATED

Belinda was, however, very quickly proved wrong about the complications in her life decreasing. No one except Melissa ever went to visit Toby on a Sunday. They wanted to give her some time alone with her son, in case there were things she wanted to say to him, or in case she wanted to have a bit of a cry without anyone seeing her.

The day after Jim told Belinda about his feelings of guilt regarding Melissa, April rang Belinda to ask her if she would come over to the flat. She sounded upset and said that Scott was attending a very sick patient and she wanted someone to talk to. Belinda wasn't happy about this at all and hesitated before she replied.

"Oh, please, Belinda. I need you. Please come over," April pleaded.

"Okay then," Belinda told her reluctantly. "I'll be over in a little while."

She made her way slowly towards the flat, wishing she was anywhere but here at this moment in time. She didn't want to see April and she definitely didn't want to see the flat she shared with Scott. She knew her sister would be starting to gather up baby things by now and wearing loose tops.

As she reached up to ring the doorbell, the door suddenly opened and April threw herself into her sister's arms.

"Oh, Belinda. I can't bear it. I can't bear it," she sobbed against her shoulder.

"What is it, April? What's happened?"

April drew her inside the door and then ran through to the lounge, with a puzzled and concerned Belinda following her.

April threw herself down on the couch dramatically and put her hands over her face.

"I've lost it, Belinda. The baby. I've had a miscarriage!" she exclaimed.

"Oh my God," Belinda said, putting her hand over her mouth. "We have to tell Scott – and shouldn't you be in hospital?"

"No, no. It was at too early a stage for that. It just came away when I went to the toilet. I can't believe it."

"Oh, I'm so sorry, April. I don't know what to say."

Belinda went over and sat down beside her sister, holding her as she sniffed and blew her nose.

"But you really have to go to the hospital, you know, to get checked out," she advised.

April shook her head violently.

"No. No, I don't want to go right now. I'm too upset. I'll go later on, when Scott gets back home."

"Well, if you're sure. I'll stay with you till he gets here. Have you rung him?"

"God, no, not when he's working. He's very strict about that, you know." She sniffed and blew her nose again.

"But surely he'd want to know –"

"No, I can't tell him till he gets back, Belinda. I wouldn't mind a cup of tea, though – and maybe something to eat, too, if you wouldn't mind?"

Belinda stood up, glad to be able to escape to the sanctuary of the kitchen. She was shocked and upset, but couldn't help also feeling something akin to relief, too. She knew she shouldn't be feeling like that, but she simply couldn't help it. She never lied to other people and she seldom lied to herself. She chewed on her bottom lip while she brewed a pot of tea and made some salad sandwiches. It struck her as a little strange that her sister wanted to have a meal. She was quite sure if she had just lost her and Scott's baby ,she would be too devastated to even think about eating. And she would want to go straight to hospital, too, to have it confirmed, in case she had been mistaken about the miscarriage. What on earth was Scott going to think of them if he arrived back home to this terrible news and found the two of them sitting calmly munching sandwiches and drinking tea, she wondered? She didn't know what to think. She and April had always been two very different people.

*

Scott arrived home just as they were finishing their lunch. He looked really taken aback when he saw Belinda.

"Oh, Scott. I'm so glad you're home!" April gushed as she stood up, brushed some crumbs from her clothes and threw herself into his arms.

Scott looked puzzled.

"What is it, April? Are you okay?"

She shook her head melodramatically and gazed up at him. "No, I'm not. I've lost the baby, Scott. It's gone," she told him.

He stared at her and blinked.

"What! When did all this happen? How do you know? We have to get you to the hospital –"

"No, I don't want to go there, Scott. I just want to stay here. Will you just hold me, please?" she whimpered.

Belinda eased herself up from her chair. "I think I'd better be off now. I'll see you both later. Hope you feel better soon, April," she said. She looked at Scott as she left the room and mouthed "I'm sorry."

He nodded and turned back to April. He drew her over to the couch. He sat and held her for a few moments. He didn't know what to say. "If you won't go to hospital, I'll ask Gavin to come over and see you," he suggested gently. Gavin Maitland was their G.P.

April nodded her agreement and he lifted the house phone and called the doctor, who had been his friend since they'd studied medicine together at university. Gavin said he was in the middle of afternoon surgery but would come over to see April as soon as he had finished.

"Obviously, if there's any excessive bleeding —" he began, but Scott cut him off.

"I know, Gavin. I'll get her straight to hospital if anything like that starts happening, whether she wants to go or not!"

He hung up and went off into the kitchen to make some more tea for April. He switched the kettle on and then took a bottle of vodka from the cupboard and poured himself a small drink. He swallowed it down in one go. He needed to settle himself down. He couldn't drink any more than that in case April needed him to be able to drive later on. He didn't know what to feel. The thing that seemed amazing to him was that it didn't seem real. She hadn't really been showing yet and he had never dwelt on the eventual outcome — the baby itself. So, there was no real sense of loss. He just felt numb. A little voice at the back of his mind was starting to whisper to him that there was light at the end of the tunnel now; that this meant he was no longer obligated to marry April. But as soon as that thought entered his head he felt really bad about it. What kind of man does that make me, he wondered? April's just lost our child. How can I be so cold and callous? He felt his mind being swamped with the most colossal sense of guilt. He mustn't let her see how he was feeling. He must do everything he could to try to comfort her.

He arranged the tea things on a tray and carried them through to the lounge. As he opened the door and walked through April very quickly put down her mobile phone, looking rather guiltily up at him.

"Who were you phoning?" he asked.

"I – I was going to let Mum know what's happened," she lied, "but then I thought, well Belinda will do that, won't she? No point in getting all upset again for nothing, is there?"

She looked a little flustered and that was very unlike her. He had a strong intuition that she wasn't telling the truth, but he had no idea why she would feel the need to lie to him, or why she would be phoning anyone she didn't want him to know about, so he dismissed this as a silly notion. He fussed over her and she eventually settled down quietly again, lying on the couch with the duvet wrapped around her while he flicked through the channels to try to find something she would enjoy watching.

"You know, April, he told her, "I hope you don't think I'm being callous or anything, but you really ought to have a D&C to make sure everything's cleared away."

She looked stricken. "Scott, that's our child you're talking about!" she said accusingly.

He cringed. "Sorry, love, I'm just thinking of your welfare," he assured her.

"Okay, I'll see what Dr Maitland says," she promised.

As if on cue, Gavin Maitland arrived at the front door. Scott ushered him in.

"She's in the lounge, Gavin," he said.

"How is she?" the doctor asked.

"She's a bit tearful, as you'd expect, but bearing up," Scott replied.

"And you, Scott? How are you?"

"It's happened and there's nothing we can do about it now," Scott answered.

Gavin raised his eyebrows speculatively but said nothing. He went into the lounge, bag in hand, to attend to his patient.

When he came back out of the room, he was frowning.

"Is everything okay?" Scott asked, noting the perplexed look.

"Er, yes. Fine. She's just fine, as far as I can see," he told him. He didn't linger but moved swiftly towards the front door.

"I can call you if I'm worried about her, can't I?" Scott asked.

"Of course, Scott, but I'm sure she'll be fine," Gavin answered curtly. He was following procedure in respect of patient confidentiality, but Scott was his friend of old and he was finding it difficult to say nothing. He was quite sure there had never been any pregnancy in the first place, but he was unable to say so. In any case, he told himself, it was none of his business and Scott would probably never be any the wiser. He left hurriedly and Scott went back into the lounge.

"What did he say to you, April?" he asked, leaning over the back of the couch and stroking her hair gently.

"Nothing much. But I don't need a D&C, so we can just get back to normal now, can't we?" she said, looking up at him pathetically.

He frowned, thinking this to be a rather fast readjustment, but told himself she was probably still in shock to a certain extent. It probably hadn't entirely sunk in yet. He lifted her up and carried her through to the bedroom. He snuggled her in cosily and went back into the lounge to pour himself another drink – or two. He would just have to call a cab if any emergencies arose later in the evening.

April had stuffed her mobile into the pocket of her gown and as soon as Scott disappeared she drew it out and hit Max's speed dial.

"Hi there," he said, clearing his throat and sounding a little cagey. She told him what had gone on that day.

"So now I don't have to pretend to be preggers any more, thank goodness," she finished quietly.

"But don't you think he might try to wriggle out of the engagement now?" he asked.

"No, I don't, actually. I'm really good at the emotional blackmail thing and I had to do this anyway, because I couldn't pretend any longer. He *is* a doctor, you know. He'd have been starting to get suspicious quite soon. I know what I'm doing, Max. Trust me. He's still on the hook."

"You're some piece of work," Max said admiringly.

"You can show me your appreciation sometime soon," she told him in a husky voice.

"You bet I will," Max agreed. He ended the call and turned towards the girl lying beside him, who drew him a suspicious look.

"Who the hell was that?" she demanded sharply.

"No one special," he answered smoothly, shaking his head and smiling at her.

He could soon ditch this one if it looked like April was going to hit the jackpot, he told himself. He thought that scenario was unlikely, but he always liked to keep his options open anyway.

28 THE BEST-LAID PLANS

Scott brought April breakfast in bed the following morning. He felt it was the least he could do. He was surprised by how well she looked. She was a good colour and she had slept like a log, snoring gently for most of the night. She smiled at him as he handed her the tray. He'd made a bacon roll and a cup of freshly brewed coffee for her this morning and she raised her eyebrows at him. He wouldn't normally have cooked bacon, as he didn't believe it was a healthy breakfast.

"You're really spoiling me now," she commented, smiling contentedly.

Her upbeat attitude made him even more suspicious than he had been previously. He frowned, making her remember to look sad. She promptly stopped smiling.

"I'll see if I can manage it," she told him, "even though I'm not really all that hungry."

He gave her a steady, speculative look and then went out of the room. That feeling gripped him again – the feeling that something wasn't quite right and that she wasn't being entirely honest with him. She was far too cheerful for a woman who had just lost her first baby. He had seen quite a few women in that same situation and she wasn't behaving like any of them had.

As he poured himself some All-Bran, he wondered if he was being unfair to her because he wasn't in love with her. Was he letting his growing feelings for her sister cloud his judgement, he asked himself?

As the morning progressed, he began to wonder how long he would have to wait before he could extricate himself from this relationship. This made him feel like a heel, but he had always tried to be honest with himself. He strongly suspected that April had cornered him into proposing to her. He had put the wedding date off by saying that they would have to wait until his parents came back from their cruise, but they were back home now and April knew that, too. They had never actually set a date or booked anything, so there was nothing to cancel. But then, why would she pretend to lose the baby now if she wanted to con him into marrying her? He became more and more puzzled and indecisive as he wondered what to do next. He certainly wouldn't say anything to April at the moment, but it would have to be faced some time soon. As he washed up the breakfast dishes, He made up his mind to give it a couple of weeks and then tell her that he didn't think they should get married after all.

He sighed heavily just as April came into the kitchen. She always seemed to know when the clearing-up was finished, he thought unkindly, and felt bad because he should be feeling more sympathetic towards her at a time like this.

"Hey, Scott," she said in a cajoling tone, putting her arms around his waist as he stood at the sink. "Maybe we could go out somewhere today, to cheer me up," she suggested.

"Sure, if you're feeling up to it," he answered, screwing his eyes up a little and wondering if she was made of stone. She didn't seem to be fazed at all by what had happened to her – if in fact anything had happened at all.

"I'm still really tired, but maybe some fresh air would do me good. Maybe we could go to the park and then have lunch somewhere? It *is* Sunday, after all," she reminded him.

"Okay, April, I don't see why not. It's not a bad day. You get yourself dressed and then we'll go out. But I have to be back in time to take Belinda over to the hospital," he reminded her.

As she turned to go back into the bedroom to get dressed she pressed her lips together in annoyance. He was altogether too keen on running around after Belinda these days and she was getting very fed-up with it.

She really is too cheerful too soon, he told himself, and he was quite sure she wasn't simply putting on a brave face. He was used to reading people and her behaviour wasn't consistent with a very recent miscarriage.

They set off shortly afterwards and walked through the park. They sat down on one of the benches for a while – the same one he'd sat on with Belinda, the day they'd kissed, he remembered. He smiled sadly at the irony of it.

"Don't be upset, Scott," April said softly, nuzzling his neck. "We'll have other kids. Not right now, but some day," she said wistfully.

Scott froze and stared above her head into the distance. He hadn't been expecting that. He didn't know what to say, so he decided not to answer her. His heart sank as he realised sadly that perhaps it was going to be a great deal longer than a couple of weeks before he could break it to her that there wasn't going to be a wedding or another pregnancy, not if he could help it. He was still as trapped as ever, he realised, in a cage of his own making. When he'd asked her to move in with him, he'd been dazzled by her stunning looks and rampant sexuality and he'd been trying to convince himself that he didn't feel anything for Belinda because she had started seeing Jim. He was paying the price for that now.

*

Scott's plans to pick up Belinda that evening were scuppered when she sent him a text telling him that Jim was taking her to the hospital. She explained that Melissa was able to drive herself back and forth now instead of Jim driving her there.

He rang her in reply because he wanted to hear her voice.

"I think I'll maybe pop over there later for a while myself, just to see how Toby and Melissa are doing," he told her.

"Okay. Well, we'll see you later then," she replied. The "we" grated on his nerves, and he thought her voice sounded strange and stilted.

"Is everything okay with you, Belinda?" he asked.

She hesitated for a moment before replying.

"Shouldn't you be staying with April at the moment?" she asked.

He bristled at the implied reprimand.

"April's fine. She's coping just fine," he replied stiffly. "I wouldn't leave her if she wasn't."

Belinda remembered how her sister had scoffed a plate of sandwiches just after she'd told her about the miscarriage.

"Right, see you later then," she said, her voice softening a little as she assumed he probably needed to get away from April for a couple of hours for a break. It must be a difficult time for him, too. And she knew that focusing on someone else's troubles often puts your own anxieties into a clearer perspective.

When they met later on in Toby's room, Belinda thought Scott looked tired and strained, and she was sorry for snapping at him earlier.

There was still no change in Toby's condition. Scott spoke to Jim and Melissa for a few moments and then asked if anyone would like a tea or coffee. He seemed to have assumed the role of coffee provider these days.

They all nodded, and Belinda smiled at him as she said she would like a drink. Jim caught the fond look that passed between them and he clenched his teeth. He was determined now that he wasn't going to let Belinda go. She'd told him about April's miscarriage and he was anxious to make it clear to Scott that Belinda wasn't available. She was his and she was going to stay his. He refused anything to drink and stood up to follow Scott out into the corridor.

As the room door swung closed behind him, Scott stood still and faced him.

"Is there something wrong, Jim?" he asked.

"I just wanted to say sorry about what happened – with the baby," Jim replied, and added, "but I'm sure there'll be plenty more in the future, once you're married."

Scott simply nodded and looked Jim straight in the eye. He wasn't stupid and he knew exactly what Jim was trying to tell him. He walked off to get the drinks with a heavy heart. He wasn't even going to be able to get Belinda to himself any more. He might not have told *her* how strongly he felt about her, but he was in no doubt now that Jim was two steps ahead of him in that department. Their predicament was getting more and more complicated, even after he'd thought it couldn't get any worse. He was engaged to April and in love with her sister; and Belinda was engaged to Jim, who was obviously determined to stay engaged to her.

He tried to remind himself that Melissa's current plight was infinitely worse than his, but that just made him feel even more miserable. How had all this happened? How had everything got into such a tangle? And he wondered if any of it would ever be resolved. He couldn't see any way forward in the immediate future.

A little later, as he walked back along the corridor with the drinks, he made up his mind that for the time being he would concentrate on trying to comfort Melissa as much as possible and let everything else settle down for a while. But the time would come, he promised himself, when he would have to speak, not only to April, but also Belinda. He didn't know when that time would be, but he had to at least try to find out if she felt strongly enough about him to end her engagement to Jim. They all had important, life-changing decisions to make and this was no time to leave vital things unsaid. He would bide his time, but not indefinitely. He handed the women their coffees and brought a seat over to sit down beside Melissa. He had accepted that he couldn't do anything about his own situation right then, but he could try to lift some of her burden and see her through this dreadful time. At least it was something positive to aim for – a little comfort in the midst of all the emotional upheaval of their lives.

29 THE ROAD TO DESTRUCTION

A few weeks later, towards the end of June, Scott was unexpectedly presented with the opportunity to speak to April about their wedding plans.

It was a Saturday night and the two of them were sitting together watching a 'chick flick' on television. He particularly disliked that type of film, but he had fallen into the habit of giving in to April's wishes almost all of the time, ever since the 'miscarriage' had happened. As soon as the film had ended, she turned towards him and said that she would like to talk to him.

He raised an eyebrow and waited silently for her to speak. He was quite sure that he wasn't going to like what she had to say. He usually didn't. She took a deep breath and asked him if they could please come to a decision about their wedding day.

"Your parents are back home and I'm over the miscarriage now," she pointed out. "So, I don't see any reason to wait any longer, do you, babe?"

When Scott simply looked at her without answering, she looked stricken and put her hands over her face.

"Please don't say that you don't want us to get married any more!" she begged. "I don't think I could bear it."

Scott didn't know what to do. He was caught between a rock and a hard place. He put his arm around her shoulders and drew her towards him.

"Look, April, the fact is –" he began, but he stopped speaking because she began to wail.

"I don't believe it. I don't believe you're going to dump me because I lost the baby," she bawled.

He was horrified.

"Of course I'm not. It's not that –" he stuttered, uncertain how to proceed.

"So you still want us to get married then?" she asked, giving him a pitiful look.

"Well, I think we should wait for a while before we set any dates," he replied, trying to play for time. He didn't want to be cruel and just end things with her without any warning.

She relaxed a little and blew her nose. "Okay. I'll be patient a while longer," she told him, adding, "You know, I know you've been leaving me alone lately because of what happened, but it's okay for us to get back to normal now. In bed, I mean. I'm really all right again now. And I'm on the Pill again, too, so it's quite safe."

Scott had no intention of having sex with her again, but he didn't know what to say. How could he get out of this situation without actually ending things with her, he wondered? He told her to go off to bed and he would join her shortly, but he had no intention of doing so. Neither did he believe that she was actually taking the Pill. He wasn't going to get caught with the unplanned pregnancy situation again. Also, his feelings for Belinda had consolidated into certainty recently, and he now knew for sure that he didn't want to be with anyone else. He had decided that if he couldn't have Belinda, then he would stay single. He sighed, poured himself another drink and settled down to watch some late-night television.

As she lay in their bed, April wasn't worried at all. He was a man and he couldn't stay aloof and do without sex for very much longer. She was quite sure she would be able to coax him back into their relationship and then she would simply announce to everyone that they had set the date for their wedding. She knew he wouldn't want to humiliate her by contradicting her, and in this way, she would get where she wanted to be by small steps. Little by little she would draw him in again. She had decided on the middle of August. And she had picked out her gown, too. It was safely tucked away at the back of her wardrobe. She looked absolutely stunning in it and she was well aware of that. It had cost a fortune, but she was sure he wouldn't mind. He was loaded, and she was determined that she would soon have half of all that. She was going to treat herself to some very sexy gear very soon and he wouldn't be able to resist her. She smiled as she drew the duvet up over her head. She would put her new plan into action the very next day. He wouldn't stand a chance.

*

Jim continued to pick up Belinda most evenings for a visit to the hospital. He was finding it very difficult to see Melissa so unhappy, but he couldn't get close to her now because of the sense of guilt he felt over Cam's death. He knew his guilt was illogical, but that didn't make it go away. Getting close to Mel now would have felt like a double betrayal. He missed his friend every day and couldn't shake the conviction that his feelings for Melissa had somehow brought about this terrible situation, even though he knew that wasn't a logical conclusion. She wasn't coping well with either her grief over Cam or little Toby's illness. He doubted if anyone would have dealt with her circumstances well, but it was made worse by the tremendous love she had felt for both her husband and her son. He felt completely helpless and he knew he would be in a terrible state if he didn't have Belinda to comfort him and to keep his anxieties from escalating.

They were en route to the hospital, as usual, on a rather chilly evening, a couple of weeks after the funeral. Belinda was rather quieter than she normally was, and when Jim emerged from his own thoughts for a few seconds he realised that she was looking very sad and alone. She seemed to be as engrossed in her own thoughts as he was. He made up his mind to speak to her after their visit and try to cheer her up a little.

They parked the car and made their way silently to the door of Toby's room. Jim squeezed Belinda's hand and gave her a little smile. They went inside and stood quietly at Toby's bedside. Melissa turned round and smiled sadly at them. She looked very pale and tired, and was thinner than ever. They didn't ask her if there had been any change. They knew there hadn't been. Later, when they said they were going home, Melissa said she was going to stay with Toby for another little while and would get a taxi back home.

In the middle of the drive home, Jim drew to a standstill in a lay-by and turned towards Belinda.

"Belinda, I want us to set a date for our wedding," he said suddenly. He had meant to lead up to it gently, but instead the words just came out in a rush.

She looked shocked.

"Jim, I don't think this is the time to be setting wedding dates" she began, frowning in dismay.

"I can't stand any more of this doom and gloom. I have to have something to look forward to. Please say you'll think about it. Please."

Belinda was silent.

"Has there been any change – with Scott and April?" he asked her, knowing full well that there hadn't been.

"No," she replied. She bit her lip. She knew what he was doing. He was reminding her of the fact that there was no pregnancy now but Scott and April were still living together – and were also still engaged. She closed her eyes, trying to face the facts that she'd been avoiding since the miscarriage. Scott obviously did love April and he wasn't going to end things with her. It was painful but Belinda had to admit that she'd been kidding herself. Jim understood the situation and was prepared to marry her anyway, so she wouldn't be being unfair to him if she agreed. She looked across at him and nodded.

"Okay, let's do it. Let's set a date, Jim, but not till some time next year. I want Melissa to be fully recovered from everything she's going through right now. We can set a date, once we see a minister and get it organised, but only tell family members. Don't speak about it to Melissa yet. She's got too much on her mind right now to be happy for us. And she might feel miffed that we're making wedding plans at a time like this."

Jim sighed in relief and hugged her tightly.

"Don't worry. I won't mention it to Mel," he assured her.

When Belinda went inside her house her parents and June were sitting in the lounge quietly watching television. She told them that she and Jim were planning on getting married in June or July the following year. They were delighted and congratulated her happily.

*

The following morning, Belinda dragged herself wearily out of bed and started to get ready for work. She'd nodded off again after switching off her alarm and was now probably going to be late – again. When she emerged from the shower, she lifted her mobile phone from the dressing table as she had heard a text message being delivered. She gasped as she read what it said and put her hand over her mouth. It was from Melissa. She said she wasn't going to go to the hospital to see Toby any more. There was no point. He wasn't going to get better. She ended the message by saying that it was fine with her if Jim and Belinda went to see him as much as they wanted to.

Belinda was stunned. She couldn't believe it. She got dressed, dried her hair very quickly and ran out of the front door without any breakfast. She ran very fast and just managed to catch her usual bus to work. Janine had told her if she was late again, she would be on a warning. She sat on the bus and worried about Melissa's decision and the state of mind that it revealed. As she jumped off the bus and ran into the salon, she decided she would go over to the house after work and pay Melissa a visit. She needed to know why she was giving up on Toby like this and she needed to tell her that she would try to help her in any way that she could.

Later that day, when Belinda arrived at the door of Melissa's house, she took a deep breath before she rang the bell. She had to ring it several times, pressing it persistently, before Melissa finally came to the door. As soon as she opened it, Belinda pushed it wider and stepped inside the house.

"Belinda, what are you doing here?" Melissa demanded, shaking her head in irritation.

"Mel, I'm not letting you do this. You can't give up hope. You can't give up on your wee boy –". Her voice broke and tears flooded her eyes.

Melissa shrugged her shoulders and walked back into the lounge. She lay down again on the settee, where she'd obviously slept all night, and simply lay there staring into space.

She looked ill and Belinda didn't know what to do. She didn't know what to say to elicit a response from her.

"Have you eaten anything today?" she asked. Melissa didn't reply.

"I'm going to make you an omelette or something," Belinda told her. Melissa didn't argue with her, so she went off into the kitchen to prepare the meal. She took some peppers and chopped onion from the freezer and added them in. Whilst it was cooking she arrived at a decision. She was well out of her depth here and she knew she needed help, otherwise her friend was going to end up in hospital along with Toby – or worse! She took the meal through to Melissa and sat down beside her, trying to coax her to eat some of it, at least. She did eat a few bites and then lay back down again. Belinda went into the kitchen and drew out Melissa's mobile phone from her jeans pocket. She had lifted it from the coffee table while Melissa had had her eyes closed.

Melissa's parents were at home and it was her mother who answered the call. Belinda explained the situation to her and she said they would come to see her as soon as they could. Belinda felt very relieved and was sure that this would help Melissa tremendously. She took the phone back into the lounge and Melissa didn't even notice her putting it back on the coffee table again. Then she washed up the dishes because she knew that they wouldn't get done otherwise.

Belinda slipped on her jacket and leaned over the back of the settee to say goodnight to Melissa, but she was asleep. Her beautiful blonde hair lay in an untidy mass over her shoulders. It looked as though she hadn't washed it for a week or so. And Belinda knew her friend had no intention of returning to work or of resuming anything like her normal lifestyle. She knew instinctively what Melissa was thinking. She had given up. She thought her life was over and wasn't worth saving. Depression was beginning to get the better of her.

Belinda left the house quietly. She locked the front door and then posted the key back through the letterbox. She was even more worried than she had been when she'd arrived. She would have to keep a sharp eye on her friend from now on. She would ring the house tomorrow to see if Mel's parents had been in touch about visiting her. And if that didn't work, she would have to think of something else. Belinda knew with a dark certainty that Melissa was on a downhill slide and that she wouldn't recover from it by herself. She wasn't going to let that happen. She resolved to do whatever she had to do to draw her away from this self-destructive path.

30 NO-MAN'S-LAND

The following day, Melissa walked slowly across the car park of her local Tesco. It was a bright, sunny morning. Her mum had rung her and told her that she and her father would be paying her a visit the following day. This unexpected news had made her drag herself up off the settee and go off to get some shopping in. The plastic shopping bags clunked against her legs as she walked, but she didn't seem to notice it. She didn't seem to be aware of anything much – the sunshine, the cars going past her in the car park or the whistles of the workmen on a building site across the road as they eyed her up. They were on their lunch break and their catcalls were lively. Melissa barely heard them. As she loaded the plastic bags automatically into her car boot her wedding and engagement rings caught her attention as the strong sunlight made them sparkle, and her eyes misted over with tears. But that was nothing unusual; tears were never far away from her eyes these days.

She couldn't stop thinking about Cam and still couldn't believe he was gone for good and she would never see him again. She was now also quite certain that Toby would never recover. He would never open his eyes again, and it seemed to her as though she had lost him, too. She had sunk into a deep well of grief and couldn't forget about her lost family even for a moment. She didn't want to forget them. Forgetting them was the last thing she wanted to have to do. She was still taking the anti-depressants the doctor had given her, but they didn't seem to be working so far. She didn't even want to feel better or to get better. She had stopped going in to work, but had no desire to do anything else either. She knew that, as an accountant, she could do her work at home, but she just couldn't face it. She had lost her past, she didn't care about her present, and the future was just a blank, empty space filled with loneliness and despair.

When she arrived home and started unpacking her shopping, the phone began to ring. It was a call from Belinda, who asked if Melissa would come and meet her in town. Melissa told her that she had just come home and didn't want to go out anywhere. Belinda said she would come over to the house and bring a bottle of wine with her. Melissa told her not to bother, but Belinda insisted she would come anyway. Melissa hung up the phone and sat down with a cup of coffee, not even bothering to put away the rest of the shopping.

She was sitting staring into space, gripping the warm cup as if she thought it was somehow going to try to escape from her. She sat there like that, not moving an inch, until the coffee went cold in the cup.

About twenty minutes later Belinda arrived. Melissa could hear her walking up the path, but she didn't get up. She knew the door was still unlocked. Her friend walked round to the back door and came straight into the kitchen.

Belinda stood with her head on one side looking at Melissa sitting at the kitchen table staring ahead of her. She could see right away that there had been no improvement since she had seen her last. In fact, she looked worse, if anything. Belinda put the wine bottle down on the worktop and rummaged in the cutlery drawer for the corkscrew. As she did so she looked at the bags of shopping still lying unopened on the surface of the kitchen island. She bit her bottom lip and frowned. Without saying anything, she began to put the food away into cupboards and some of it into the fridge, and then she took two large, gold-coloured wine goblets, which reflected the colour of the golden oak doors of the kitchen cupboards, and poured them each a large glass of wine.

"You not feeling any better today then?" she asked Melissa as she handed her glass to her.

Melissa shrugged and took a little sip of the wine.

"No. Why would I?" she asked.

Belinda shook her head sadly. She didn't even ask about Toby because she'd been to the hospital the previous evening and she knew his condition hadn't altered.

"Mel, you can't go on like this, honey. You'll make yourself ill. You need to think about Toby, too. What if he wakes up and you're not well enough to look after him?"

Melissa simply shrugged again, staring blankly in front of her.

"He won't," she whispered.

Belinda winced, trying to squash down her agitation because she didn't want to upset Melissa or make her feel pressured. But something obviously had to be done – and soon – otherwise the situation would deteriorate into a tragic ending for her friend, and for Toby, too. She took a deep breath and launched into the speech she had prepared on the way over.

"Mel, would you do me a favour? Would you try and get some help? I've made enquiries and there's a group that meet up in the Community Centre every Wednesday evening. They've all suffered bereavement of one sort or another. The idea is for them to try to help each other to cope with their feelings. I know it's the last thing you feel like doing, but I'm getting really worried about you. Please say you'll give it a try – for me. Please."

Melissa looked at her friend and shook her head slowly.

"You know I'll keep nagging at you until you agree to go," Belinda pointed out in desperation. She could feel tears pricking at the backs of her eyes.

Melissa sighed and Belinda beseeched her again. "Please, Melissa. Do it for me, even if you don't want to go."

Melissa still said nothing.

"Will you at least think about it?" Belinda implored, her anxiety tightening her insides into a painful knot.

Melissa nodded half-heartedly and Belinda had to be content with that. She relaxed a little and topped up their glasses.

"Have you had anything to eat yet?" she asked kindly, knowing the answer before Melissa shook her head.

Belinda sighed and stood up to go and prepare something for both of them. As she moved around the kitchen, she wondered how Melissa was ever going to manage to go back to work again and resume her life. It occurred to her that maybe Mel wouldn't ever manage to go back to work. And she still couldn't quite believe that she would really abandon her son. It was so out of character, but she was obviously going into a decline and needed some kind of help to pull her back from the edge.

Belinda dug out the wok and drew some chicken from the fridge and some stir-fry vegetables from the freezer. She had brought a chocolate sponge cake with her and she set about rustling them up a quick meal. She strongly suspected that there were nights when Melissa didn't bother to feed herself at all. She was becoming extremely thin and her face was almost haggard now. Her mental state was bad enough, Belinda knew, without her becoming physically ill into the bargain.

Still, she had agreed to think about going along to a group meeting, so that was something, at least. When Belinda put their plates of food down on the table, she decided to talk about something else, in the hope of taking Melissa's mind off her own life for a little while.

She decided that it might be a good idea to tell her about her feelings regarding April's fiancé and her inability to decide whether or not to marry Jim, although she knew none of the emotional turmoil in her own life came anywhere close to the distress her friend was going through.

"Jim and I are having a bit of a rough time just now, you know, Melissa," she began, trying to sound as convincing as possible so that the other woman wouldn't smell a rat.

This had a little bit of an effect. Melissa raised her eyebrows and blinked in surprise.

"That's surprising," she commented, frowning a little. "What's up? You usually get on great together," she added, looking puzzled.

Belinda didn't want to lay it on too thick because that would only make Melissa feel that everyone in the world was miserable and that wouldn't help her at all; so she simply shook her head and claimed that she didn't know what to do for the best. She admitted that she had feelings for Scott, and she added that she suspected he felt the same way about her.

Melissa raised her eyebrows, but then she nodded.

"I thought there was something simmering between you two the last time you were both at the hospital. You should try and get a chance to speak to him about it, you know."

This was the most Melissa had said since the day of the accident and Belinda had to work hard to conceal a little spurt of satisfaction that her plan seemed to be working. She lowered her head and her eyes and tried hard to look worried.

Melissa looked straight at her and added, "It's no good just wishing and surmising. You need to know how he feels. It's the rest of your life, marriage -". She broke off abruptly and closed her eyes. The realisation suddenly hit Belinda that no matter how hard she tried to steer clear of the subject, Melissa's loss was always going to float to the surface. She was gazing in front of her once more, lost in her own pain. Belinda sighed and tried to capture her attention again.

"What should I do, Melissa? I don't know how to deal with this," she pleaded.

"Well, I would sit Scott down and get to the bottom of it all, Belinda," Melissa advised her, after thinking about it for a moment or two. "Even if he doesn't want to talk, make him do it. Because it will all build up and get out of hand if you just ignore it and hope it'll go away! If he's got feelings for you, too, you need to know where you stand with him."

"Okay, I will, Mel. I'll ring him when I go home tonight. I'll ask him to meet me tomorrow to discuss things."

Melissa nodded, a sad smile curving her lips as she sat back against the cushions, enveloped within her own no-man's-land of misery once again.

Belinda decided she'd at least made a little progress and that it was time to go home. She told Melissa to give her parents her best wishes the following day and then she let herself out of the house, locking the door behind her. As she made her way home on the bus, she decided to act on Melissa's advice and contact Scott so they could discuss things. She took her phone out of her pocket and sent him a text. They arranged to meet the following evening at the hospital and then go for something to eat and a chat afterwards. Belinda just hoped that she wouldn't bottle out of asking him what plans he still had with April. They were going to be seeing a lot of each other in the future, one way or another, and she didn't want things to be awkward and difficult between them. It was up to her to bite the bullet now and then at least she would know what to do for the best. The time for uncertainty had passed. She had to know. She was in as much of a no-man's-land as Melissa, for very different reasons, and it was time to do something about it.

31 THE BEST POLICY

The following day, Belinda wasn't looking forward to her talk with Scott that evening and she felt very distracted all day at work. She kept trying to rehearse what she would say to him and was trying to decide how much she should reveal to him about her own feelings before she knew the extent of his feelings for her. It was quite a dilemma and she kept changing her mind about the best course of action. She had a throbbing headache by lunchtime. She took a couple of headache pills after she'd eaten her lunch and tried to take her mind off her own troubles during the afternoon by pondering on how Melissa's parents would be getting on in trying to lift their daughter's spirits.

Across town in her house, Melissa was struggling to cope with her parents' visit. She knew they were worried about her and she guessed that Belinda had probably rung them to enlist their help in cheering her up. Unfortunately, they didn't want to talk about Cam because they missed him so much themselves and they felt that Melissa should try to put the past behind her and move on. But all she wanted to do was talk about him. She went through to the bedroom to get her photograph albums from the top of the wardrobe. She took them into the lounge and asked if they would join her in looking through them. They did so, reluctantly, but after a very short time her mother stood up and went out into the hall. She was upset and she was blowing her nose on a tissue when her husband came out to see if she was all right. He put his arm around her shoulders and she began to cry in earnest.

"I can't do this, George," she said tearfully. "I just can't. It's making me feel as bad as Melissa and it's not helping her. It's making her dwell on Cam even more than if we weren't here."

"I know," he replied. "I think it's too soon for us to give her any help. It's all still too raw. I think we should go back home and wait until she gets over it a little bit before we come back. There's no point in the three of us getting depressed over it, is there?"

She nodded and sniffed and they went back into the lounge together.

"I think we're going to be heading off now, love," George told her.

She didn't look up from her photographs.

"I can stay with you for a while longer, if you want me to," her mother offered half-heartedly, earning a frown from her husband as she did so.

"No, Mum. It's okay. I'll be fine," Melissa assured her. "Just you get off home now and thanks for coming. It was nice to see you both."

She bent over the photo album again and by the time she looked up her parents were at the front door, preparing to leave. She stood up and forced herself to go and wave goodbye to them, because if they thought she was in a bad way they wouldn't leave. She tried to smile, but didn't quite manage it. When they were gone she went back into the lounge and opened up her laptop. She had a whole collection of photos she hadn't looked at for a long time. Most of them were of her and Toby, because Cam had been the photographer of the house. But all of them reminded her of him, whether he was pictured in them or not. She could almost hear him telling them to say 'cheese' – and sometimes he used to say "Say Gorgonzola" to make Toby laugh. She clicked on the file that contained their wedding photos and drew the box of Kleenex over next to her. When she was finished looking at these photos, she decided, she would dig out the DVD of their wedding and put it on the TV, and then she really would be able to hear his voice, if she could bear to listen to it. The phone rang, but she ignored it. It rang and rang for ages, so she took it off the hook and sat back down to resume her trip down memory lane.

*

While Melissa was speaking to her mum and dad, Belinda had been doing her best to speak to Scott. They said very little to each other at the hospital. Luckily Jim was otherwise engaged that evening; so it had been easy for Scott to come and pick her up and take her in to see Toby without anyone questioning the arrangement. The two of them sat by his bedside in virtual silence. After a while, Belinda asked Scott if he had heard anything more about the little boy's recovery. He shook his head sadly.

"Are we still on for this little talk over dinner?" he asked her.

She nodded and tried to smile, but she was feeling increasingly tense about it and had completely forgotten all the statements and questions she had practised earlier. Everything was getting muddled up in her head now.

They left the hospital and drove in silence until they reached the McDonalds restaurant they used to go to until Jim had started picking her up. However, it was quite busy and Belinda began to frown.

"It's really noisy tonight, isn't it?" she commented.

"We can go somewhere else if you want. I know a Beefeater place a few streets from here. They serve good food and it's usually fairly quiet on week nights. Want to try that?"

Belinda nodded and they went back out to the car. The Beefeater wasn't far away and it didn't take them long to get there. They were seated in a cosy little alcove in the corner and the lighting was soft and mellow. Belinda felt much more relaxed as she took off her jacket. The nights were starting to get a bit chilly now and the restaurant was warm.

"Oh, it's so nice and warm in here!" Belinda said, feeling much more at her ease than she had felt at McDonalds.

"Yes, it is nice, isn't it. Helps the digestion if you're feeling warm and relaxed while you eat," Scott commented.

Belinda laughed.

"You're such a doctor, Scott!" she said, softening the comment with a friendly smile.

He looked at her without replying and she felt as if she could look into his soft brown eyes for a very long time.

The waitress standing beside their table cleared her throat and reeled off the specials for that day.

"Would you like a drink while you're waiting?" she asked, writing down their food order and gathering up their menus.

"I'll have a non-alcoholic beer," Scott replied.

"And I'll have a pint of cider," Belinda said, to Scott's surprise. He raised his eyebrows.

"That's not like you, Belinda," he said, looking at her quizzically.

"Bit of Dutch courage, actually," she admitted, then added, "Can we eat first and then talk?"

"Sure," he said, shrugging his shoulders as if he wasn't bothered, but in truth he was really curious about what she wanted to discuss with him. He wondered if things weren't going so well with Jim, as he was conspicuous by his absence this evening, but he didn't want to jump the gun by asking. Maybe it wasn't about that at all. He knew he would just have to be patient until Belinda was ready to talk.

The meal arrived quickly and both of them wolfed it down, as it was well into the evening and they were both very hungry. Belinda had finished her cider and Scott ordered her another one. She was drinking quite quickly and her cheeks were a little flushed now. Neither of them had ordered a sweet, so he decided it was time for them to start talking.

"So, what did you want to talk to me about, Belinda?" he asked, getting straight to the point.

She took a deep breath. It was now or never.

"Scott, do you remember that Sunday morning in the park?" she asked.

"Course," he said, looking rather sheepish. "Not my finest hour, I must admit."

"So you regret it then?"

"No, I don't – I didn't mean that. It's just that I'm living with April and I shouldn't have kissed you."

"I know, and you're getting married sometime soon, aren't you?"

"Yes, I suppose we will be," he agreed on a sigh, feeling guilty about not being entirely honest with her. He knew he couldn't tell her he wasn't going to marry April until he had told April herself.

"Scott, am I right in thinking that you're not exactly thrilled about the idea of marrying my sister? I mean, she's not pregnant any more, if she ever was in the first place, and not long ago you told me –"

"That I wanted to be with you. Is that what you're asking – if I still feel the same?"

"Well, yes, I suppose I am," she agreed lamely, looking down at the table in embarrassment.

Scott looked perplexed for a few moments, and then he ran his hand through his hair in exasperation.

"Belinda, you're not wrong about that. I told you before that I want to be with you, but I don't know what to do. I'm engaged and she's your *sister*! It's an impossible situation. I don't want to hurt anyone, but it looks like I'm going to have to. And I don't want you and your family to fall out either."

Just as Belinda was about to ask him which of them he was going to have to hurt, her mobile rang. It was Melissa's mother.

After speaking to her for a few moments, Belinda rang off.

"Scott, I'm going to have to go. That was Melissa's mum. She's very worried about her. It was too much for her seeing her daughter so depressed. Her and Mel's dad have gone back home again. I need to drop by and make sure she's okay. Would you mind dropping me off there?"

"Of course I will, and I'll come in and see for myself that she's all right."

"Thanks so much, Scott. Sometimes I wonder what I'd do without you," she added quietly.

He helped her into her jacket and they left the restaurant. They reached Mel's house in no time, as the roads were quiet now. They knocked at her door for ages, getting no reply, and then Belinda decided to try the door. It wasn't locked and she breathed a sigh of relief as she stepped inside, with Scott immediately behind her.

Melissa was sitting on the floor with her laptop open on the coffee table. She had fallen asleep and her face was pressed down on the keyboard. Scott gently lifted her head and she opened her eyes a little, then closed them again. He gave her a little shake and put his hand underneath her chin.

"Melissa, are you okay?" he asked.

She nodded. Her eyes were wide open now and she was frowning.

"I thought you'd gone home, Belinda. What are you doing back here? Why can't people just leave me alone?" she complained.

Scott answered her. "We're not going to leave you alone, Mel. I'm going to come and take you out tomorrow – to the group that Belinda told you about. You need to talk some of this out. And Belinda is going to stay here tonight, aren't you, Belinda?"

She nodded and went through to the kitchen to make some coffee. As she did so, she could hear Scott speaking gently but firmly to Melissa. Belinda sniffed tearfully and blinked as she put the mugs on the tray to take through to the lounge. If anyone could help Melissa, it was Scott. Jim had virtually deserted Mel, for reasons of his own, and Belinda herself wasn't making any headway with her. She had meant what she'd said earlier that evening in the restaurant. There were times when she didn't know what she would do without Scott. He was supportive without being overbearing or patronising, contrary to her initial impression of him.

As she took the tray through to the other room, she knew that she was even more deeply in love with him than she had been before, but she still didn't really know where she stood with him. She would have to wait until she was alone before she could mull over everything he'd said to her and try to decide exactly what she meant to him. Her plan to tell him everything and establish where she stood with him had gone awry, but at least she had tried. And he now knew that she was definitely interested in being with him, whether it upset her family or not.

However, at that time, Melissa's plight was the most important consideration, and Belinda decided to stay with her and to help her as best she could until she could begin to see some light at the end of the tunnel. She would ring the salon the next morning and arrange for some time off. She was due a couple of weeks' holiday, and she could take at least one of those now, when her friend needed her most. She felt more confident that Melissa would soon be on the mend, now that Scott was going to be helping her.

32 STALEMATE

When Scott arrived home very late in the evening after visiting Melissa, April was sitting up, waiting for him. She came over to him and kissed him on the mouth as soon as he came through the door. He was surprised but wary. He hoped he wasn't going to have to be rude to her if she had decided they were having sex that night. He knew her quite well by now and had a feeling she wanted something from him, but he wasn't sure what it was. They sat together on the settee watching television and drinking hot chocolate. April wasn't speaking much, but he was sure she was about to start talking about getting married again. However, when she did speak, it wasn't about that.

"Hey, did I mention that Belinda and Jim have set a date for their wedding? July next year!" she said airily, making it sound more definite than it actually was.

"Oh, have they?" was all Scott could say in reply. So much for Belinda being interested in him, he thought. She's doing a good impression of being much more interested in Jim!

"Scott, I was hoping we could go over to see Mum and Dad some time this weekend. I know you've got something on, on

Saturday morning, but maybe we could go over there in the evening?"

Scott was very relieved that she wasn't going to start talking about wedding dates herself.

"Well, of course we can, April. We can go over there any time you want," he answered, smiling in relief.

April smiled back at him and snuggled into his side. Not for the first time, she wondered how he could manage to be so clever and so gullible at the same time.

*

During the rest of that week, Scott went over to Melissa's house each evening to see how she was doing. He and Belinda had spoken at length about Melissa's state of mind and he was as sure as she was that Melissa wasn't recovering from her bereavement. She wasn't making any progress at all, as far as he could see. He had driven her to her first group therapy session at the Community Centre and had picked her up when it was over, but it didn't seem to have made any impression on her at all. She was obviously merely going through the motions in order to avoid confrontation about it. Also, she looked very unwell. He had asked her several times to either visit her G.P. or allow him to do some tests to make sure she was well physically; but she had just shaken her head, her eyes glazed and lifeless. The spark had gone out of her existence and nothing short of a miracle was going to give her back the will to live. He had previously hoped that Toby being in a coma would give her something else to focus on until the grief started to ease off, but it looked as though Toby's condition was only adding to Melissa's distress and the stress of it all was taking over her mental health.

By Friday evening, when Belinda had taken almost a week off her work to keep Melissa company, she and Scott were both still very worried about her. She didn't seem to want to eat anything or do anything, and her face looked even paler and more haggard than ever. She was very tired all the time. At one point she lay down and fell asleep on the settee and Scott and Belinda went into the kitchen to talk about the situation.

Belinda couldn't contain her exasperation any longer.

"What are we going to do about her, Scott? I'm all out of ideas. Nothing seems to be working and she's obviously becoming ill now. Can you think of anything we can say to get through to her?" she asked him anxiously.

He shook his head, staring at the kitchen flooring as though the answer could be found within its shiny, marble-tiled surface.

"I don't know, I just don't know," he replied, racking his brains for some inspiration. I know a psychologist and a psychiatrist, but I don't think any stranger could make a connection with her the way she is now. But at least we know that she trusts us two and she listens to us and tries to do what we suggest. She's just so miserable that nothing is getting through to her. The stress is winning. Once clinical depression sets in, it can take a while to start lifting. And the fact that she has absolutely nothing to look forward to in life at the moment is making things ten times worse.

Belinda turned round towards the worktop and began to take mugs and coffee out of the cupboard.

"I still can't believe that she's stopped visiting Toby. I don't understand that. She adores him and she was a devoted mother before all this. I can't believe she's really given up on him, not deep down. She can't have. And I'm sure she's gone downhill faster since she stopped going to the hospital," Belinda pointed out sadly.

Scott mulled this over for a few moments before he spoke again.

"Yes, you're right, Belinda," he agreed. "Hmm, maybe that's the answer, you know. If we could just get her to come with us to the hospital to see him again, I'm certain she'd start to feel a little bit of hope and concern for him – and that would give her something else to focus on other than her own misery. What do you think? Do you think I could persuade her to go and see him again?"

"I don't know. It's worth a try, I suppose. I've already tried, but she doesn't even answer me when I talk about him. But she listens to you. There's no harm in giving it a try, is there? We've got to do something!"

She poured out their coffees and they sat down facing each other across the beautiful glass kitchen table.

"So, how are things with you and April?" she asked tentatively.

"Same as ever," he answered, lowering his eyes. Then suddenly he looked up and gazed directly at her. "And you and Jim? April mentioned the other day that you two have set a date for your wedding."

He looked annoyed and she didn't blame him for that. He must think she was playing some sort of game with him.

"He kept pressuring me and I gave in eventually, Scott. I know I shouldn't have done that, but I felt so sorry for him. His social life revolved around Cam and Mel and now he's so alone – and on top of that, he feels guilty about his feelings for Mel. And he kinda blames himself for Cam's death."

Scott's eyebrows shot up. "You're kidding! I didn't know that. God, how awful for him. But you can't tie yourself to someone for life because you feel sorry for them, Belinda."

As he spoke the words, he knew that what he was doing with April wasn't a million miles away from Belinda's situation with Jim. They were both playing for time. He fell silent, drinking the last of his coffee thoughtfully. Then he stood up and went through to the lounge to see if Melissa had wakened up yet.

Belinda washed up the few dishes that were in the sink as it wasn't worth switching on the dishwasher for a few cups and plates. And as she did so she could hear Scott speaking in coaxing tones to Melissa. She frowned, at a loss to know what they could try next if Mel didn't agree to visit Toby again.

She turned away from the sink, drying her hands on the tea towel as Scott came back into the kitchen and closed the door behind him.

"She's agreed to come and visit Toby again tomorrow! I think she's really missed him this week," he announced.

"Oh, brilliant! That's brilliant, Scott. I knew if anyone could persuade her you could!" she told him, her relief and the all-consuming love she felt for him showing in her animated face.

They moved together without even knowing they were going to do it. They put their arms around each other and Scott tilted her face up and lowered his head. But before their lips met, they heard Melissa heading towards the kitchen door and they sprang apart guiltily. She came through the door with her head down, as usual, and went across to the sink, pouring out a drink of water for herself and then said she was going off to bed. She didn't seem to notice that she had interrupted anything.

Once she had left the room, Scott cleared his throat. "I really ought to be going, Belinda. It's getting late and I've stuff to do in the morning."

She nodded and they both went into the hallway to find his jacket. He shouted goodbye to Melissa up the staircase, but didn't get any reply, and then he left without saying anything else. Belinda closed the front door and went through to the lounge. She didn't switch on the television; she just sat quietly and thought about Melissa's situation, her own situation and Scott's circumstances. It was stalemate. Nothing was moving, nothing was improving, and she had no idea what to do to remedy things.

*

As soon as Belinda had left, Melissa went upstairs to her bedroom and drew out her photograph albums again. She wanted to soak the images up and keep them in her head. Sometimes she had used to get annoyed at Cam because of the number of photographs he took. He was a keen photographer and was always snapping away, especially when they went on holiday. She often used to turn her back on him as he took the pictures because it was beginning to annoy her. But there were endless, wonderful pictures of Toby, from birth onwards. Now these same pictures were her lifeline, her only source of comfort. She spent a long time looking through them from beginning to end, then she put the light out and crept into bed, holding the books against her chest. She didn't even bother to get undressed. There didn't seem to her to be any point. She lay there in the dark and thought ahead to the next day – another empty, meaningless, painful day; and she prayed that it would never come.

She prayed to God to take her soul that night so that she could be with her family again. The dark emptiness of the rest of her life stretched out before her like a lonely, gaping abyss that could never be filled. She couldn't bear it. She couldn't bear it any longer. They had been so happy, she and Cam, not just in the golden glow of hindsight but in reality. They both came from financially comfortable backgrounds, and with Cam's Directorship salary and her own earnings, had been easily able to afford to buy this lovely, two-storey house of theirs before they were even married. Their friends and families had showered them with expensive gifts and they had had the house decorated and fitted out with furniture in no time at all. Melissa had been blissfully, perfectly happy throughout her six-year marriage to Cameron. They had been perfectly suited to each other and he had been as happy with her as she was with him. She had used to look at other couples, noticing their snappiness with each other and their dissatisfaction with their relationships. She and Cam hadn't been like that. Everyone had remarked on how happy and well-suited they were. She used to always feel she was the luckiest woman alive – simply because she was!

Now there was nothing left. It had all been snatched away from her by God or gods, unknown, or by Fate, whatever that was. She had been brought up to believe in one true God, an all-knowing, all-loving God who sometimes worked in mysterious ways. She had been told, and had always believed, that there is a plan and a purpose to life and that there is no point in trying to fight your destiny. She didn't know what she believed now, because the beliefs she had grown up with no longer made any sense to her. Maybe there was no rhyme or reason to anything. The cruelty of what had happened to her family and to her was unbearable and unfair – and she didn't see how she could possibly develop any kind of acceptance of it no matter how long she lived. Why had she not died with them, she wondered now? It felt to her as though Toby was already gone, already lost to her. If she had died, too, then they would all have been together again. And if there was nothing beyond death, then at least there would be the peace of oblivion – instead of this searing, tearing pain of a loss that couldn't be eased – ever. Why was she still alive? Why had she been unwell with her headache and stayed behind that day? She had always gone with Cam and Toby to the swimming pool on a Saturday. Every week, the three of them had gone there together. She should have been with them. It made no sense to her. There was nothing left for her to live for, so why was she still here? If there was a God, what reason did he have for leaving her still alive, without her husband and her beautiful, precious child? There couldn't be any reason, she deduced – none at all. It was senseless, she concluded, as hot tears slid down her cheeks onto her pillow.

People she knew had kept telling her, at the funeral and immediately after it, that at least she was all right for money, that she didn't have to worry about that. She found that quite logical but also irrelevant. Being short of money wouldn't even have penetrated the fog of grief and sadness that enveloped her heart and soul. Having money was no consolation. Nothing could console her now. She knew what she needed to do, but she wasn't sure if she could inflict that kind of loss on her parents, having suffered so much pain herself. She was trapped. Trapped by caring about them and by not caring about herself, in equal measure. That feeling of being trapped formed the crux of her depression.

Her mind wandered back to her previous happiness again, to the last few weeks when her family had still been with her. She and Cam had just decided to have another child. She had had a difficult pregnancy and birth with Toby, and it had taken her some time to get over that and to want to do it all over again with another child. But when Cam had asked her if she was ready to go down that road again, she had said yes immediately and their happiness had been complete. *If only we had decided to do that sooner*, she thought, *then I would at least have something to cling onto, some reason to go on; a part of Cam would still be with me.* But that decision had been reached between them only a week before the accident happened. She wondered yet again how life could be so cruel as she slid into the darkness of a turbulent, dream-filled sleep. But there were no answers to be found – in wakefulness or in sleep. Nothing made sense to her any more and she was certain it was never likely to do so for her ever again.

33 THE EVE OF DESTRUCTION

The following morning was a Saturday. Scott made a trip out to see some of his seriously ill patients and arrived back home around lunchtime. He was hungry and was surprised to find that April had made a large pot of soup and was busy cutting up some crusty bread to have with it.

"My, you're getting very domesticated, April!" he remarked.

"Well, why not?" she answered, smiling at him sweetly.

"I didn't know you did any cooking," he said unwisely.

She turned away from him before replying.

"Didn't spend all those years with Mum without learning something, you know," she parried.

He began to butter the bread, wondering how he was going to extricate himself from this relationship without blood being spilled.

*

Later on that evening, when they arrived at the Carters' house, Scott was still trying to figure out how to broach the subject of them not actually getting married at all. But he couldn't concentrate on it; all he could think about was that he would get to see Belinda again. He had stopped feeling guilty about that now. He couldn't help his feelings and decided that there was no point in pretending any longer. He had made up his mind. He was going to end things with April that night when they got back to his flat, whether the words came easily to him or not.

Mr and Mrs Carter made them both very welcome and when June and Belinda joined them, they all sat round the large kitchen table together, just like the first time April had brought him home to meet her parents.

Belinda seemed to be remembering this, too, as she kept stealing little looks at him while they ate. He smiled back at her. Suddenly there was silence in the room and a feeling of awkwardness. While Mrs Carter poured out teas and coffees, they all made their way into the lounge to relax on the large, comfy sofas.

As soon as Elspeth had brought the tray through and given them all their drinks, April said she had an announcement to make. Everyone looked at her, including Scott.

"Scott and I have set a date for our wedding – in August!" she announced. "We've decided on the 1st of August."

There was a stunned silence from Scott and Belinda and a noisy round of exclamations from everyone else. When Scott finally managed to drag his eyes away from Belinda's shocked face, he stared hard at April, trying to figure out what on earth was going on in her mind. He downed his coffee quickly and said that it was time for them to be going. April tried to protest that it was too early, but he took her by the arm and guided her firmly out into the hallway, where he shoved her jacket at her and pulled open the front door. He had marched her halfway down the path before Mr and Mrs Carter even got to the doorstep to wave goodbye to them.

Scott opened the car door for April and closed it loudly the instant she was seated. He got into the driver's seat and drove off without a backward glance at the house.

"Do you think there's something wrong between those two?" Elspeth asked her husband.

"I should say so," he replied, nodding wisely, as they went back inside and closed the door.

*

In her bright, sunny little house, Melissa had awakened that morning knowing exactly what she had to do. It was Saturday, and she knew that she still needed to get more tablets from the chemist. She had quite a few, but not enough to do the job effectively, with no chance of recovery. Belinda would be coming over to the house about 11 o'clock and Scott was going to be with her. The three of them were going to the hospital to see Toby. She had to say goodbye to him, but she would see him again soon, she knew. He wasn't going to recover, so she had to go and be with Cam and they would wait for their little boy to join them. Then they would all be together again – her lovely, special little family. She felt calmer now and even managed to eat a slice of toast for her breakfast. It made her feel nauseous, but she forced it down. When Belinda and Scott arrived, she smiled at them and was able to tell them honestly that she had eaten some breakfast. However, they didn't look as pleased as she had expected them to. There was obviously some tension between them that morning, she realised. Oh well, it would sort itself out, she decided philosophically. It was obvious to her now that they were meant for each other.

The three of them headed off for the hospital. Toby still lay unmoving and was looking quite pasty. Melissa smiled at him as she held his hand and murmured softly to him that everything was going to be all right now.

"I think she's turned a corner at last," Scott whispered to Belinda as they watched her comforting her son.

"Oh, I really hope so," Belinda agreed.

Scott dropped the two women off in the town centre an hour or so later as Melissa said she had some shopping to do and Belinda needed to go into the Building Society in Renfield Street.

APRIL'S MAN

Scott headed straight home. He was furious with April and intended to have a serious talk with her. They had done quite a bit of shouting earlier on, but hadn't arrived at any conclusions about their relationship. He still couldn't believe that she had been high-handed enough to announce a date for their wedding without even consulting him! Enough was enough, he decided, but he couldn't stop a strong feeling of guilt from creeping into his thoughts again. She had done nothing wrong, really. He just didn't love her. He realised now she had manipulated him into asking her to move in with him. And he was at fault also, for not being honest with her, or with himself.

He parked his car absent-mindedly in the driveway and frowned deeply as he approached the door of the flat. He hated confrontations and was sure that April would weep profusely and beg him to relent. But this couldn't go on, he knew, and it was time for actions, not words. He marched straight into the lounge, found it empty and tried the kitchen. It was empty, too. He had a quick drink of water to take the sudden dryness from his throat and turned to go towards the bedroom. He walked a little way down the hall and then stopped dead in his tracks. He could hear April's voice in the bedroom – and someone else's, too! He couldn't believe his ears. She was in their bedroom with someone else. It was definitely a man's voice. Maybe there was some innocent explanation, he told himself. This couldn't be what he thought it was.

He crept the rest of the way towards the door softly to make sure they didn't hear him and threw the door wide open. He knew he would never forget the scene that met his eyes as long as he lived. April was sitting on top of the pillows, wearing nothing but bright red lipstick with a purple feather boa wrapped around her neck. A male he had never seen before was drawing the ends of the feather boa backwards and forwards across her breasts. He was naked, too. Scott was struck dumb. It was a moment or two before April noticed him standing in the doorway. She gasped loudly and clamped her hand to her mouth. The man turned round and stared at him, then he silently stood up and began to get dressed. This procedure took him a few moments as his clothes were strewn all over the floor.

"Scott, this isn't the way it looks," April was stuttering. "I can explain – please let me explain. This is a shoot. Max was simply taking pictures of me and we got a bit playful. There's nothing going on. Honest!"

Scott found his voice again at last. It was suddenly painfully obvious to him that she had been quite deliberately playing him for a fool. He couldn't believe he hadn't seen it before.

"April, pack your things and get out," he said tersely. There was no point in saying any more to her. Angry and humiliated though he was, he wasn't actually hurt because he didn't really care for her any longer, anyway. This was his Get Out of Jail Free' card and he was going to use it.

He walked towards the front door and opened it. He stood beside it and glared at Max as he sloped past him and went out through the door. They said nothing to each other. There was nothing *to* say.

He slammed the door shut and marched into the bedroom again. April had pulled her robe around her and was sitting on the edge of the bed, sobbing her heart out. He hadn't the energy or the inclination to argue the toss with her, so he took her two suitcases from the cupboard in the hall and started to pack her things for her. This made her cry all the harder.

"Please, Scott. I told you, it isn't what you think. I'd never do that to you – you know that. Please listen to me," she pleaded.

"Don't insult my intelligence!" he barked at her and continued to pack her clothes and jewellery as fast and as untidily as he could manage to. He couldn't wait to get rid of her. By the time her cases were full, she had calmed down a little. She decided to have one more try at convincing him she was innocent.

"Scott, I think you at least owe me a chance to explain, you know. After all, we *are* engaged and we almost had a child together, didn't we?"

"What was that guy's name, April?" he asked her.

"Max," she told him very quietly.

"Well, maybe you'd better go and try out your little pregnancy story with Max, April, because your lies won't cut any ice with me any more."

So saying, he turned on his heel and lifted the large suitcase out to the boot of the car. When he came back she folded her arms and refused to budge or to lift up the smaller case.

"Go out to the car," he ordered.

"No way," she said stubbornly, adding, "Anyway, I'm not even dressed. You've packed all my stuff away!"

"Well, unless you want to walk home like that, I suggest you get into the car," he said warningly.

She stood up and sniffed huffily.

"This is ridiculous!" she began, but he pushed her along the hall and out of the front door, which he locked behind him. He made a mental note to have his locks changed as soon as possible. He got into the car and waited for her to join him. She continued to stand outside the door.

"Okay, have it your own way. You can walk home," he growled, slamming the car door shut and starting up the engine.

She stood her ground, so he moved off and drove to the end of the driveway. She came running after the car, holding her gown closed at the same time. She got into the car, her face aflame, and as soon as they arrived at the Carters' house he jumped out, dumped her bags on the ground and drew her out of his car by the arm.

"Let go of me! You're hurting me! Let go!" she squealed. Her mother had come outside to see what all the commotion was about.

"What on earth's going on?" she asked.

"Why don't you ask your darling daughter?" Scott said through gritted teeth, then turned and threw himself back inside the car. He drove away, heaving a huge sigh of relief, mixed with exasperation, as he sped off. He glanced in his rear-view mirror and saw Mrs Carter putting her arms comfortingly around her daughter, who was sobbing loudly. He smiled cynically. April was bound to spin her mother a pack of lies, but he would soon put the woman straight regarding her eldest daughter's behaviour the next time he saw her.

34 TRAPPED

While Scott was expelling April from his home, Belinda and Melissa were walking up Renfield Street. Melissa said she wanted to go to Boots and then the Building Society and Belinda nodded, linking arms with her as they walked.

"There's no need for you to come in with me, Belinda," Melissa assured her. "I'm just getting some strong painkillers. These migraines are getting a lot worse."

"That's okay. I'll come in anyway and have a look at the make-up while you get served. I've been needing a new lip gloss for ages and I keep forgetting to get it," Belinda said innocently, hoping she sounded convincing. She wasn't really looking for lipstick; she was just making sure that Mel was all right.

They went into the shop together and Belinda happily browsed through the selection of lipsticks and used a Tester or two while Melissa waited in the queue to get served. Belinda stole a surreptitious look at her friend's reflection in one of the shop's mirrored panels. She had a little more colour in her cheeks today and Belinda thought the visit to Toby had seemed to soothe her spirits. She hoped that Melissa had in fact turned a corner in her recovery, as Scott had thought. She turned away from the mirror as Melissa headed back towards her.

"Can't see any lippy I fancy," Belinda commented while she held the door open for Melissa.

"Okay. We'll just go to the Building Society and get back off home then," Melissa suggested. She was anxious to get home and get on with what she had to do. She didn't want Belinda to pick up on her plan before she had a chance to carry it out.

The Building Society was just a few doors away, so it didn't take them long to get there. It was open on Saturday mornings, which was why she had opened an account there. It was a small branch office and there were only two tellers. The girls stood together in the right-hand queue, the one nearest the door. The queue they were in seemed to be moving more slowly than the one on their left.

"All this waiting in queues is making me tired," Melissa commented, adding, "Think I'll get off home by myself after this, Bel. I'm needing a wee nap this afternoon."

"Yeah, fine. I've got a few things to do before I go back to work on Monday anyway," Belinda replied. She was a fairly patient person, but even she was beginning to feel agitated at the delay. There seemed to be some sort of problem at the desk. The queue they were in had stopped moving altogether now.

As they stood there together, Melissa's attention was caught by a little boy running backwards and forwards between the two lines of people. He was fair-haired and reminded her of her Toby. She looked at him longingly and made up her mind to ring the hospital again as soon as she had finished at the building society – just on the off-chance that there had been a change in his condition. She didn't seem able to drag her gaze away from the little boy's face. She was so focused on him that she failed to notice when the quiet buzz of noise in the room was abruptly replaced by total silence. She became aware of some sort of commotion at the front of the queue and she forced her gaze away from the little boy and looked at the desk. Someone gasped and then a gruff voice addressed one of the tellers, demanding that she hand over whatever money was in the drawer.

The teller froze. The man who had spoken was holding a gun, some sort of pistol. He wasn't pointing it at the teller directly, but the very sight of it was enough to induce a state of panic in her. He demanded money from her again and told her to keep her hands where he could see them so that she wouldn't be able to ring the alarm.

Everyone stepped back, away from the armed man, in a communal reflex action.

It then became apparent that there was a second man, also holding a gun, and demanding money from the other teller. The other teller was a middle-aged man, who looked every bit as stunned as the female teller. Emerging suddenly from her momentary shock, the female teller began to gather together the piles of cash in the drawer beneath her desk and stuff them into the bag on the desk. The alarm switch was very close to her hands, but she knew she couldn't use it without the gunman seeing what she was doing. He was watching her like a hawk and she couldn't risk it. She darted a quick look towards George – the other teller. Unbelievably, he had now folded his arms across his chest and was glaring at the gunman facing him. The female teller swallowed and looked away. She had no intention of not doing everything these men demanded of her, and she couldn't believe that George would be stupid enough to look into the barrel of that gun and refuse to do as they asked. But he was. Everyone still standing in the building society turned en masse and headed for the door. Quite a few people, including the little boy and his mother, had already turned and run from the building, responding to a strong instinct to flee from danger.

The second gunman was still waiting for George to start packing money into the carrier bag he had thrown across the desk towards him. However, this wasn't happening. Melissa and Belinda, and all the others still in the building, ran towards the door, but were halted in their tracks as they arrived at the exit. The first gunman had realised they were going to have trouble getting their money and had got there before them and locked the door. He didn't want any new clients coming in and making things even more complicated, and he didn't want anyone else to get out and raise the alarm.

The Building Society customers turned and looked at each other – they were trapped! Everyone turned towards the desk again and watched in stunned silence as they became aware that the teller was still defying the robber by refusing to do as he asked.

"Get a move on!" the second gunman shouted at George, who remained stubbornly silent and unco-operative.

As the teller continued to defy him, the robber lost patience and raised his gun. He pointed it directly at George and yelled at him again.

"Get on with it, you old tosser! Do it! Or so help me I'll use this on you!"

George still refused to budge. The robber was backed into the proverbial corner. He had to do something or he wouldn't get his money. There was no way they had enough money to split between the two of them – or three, if their getaway driver was still outside. If this teller didn't cough up, he knew he would get nothing. He fired a shot, intending to hit the teller in the shoulder. But something had gone wrong. Everyone screamed in horror. George had moved towards the alarm button just as the shot was fired and he was now wounded in the chest. He keeled over, fell from the chair and hit the floor. The first gunman looked shocked, too, but quickly recovered himself, grabbed his bag of cash and tried to usher the other gunman out of the building. They had intended to get the Branch Manager to get the rest of the money stored in the building society office for them, as well as the stuff under the desks, but there was no time to get any more money now. They had to go. He had seen George pressing the alarm and was well aware that they didn't have much time now before the police would arrive.

"We have to go – we have to go now!" he yelled at his partner in crime.

"No way – not till I've got my money!" the other man declared. He leapt over the barrier, ran behind the counter and dragged the drawer open to empty the notes out by himself. After a couple of minutes, the first robber began to be aware of police sirens in the distance and ran round the desk himself to try to get his mate away and get him out of the place before the police vehicles arrived on the scene. He looked down at the immobile body on the floor and swore. This wasn't meant to happen. They had agreed that they wouldn't use the guns. They only needed them to make the tellers afraid so they would hand over the money and then they would be out of there. They had loaded the firearms in case they had to fire any warning shots. A few minutes was all it would take and they would be gone before the police arrived. That had been the plan, but it had all gone wrong. He decided he would just have to leave Jerry behind and make his escape by himself. However, he soon became aware that even that was no longer an option.

Melissa had felt a strong urge to turn and leave the crowded room when she'd first entered the Building Society, and now she started to feel total panic as she realised that they were, to all intents and purposes, completely trapped. Her feelings escalated very quickly and she was finding it hard to breathe. She felt like a claustrophobic trapped in a lift that had become stuck between floors. The first gunman shoved her and Belinda roughly out of his way and went across the room to join his partner.

The first robber, who seemed to be the leader, knew that the police were on their way and that they weren't going to be able to make a getaway. He was quite sure their driver would have taken off by now, anyway, as he would have worked out that something had gone wrong. He was glad he had locked the door when he did. They were going to need hostages so that they could bargain their way out of this mess.

He yelled at all of them to sit on the floor with their backs against the far wall of the room, facing the front door.

Melissa, who was standing in a daze, was roughly shoved in the centre of her back towards the other customers, who were now huddled together against the wall. She stumbled onto the floor as the man shoved her forward again, with some force. She sat down heavily, her eyes round with fright and astonishment as she fully faced the fact that they were now in the centre of a hostage situation. Panic welled up inside her again and she put her hand over her mouth to stop a loud groan from escaping her lips. Although Belinda was sitting immediately beside her, in terrified silence, she had never felt so alone in her life. She just wanted to get out of there and she knew it could be some time before that happened. She tried to contain her feelings, but moaned loudly without realising she was doing so.

The lead gunman yelled at her to keep her mouth shut and sit still. He hadn't seemed to actually register her as a person – she was simply a nuisance – one more to add to the hostages already sitting trembling on the floor. She obeyed his orders without any hesitation. If she had felt closed in as she had entered the building, it was nothing to how she was feeling now. All she wanted to do was to get out of there, but she knew she had lost that chance – they all had. She watched as the man who seemed to be in charge of things proceeded to barricade the door with a heavy desk.

Melissa swallowed hard and tried to calm herself down a little. The effects of her last tranquilliser had worn off and she felt ill. The two men began to confer with each other, but were still holding guns on their hostages. Melissa slowly turned her head and looked at the other people who were trapped along with her. There were approximately a dozen of them, she estimated, and they all looked absolutely terrified. There was a young, smartly dressed man, a young blonde girl, an old married couple and two sisters who were so alike they could be twins. The two girls were holding each other and sobbing softly. There were also three or four single people there, of varying ages, who didn't seem to be with anyone and were therefore sitting in silence, trying to keep their heads down. Sarah, the female teller, was beside the other three members of staff sitting in the centre of the crowd. The backroom staff, including the Branch Manager, had been hauled out of their rooms by the leader and told to sit down and shut up. Every time they tried to communicate with each other the raiders would silence them by walking towards them or pointing the guns in their direction. The gunmen soon decided to separate the staff members, in case they got any ideas about tackling them.

There was also a young-ish man sitting on his own, slightly apart from the others, who seemed to be looking at the gunmen and trying to assess the situation. Melissa thought this was a very cool-headed thing to be doing at that point in time, considering that it was such a recent event. She could almost see his mind working overtime assessing the set-up, and so could the robbers. They kept looking over at him and were clearly discussing what to do about him. The leader was obviously warning the other man to keep an eye on him in case he decided to take matters into his own hands.

The raiders were substantially outnumbered, but the guns they held in their hands held their captives in thrall very effectively. Nobody was going to argue with a gun, especially after the teller had been shot. Even though this was Glasgow, where it was not unheard of for someone in such a situation to have a go at tackling anyone committing this kind of offence, it was too soon after it had all begun for the men to really contemplate any of the hostages taking such an action or which direction it was likely to come from. But they knew that people could behave in surprising ways when their back was against the wall, surprising even themselves sometimes, both in good ways and in bad.

Melissa took a very slow, deep breath and tried to summon up all of her emotional strength. She had recently felt that nothing would ever penetrate her ongoing depression, and so far she had been right; but at that moment in time she was aware of a small frisson of nervous apprehension, and it made her blink in surprise. Something had got through to her at last. The only thing she ever thought about these days was wondering why she was still alive because she had always believed that everything happens for a reason. However, she was sharply aware that she was not worried for herself, for her own survival. She was anxious on behalf of Belinda and the other people in the room – people she had barely even noticed as she'd stood in the queue behind them waiting to get served. She didn't want them to be in this situation, especially the younger ones. She kept looking at a young woman holding her little girl in her arms, and she immediately thought of Toby again. Her eyes moistened with tears. She hadn't felt anything for such a long time that she was amazed that her feelings were coming to the surface again. Antidepressants and tranquillisers had subdued her emotions to the extent that she had been sure nothing would ever get through to her again. She had thought she was done with crying and feeling bereft, but here it was again, threatening to swallow her up in its intensity. Her lips trembled a little and a frown settled in the centre of her forehead.

She glanced sideways at Belinda, who was sitting silently, biting down on her lower lip to stop it from trembling. Melissa watched with trepidation as the lead gunman walked over towards the group of people huddled together against the back wall of the room. She could almost feel everyone moving slightly closer together as he did so, except for the young man, who was sitting a little apart from them all. He looked as though he was prepared for anything.

The lead gunman stood in front of them, his gun hanging almost casually at his side. Suddenly he spoke, his voice grating and contemptuous.

"What? No have-a-go heroes? You're a sorry lot, aren't you? Call yourselves Glaswegians? What a joke!" He gave a short, mirthless laugh and stood waiting for his words to have an effect. He knew that people in this type of situation tend to behave in fairly predictable ways. First the fear grips them and holds them immobile; then they wait to see just what their captors are made of; and then, finally, they will try to work together to overpower or outsmart those holding them captive. He was testing the water, trying to figure out if any of them had the gumption to challenge him.

Melissa looked away from him towards the other hostages. She wondered if anyone would be foolish enough to answer him. She looked at the young man who sat a little to the side, but he was calmly waiting for the robber to continue, and was also looking round the little group, making eye contact with them and shaking his head a little to try to warn them not to respond. It was obvious to him that the robber was trying to draw them out, to see who was going to cause him problems during their captivity.

"We've got a while to wait for the police to get their act together, haven't we?" the robber pointed out. "I hope none of you are going to get any stupid ideas in the meantime. This isn't the movies, you know, and these guns are real, as you can see," he sneered, pointing to the body behind the desk.

One of the male staff snorted, making the robber look directly at him.

"Would you like a demonstration, then?" he asked, holding the man's gaze.

The man swallowed and looked down at the floor, shaking his head in reply.

"I thought not," said the gunman, smirking to himself as he surveyed them all. "I want each of you to move away from the person next to you," he commanded. "At least a foot of space between you!"

Nobody moved.

He raised his gun and pointed it at them. Everyone moved instantly, scrambling over one another in their haste to make some floor space appear between them and the person next to them. The young sisters seemed to find this difficult and only managed to leave a few inches of space between them. They held hands and couldn't seem to separate themselves, even though they were terribly afraid of the gunman. He looked at them. They were obviously no threat to him, being young, terrified girls, but he couldn't allow them to disobey his orders or he would be perceived as weak.

He strode up to them and hit one of the girls on the head with the butt of his rifle. She yelled in pain and her sister dropped her hand immediately and moved a little further away from her, hugging herself and crying. This situation was a terrible ordeal for them as they went everywhere together and always comforted each other in times of difficulty or stress. They could have faced their situation much more easily if they had been able to stay together.

The leader then ordered them all to take out their mobile phones and throw them onto the floor in front of them. Everyone did so reluctantly but quickly and he then nodded at the second gunman, indicating that he should collect up the phones.

As soon as this task was completed, the leader marched off to speak to his henchman, who had gone to stand moodily in the corner of the room. The leader drew him a look that would have felled a more sensitive man and leaned in to speak to him furiously under his breath.

"This is all your fault, you fucking idiot! We said no shooting. Which part of 'no shooting' did you not understand?"

"Fuck off," his mate replied, turning his head away, but it was all bravado, because he knew they were in a real mess now and he had no idea how they were going to get out of it – or even *if* they *were* going to get out of it.

The leader glared at him and ordered him to go over and keep an eye on the young man who was sitting on his own.

It was clear to that same young man sitting watching the gunmen closely that the leader was in full control of both the hostages and his partner in crime. He had completed his survey and now knew what he needed to do – which was precisely nothing for the time being. Waiting was obviously going to be the hardest part of this whole dreadful situation.

35 SETTLING IN

Melissa and Belinda spent the next hour in total silence, sitting with their backs to the wall in extreme discomfort. Melissa looked around at her fellow hostages and wondered how long this was going to go on and whether or not the others were coping with what was happening to them. She also wondered who would be the first to break the silent deadlock, to crack under the pressure. She asked herself how much longer she could stay like that – and, more importantly, how much longer she could hold onto the contents of her bladder! It was becoming very uncomfortable, the discomfort heightened considerably by the stressfulness of the situation.

Just as she thought she would have to be the first to ask go to the toilet, one of the young girls sitting beside her began to sob softly. It was obvious that she was trying to hide her distress, but it was becoming too much for her.

Melissa raised her right hand, very slowly and cautiously, into the air and looked over at the two gunmen. She felt like a little child on her first day at school. Both men glared at her and the edgy one, the one who had shot George, raised his weapon. She lowered her hand immediately but continued to look at them questioningly.

"What's up with you?" the leader barked out.

"We need to go to the toilet," Melissa replied, her voice croaky and uncertain.

"Who does?" he rasped, his jaw clenching visibly.

Almost everyone put their hands slowly in the air.

"One at a time then – and don't try anything or you'll be sorry," he warned, tilting his head in the direction of the teller, who was still lying immobile on the floor.

Melissa helped the young blonde girl on her left-hand side her up onto her feet, giving her a little push forward, and then sat back down again.

"I don't know where it is," the girl muttered, looking sheepishly at the armed men.

One of the Building Society staff told her that it was through the second door on the right and then along at the end of the corridor.

The edgy gunman began to follow the girl and she looked even more terrified than ever. She was almost running by the time she reached the door. The gunman walked into the Ladies just behind her and proceeded to check the whole room to make sure none of the windows was large enough for anyone to squeeze through.

In the main room, beside the other hostages, Melissa closed her eyes and tried to calm herself down. I'll wake up in a minute and this will be just another bad dream, she promised herself. She was used to bad dreams now. She never had any other kind these days. She kept her eyes firmly closed for two or three minutes, but when she opened them again, she was still in the middle of the nightmare situation and her bladder pain was now urgent. She stood up and pointed to the door, but the leader told her to wait till the other girl came back, which, luckily, the girl did right at that moment.

Melissa tried to smile encouragingly at her despite her own fear and discomfort and walked towards the open doorway. As soon as she walked through it, she began to run.

As she ran along the corridor, relieved to at least be out of that room for a few minutes, the edgy gunman leaned against the corridor wall and glared at her, watching her every step as she hurried towards the toilet. Melissa licked her parched lips and disappeared inside the Ladies.

When she came back out again, feeling considerably more comfortable and slightly calmer, she hurried back to the front room, where the others had split into two lines, one male and one female. As she took her seat on the floor again, Melissa looked at the blonde girl and smiled. She was about to speak to her when the leader barked at her.

"No talking. I won't tell you again!"

Melissa closed her mouth again but surreptitiously squeezed the girl's hand to give her some reassurance. She looked deathly pale and her eyes were large and round and stood out in her frightened face. She could feel the girl trembling a little, but she was obviously a great deal happier now that she had been to the toilet.

Melissa began to wonder what was happening outside. This wasn't a movie and she had no idea how long it would take for the police to resolve the situation. She bit her lip and tried to relax a little, but then she became aware that she was starting to develop a migraine. The little bit of distortion in the centre of her vision was gradually becoming a recognizable zigzag. She groaned.

God, that's all I need now! she thought to herself and a deep sigh escaped her.

The lead gunman glanced over at her but soon looked away again, apparently deciding she wasn't likely to be a problem, for the time being at any rate.

The young man who had been sitting a little apart from the others was now standing in the line for the Gents. As he walked off through the doorway, he turned and seemed to flick an assessing gaze onto the people dotted around the room. He shot the blonde girl a sympathetic look and then disappeared. Melissa fell to wondering why someone so young was behaving like that. It occurred to her that he was trying to form some sort of plan. Perhaps he was going to attempt to escape, but she felt that this would be a foolhardy thing to do at that point in time. The armed men were still too alert and agitated. Later, when their captors were tired, if the police hadn't organised a rescue yet, maybe they could manage something, but then they would all be tired also. She sighed and closed her eyes again. Could she risk taking a painkiller out of her handbag, which was still on her shoulder? She didn't think so; there was still too much tension in the room. She would just have to endure it. Hopefully it wouldn't be one of the really bad headaches. She didn't want to start being physically sick in the current circumstances. Things were bad enough without that!

When everyone had been to the toilet, including the two gunmen, who obviously went in one at a time, whilst the other one stood guard, things settled down a little and a feeling approaching calm began to steal over them all. Then suddenly, a desk phone began to ring. It startled them all and even the armed men jumped in alarm.

The leader marched over to the desk and lifted the handset.

He said nothing but simply listened; then he put the phone down again and narrowed his eyes as he began to address his hostages.

"If any of yous move or speak to anyone else, you're dead," he warned them, raising his weapon as he spoke. "Looks like we're all going to be here for a while."

36 MELISSA'S CHOICE

As the evening wore on, while Melissa and Belinda were settling down to an acceptance of their plight at the Building Society, Jim was pacing the floor of his flat. He'd been trying to contact both of them for quite some time. He'd intended asking Belinda to come out with him that night, but she wasn't replying to his calls or messages. He'd even tried Melissa's mobile and her home phone, but still nothing. Even if the two of them were out somewhere, he reasoned, they wouldn't both have switched their phones off. It didn't make any sense. There was something wrong. He just knew it. He didn't want to ring Belinda's home in case he scared her parents for nothing, but he couldn't just leave it. He screwed his face up in concentration, wondering what to do next, and then decided he could try Scott. Maybe he'd know something.

Scott heard his mobile ringing. He was sitting quietly, munching a packet of crisps and watching television, as it was Saturday evening, and he didn't feel like getting up and going into the hallway to fish the phone out of his jacket pocket. It was probably work, as he was on call that day, but he didn't feel like going to work. He had too much on his mind. He knew he would have to answer it eventually, though. The phone kept on ringing and he hauled himself up reluctantly to go and answer it. He frowned a little as Jim explained to him that he couldn't raise either Belinda or Mel on their mobiles.

"Well, maybe they've gone to the cinema or something," Scott suggested.

"Yeah, maybe – I never thought of that," Jim replied, sounding relieved. He hung up and Scott went back to sit in front of the television. As he did so, there was a newsflash. It stated that there had been an armed robbery at the Building Society in Renfield Street and that the robbers had been thwarted in their escape and had taken hostages. Scott looked at the picture of the street, where the police had erected barriers to hold back the onlookers. There were police cars with flashing lights everywhere and ambulances standing by. Scott frowned again as he thought about the fact that he had dropped the girls off just round the corner from that street earlier that day and the fact that Jim hadn't been able to contact either of them. He felt a chill run down his spine, but he instructed himself to be calm. He was not a man to panic and there could be loads of reasons why they weren't answering their phones.

He lifted his own phone off the coffee table and punched in Belinda's number. It rang and rang and then he was asked to leave a message after the tone. He left a message for her to ring him back as soon as she received his message, then he hung up and took a deep breath. His brain kept telling him that he was jumping to conclusions, but his instincts were telling him that Belinda was in trouble. He knew it. He could sense it, just as Jim had earlier. He stared at the television screen and he was convinced she was in there – she was a hostage! He rang Jim and told him about the heist situation. He told him to come over to his flat so that they could decide what to do. Scott knew that if his instincts were right, they were going to need each other for support in the hours to come.

*

The next few hours were the worst that Melissa and Belinda and all the other hostages had ever endured. They were tired and hungry and afraid. The police officers had sent in pizzas for them all, but most of them felt sick with fear and couldn't manage to eat more than a few bites. Melissa kept looking across at Belinda, but she was too far away for her to whisper anything to her without being heard. The lack of communication was the worst thing about their captivity.

There didn't seem to be very much in the way of communication going on between the gunmen and the police, either. Any conversations were brief and the leader was very tense now. He spoke angrily down the phone and slammed it down if he felt they weren't listening to what he was saying. He was intelligent enough to realise that the police were waiting for them to get tired and then they would swoop. The police were making all the right noises, but they knew from the statements of people who had been outside the building earlier that someone had been shot; and it was obvious to the gunman that they wouldn't wait very much longer before taking action.

George, the injured teller, had come to eventually, but was still slipping in and out of consciousness, and the leader had been reluctant to put him on the line to the police in case he tipped them off about anything. He had let him say a few words, but the man had sounded drunk because his speech was slurred, and the police said it could have been anybody's voice on the other end of the line. He knew they didn't believe him. They thought the man was dead. The trouble was that the events of the day and the continuing stress levels were making him feel really tired and he couldn't think straight. His partner was muttering distractedly to himself and even some of the hostages were starting to whisper amongst themselves. He was losing control of the situation and he didn't know what to do about it. He had made his demands for transport, but he feared that armed police would break down the door soon and they would be overpowered – or even shot. He ran his hand over his face in despair. It was a mess

– a complete mess! He would get that hothead Jerry for this, for screwing everything up. He promised himself that.

While the leader was busy trying to decide what to do next, the young man, whose name was Aaron, had stealthily slid himself along the floor until he was partially hidden from the gunmen by the other hostages, then drew out his second mobile – his work phone – from a pocket in his cargo jeans and was engaged in quietly texting his colleagues in the police force. He told them how many people were in the room, where they were located and which ones were the gunmen. He also said that the injured teller looked to be in a bad way and needed urgent medical attention. Everyone was either sitting or lying down now, as it was almost two o'clock in the morning and they were all exhausted. Aaron knew how much his information would help to reduce casualties during the rescue mission.

*

Everyone in the Carter household had been in a state of deep shock for the last few hours, ever since Scott had rung them to let them know that he thought Belinda was being held hostage in the building society. He hadn't called them immediately, in case he was wrong and was worrying them for nothing, but as the evening had worn on and still there was no news from either of the girls, he had telephoned and explained to Mrs Carter about his fears for Belinda. Her parents had simply assumed earlier in the evening that she had gone to stay with Melissa when they didn't hear from her, but now they were all sitting round the television, after ringing the police to try to find out what was going on. The police either wouldn't or couldn't tell them anything; so all they could do was watch the screen and wait for some information or some news that the siege was coming to an end. They debated with each other whether they should go and wait outside the building society for news, but decided that it could go on for some time and that also they would probably be kept better informed by the news channel than by the police at the scene.

At Scott's flat, he and Jim were both pacing the floor in a state of high anxiety. Jim was so worried about Melissa that his earlier feelings of anxiety about Belinda's safety had been swamped by his fear that something would happen to Melissa and he would never see her again. He said this to Scott, who frowned and commented that he seemed to be more worried about Melissa than Belinda.

"You're in love with Melissa, aren't you?" Scott challenged him.

Jim nodded and began to sob into his hands, both of which were covering his face.

"I can't lose her, too. I can't lose her, too. I miss Cam every day. If I lose Mel, too, I'll just want to die. I can't bear it. I can't."

Scott sat in grim silence. He knew exactly how Jim was feeling because he could think of nothing else but Belinda. The thought of losing her was unbearable and he was going to tell her that as soon as she was out of there. He no longer cared about April's feelings or about Belinda's parents and what they would think. He just wanted to put his arms around Belinda and keep her safe for the rest of her life. He knew what was coming. He knew there would be a rescue attempt and that hostages could sometimes be casualties as well as the gunmen. He was petrified. He had never been so scared or felt so helpless in his life.

The newsreaders on the news channel were beginning to talk about an imminent swoop by the police on the building society. They were not prepared to wait any longer as they knew the injured teller needed to be taken to hospital as soon as possible. And the gunmen had said they were not going to let him be taken to hospital; nor were they going to release any of the other hostages. They were sticking to their demands for transport. They hadn't asked for any cash as they had already forced the Branch Manager to hand over everything that was stored in the building. It was now or never.

"That's it! I'm going over there, Jim. Are you coming with me?" Scott asked.

"Of course I'm coming!" Jim answered instantly.

The two of them set off, united in fear, for the scene of the siege. They both knew they would remember this night for the rest of their lives, whatever the outcome.

*

Across town, in the heart of the siege situation, neither the hostages nor their captors were united in anything. Some of the hostages had fallen asleep, others were awake but silent, and a few people were whispering to each other. The gunmen didn't seem so bothered now about any of them trying anything. They knew they had more to worry about than that. Something would happen tonight – they were certain of that now. They were sitting at the opposite end of the room from the hostages, arguing with each other. The leader was being blamed by Jerry for getting them into this situation, and he responded by accusing Jerry of landing them all in trouble by his earlier reckless actions.

Belinda was trying to communicate with Melissa, but she kept turning her head away from her. Belinda knew Mel was in a very bad place at that point in time, and she hoped the other woman wasn't planning to do anything foolish. Unfortunately, Belinda was right in that summation. Melissa was indeed planning to do something very foolish. She knew she couldn't take any more of her ongoing despair and she had been making plans to end her life that very night, so she had decided to take advantage of the current situation to move things along. Since the heist had begun she had felt increasingly unwell. She felt really ill now and very weak and nervous. She kept wanting to cry all the time and there was a tight band of tension putting constant pressure on her skull. She just wanted an end to it all. She couldn't take any more. She wanted to be with Cam again and she knew that Scott and Belinda would look after Toby when she wasn't around any more. She thought about what the police were likely to be planning and made her decision accordingly. When they came through that door, she would be ready for them. She would be the first casualty – a voluntary one. She began to stare fixedly at the doorway, instinct telling her that it wouldn't be much longer now.

She hadn't been able to eat anything at all and was feeling really sick and faint. Just as she thought she would either throw up or pass out, the armed police unit burst their way through the door and she stood up, shaking from head to toe, and made to run towards their guns. But Belinda had been watching her carefully and instantly leapt up and reached over to her. She put out her hand and grabbed Melissa's arm, stopping her in her tracks. Melissa turned and looked into Belinda's face and as she did so, a peculiar feeling stirred her insides – a feeling she had had before. She told herself that it couldn't be that – and then it came again! There was no mistaking it this time. She gasped in amazement while the stand-off between the police and the robbers carried on around her. She could easily have pulled away from Belinda into the line of fire, but she had made her choice. And Cam had helped her to do it. She and Belinda put their arms around each other and crouched down as low as they could, praying for it all to be over quickly.

It should have been over very quickly, thanks to the information Aaron had supplied. However, the head gunman had other ideas. His backpack of money firmly in place, he turned and grabbed hold of Melissa and forced her towards the open doorway at gunpoint. As they moved towards the door together, he turned and fired a single shot over his shoulder. Melissa was now in terror of the very thing she had aimed for earlier that night – dying. It couldn't happen to her now – not now!

However, as soon as the robber and his hostage went through the front door, Melissa was dazzled by the lights from the array of police vehicles and a fleet of ambulances. The gunman was dazzled, too. He put his arm over his face to shield his eyes. Armed police took careful aim and wounded him. He fell to his knees – and Melissa was free! She sank to the floor and sat back against the door jamb. Jerry was dead – having been shot, it later transpired, not by the police but by his partner in crime. The gunman was handcuffed and marched towards a waiting ambulance between two of the armed officers. Another ambulance crew came inside and lifted the teller onto a stretcher. They gave him oxygen immediately. He wasn't moving but was still alive. They rushed him straight to hospital.

As the scene quietened down, the police allowed the hostages to exit the building, two at a time, and Belinda and Melissa held onto each other tightly as they left.

"Belinda, I've just realised I'm pregnant!" Melissa whispered in her friend's ear.

Belinda blinked in surprise and even managed a weak little smile. Now she understood her friend's sudden change of heart. She had something to live for again. Belinda gave her an encouraging squeeze as they stepped out into the street, the flashbulbs of the press going off all around them. The police were shepherding the hostages into the waiting ambulances. Belinda could see a television camera recording everything, and she could also see their two families waiting anxiously behind the police cordons. Jim and Scott were standing at the very front.

Suddenly, both of the young men ducked underneath the cordon and ran forward. Belinda tensed, worried that Jim was running towards her, but it was soon apparent that he wasn't. He ran straight to Melissa and held her close and Scott ran straight towards Belinda and held her in his arms, whispering to her that he would never let her go ever again. All four of them were in tears as the ambulance crew came towards them to take the girls off to hospital to be checked over.

37 STRENGTH IN NUMBERS

Scott sat by Belinda's side while the hospital staff checked her over and made sure that she was none the worse for her ordeal. Her family had gone back home to wait for her, after much general hugging and many tears from her mother. It didn't take long for Belinda to be given the all-clear and she stood up to leave, thanking the staff for their help.

"Scott, I want to go and see Melissa," she told him, adding "She's probably with Toby by now."

They set off together along the hospital corridor, their arms criss-crossed behind each other's backs. They went upstairs in the lift and when they arrived at Toby's room, they looked through the little window in the door before going inside, and Melissa was indeed there, sitting at the bedside, along with Jim. Jim looked up as Belinda and Scott walked in and Melissa looked up and actually smiled at them. It was the first time Belinda had seen her smile since Cam's accident and it brought tears to her eyes. She bent down and hugged her.

"Are you all right?" she asked. Melissa nodded.

"Have you been checked over?" Scott asked. She nodded again.

"I think we should all go home now," Scott suggested.

Jim and Melissa stood up, both of them kissing Toby before they left the room, and then all four of them headed for the car park. Melissa had several anxious messages from her mum on her phone as Jim had informed her parents of the situation as soon as he'd established that she was definitely a hostage; so she rang her and told her she fine and was on her way home.

Scott and Belinda said goodbye to Jim and Melissa in the car park and Scott drove straight to Belinda's house. The two of them sat for a little while and spoke to each other in the car before they went into the house.

"I need to know that we're going to be together now, always," Scott told her. "I never want to feel that fear and panic ever again."

He held her hand and looked directly at her, waiting for her reply.

"It's always been you, Scott, right from the start!" she told him, leaning across the seat to kiss him. She had slipped her engagement ring off during the siege and put it into her pocket. "Are you coming in?" she asked tentatively, unsure if he would do that because April would be there.

"Of course I am," he assured her. "We're together now. The past is in the past. If anybody doesn't like that, they're just going to have to get used to it. Come on, I'll see you inside and then I'm off home to let you get a good sleep. You must be shattered!"

Exhaustion was pulling at Belinda and she was struggling to keep her eyes open. They walked into the house together and Scott said hello to everyone, including April, who was sitting silently on the settee looking rather subdued. She had just been through a doubly traumatic night, worrying about her sister and also receiving a call from Max, who had decided to finish things with her and take his chances with Sylvie now that April wasn't going to be coming into any money.

After a while, Scott took his leave, letting everyone know that he would be back the next day to see Belinda. Her parents looked at each other, then said goodbye to him before he left.

"We'll all have a long chat tomorrow," Scott promised them and they nodded in agreement. There was a great deal that had to be cleared up about what had gone on between Scott and April, and between Scott and Belinda. But for tonight, the only thing that mattered to Pete and Elspeth was that their daughters were all safe and well.

Belinda went upstairs to her bedroom shortly after that, having had a quick cup of hot chocolate and a slice of toast. She smiled to herself as she slid under the duvet. It had been a dreadful ordeal to go through, but she had survived and now she and Scott were going to be together. She realised that this would be difficult for April to accept at first, and probably rather strange for her parents, too, to begin with, but she was sure it wouldn't be long before her sister would be seeing someone else. She had never really cared for Scott in the first place. Belinda closed her eyes and slid immediately into a deep, restorative sleep.

*

Jim and Melissa sat together in the lounge of her house. They were holding hands without speaking. They didn't seem to have had any need for words so far, but Jim knew that they would have to discuss things. He also knew that she must be absolutely exhausted and that she would have to rest herself before they did any serious talking. But he was determined not to let her slip away from him again. His guilt about Cameron was still there in the background, but he now knew that it was something he would have to learn to deal with. Melissa needed him and would always need him, and whether or not they ever got together as a couple, he knew he would always be there for her. He stood up and went into the kitchen. He put the kettle on and made some tea and some toasted cheese. They had often had that for supper when Cam had been alive, usually after a couple of bottles of wine.

He brought the meal through to the lounge and laid the tray down on the coffee table. He gave Melissa her cup and made sure she ate a piece of the bread and cheese, although he could see that all she wanted to do was lie down and go to sleep. He put his own cup down and put his hand underneath her chin.

"I know you're exhausted, Mel, and you need to sleep, but I'm going to be here when you wake in the morning and I'm always going to be here for you from now on, no matter what happens in the future. I want you to know that," he said quietly.

She smiled and touched his cheek with her hand.

"I know, Jim. I've always known that, deep down," she whispered.

She took herself off upstairs and he lay down on the settee, drawing his jacket over him. He fell asleep thinking that he was going to keep his word, whether she wanted him to or not. She had a great deal to cope with at that time and a lot of things to deal with in the future.

*

The following evening, Jim was still with Melissa. She invited Belinda and Scott to come over to her house and the four of them ate a takeaway Indian meal together, washed down with a couple of bottles of red wine – and a glass of lemonade for Melissa.

They weren't exactly jolly that evening; their recent experiences and the emotional roller-coaster each of them had been on had left them all rather quieter than usual. But each of them was anxious that the others should know there was no animosity about previous relationships and that the future was what was important now. Their strongest need was to support each other.

They chatted amongst themselves for a little while and then, unexpectedly, the phone rang. It was the hospital. They told

Melissa that Toby was beginning to show some signs that he might regain consciousness. She gasped and put her hand over her mouth, then told them excitedly that she would be at the hospital as soon as she could. She turned towards the other three sitting round the table, each of them now looking tense and apprehensive.

"It's Toby," she told them, her voice quivering. "He's shown some signs of improvement. I'm going to the hospital straight away!"

"We'll come with you," Belinda said.

"Oh, there's no need –" Melissa began.

"Remember what we said about supporting each other?" Belinda reminded her. "Well, we meant it."

They all happily abandoned their meal and drinks and put their jackets on while Melissa lifted the phone again, with shaking hands, to order a taxi for them.

When they all trooped into Toby's room a little later, he was not yet fully conscious, but the doctors told them that his brain activity had increased greatly and that he should be awake very soon. For Melissa, just watching as his eyes flickered open from time to time was enough. It was all she needed to see, and she couldn't understand how she could ever have even considered abandoning him. Her shock and depression must have produced a kind of temporary insanity – that was the only explanation she could arrive at. She sat down on the side of his bed and put her hand protectively over her stomach. She was determined never to fail her son or abandon him again, or the tiny child growing inside her, and she made that silent promise to them both, there and then. She was sure she was carrying a girl. Cam had wanted a daughter so much and she felt that this was his way of giving her something to live for, of giving her back her life. He had always been her hero and he always would be, whatever happened between her and Jim. She understood, at long last, why she was still alive.

The doctors and nurses were busy hovering around the bed, monitoring Toby's progress; so the others had to be content with sitting watching the proceedings at the other end of the room, but they had optimistic smiles on their faces, for the first time in a long while. This was the icing on the cake; and they each recognised that, aside from the dreadful loss of their good friend Cameron, they couldn't have wished for a better outcome.

THE END

ABOUT THE AUTHOR

Rosanna Rae is married and has three grown-up sons. She has lived in Livingston, West Lothian for over thirty years.

Some years ago, the author studied Social Science subjects with the Open University and was awarded a BA (Open) in 1990. She spent 16 years at home raising her family and then returned to full-time secretarial employment in Edinburgh. She took a writing course with The Writers Bureau in 2003 and then began writing her first novel.

A NOTE FROM THE AUTHOR

If you enjoyed reading this book, here are some links you may find useful:

Find me on Facebook: https://www.facebook.com/RR.author

Or go to my Amazon Author page for more details about my novels:

Amazon.co.uk: Rosanna Rae: Books, Biography, Blogs, Audiobooks, Kindle

If you would like to read a Chapter 1 excerpt from any of the following books, please visit my website:

http://www.rosanna-rae-novels.com

My other titles:

Karen's Affair **Jo's Dilemma**
Lynsey's Secret **Lola's Money**
Hazel's Home

These titles are also available from Barnes & Noble in paperback editions only:

rosanna rae | Barnes & Noble® (barnesandnoble.com)

These books are all stand-alone novels and do not form part of a series. They can therefore be read in any order.

Happy reading!

Printed in Great Britain
by Amazon